Carved in Stone

Margaret Manchester

First published in the United Kingdom in 2019 by
Mosaic (Teesdale) Ltd, Snaisgill, Middleton-in-Teesdale,
County Durham DL12 0RP

ISBN 978 1 9164327 4 1

Design, layout and typesetting by
Mosaic Design and Print, Middleton-in-Teesdale

About the Author

Margaret Manchester lives in County Durham, England, with her husband and two sons. She was born in Weardale and spent her childhood there.

Research into Margaret's family history discovered that many branches of her family had lived and worked in the area for centuries, either as lead miners, smelters or farmers. This sparked her interest in local history.

Whilst she studied local history and archaeology, Margaret worked as a guide at Killhope Lead Mining Museum. She was awarded a Masters degree in Archaeology from the University of Durham and went on to teach archaeology, local history and genealogy.

As well as writing, Margaret is currently the managing director of a multiple award-winning business; she is the chair of a charity that supports industrial heritage; and she enjoys spending time in her garden and with her dogs.

Dedication

This book is dedicated to my father,
Eric Adamson,
with love.

Acknowledgements

Firstly, I would like to thank my husband, Alec, for his patience and understanding while I was writing this book, and for reading and commenting on my many early drafts. I could not have completed it without his support.

I am very grateful to my sister, Linda Brown, my father-in-law, Leslie Manchester, and my friend, Ian Forbes, for reading it and providing feedback prior to publication.

The sunrise photograph used on the front cover was taken in Weardale by local photographer, Peter Elliott: www.aviewfrom.com.

The sunset photograph on the back cover shows a view of Weardale from Crawleyside, Stanhope, and was taken by Linda Brown.

Finally, thank you to Judith Mashiter at Mosaic Publishing for transforming my manuscript into a book.

Chapter 1

The Moss, Lanehead, Weardale
February, 1881

Ben Featherstone lifted the sneck and stooped to go through the doorway of the low-roomed cottage, where his mother sat in her wooden chair, snoring quietly. He took off his coat and hung it on the hook on the back of the door, and brushed the powdery snow from his hair. The fire was low in the grate; he picked up a piece of peat and dropped it onto the embers, the acrid smoke invading his nostrils, while his sheepdog, Bess, lay down on a clippy mat in front of the hearth, not bothered in the slightest that it was covered with soft grey ashes.

Lizzie woke with a start and, rubbing her eyes, she said, 'You're back early! It's still light outside.'

'Aye, there was nothing that needed doing, and there was nobody to answer to, so I thought I might as well come home.'

'It's good to see you, lad.'

'How've you been?' asked Ben, as he pulled out a chair

and sat down at the table.

'Aw, you know. I wish I could get a new pair of legs, and a new pair of hands wouldn't come in wrong either,' Lizzie laughed as she tried to straighten her arthritic fingers. Then shaking her head, she said, 'It takes me twice as long to do everything these days, but there's no use complaining. What about you? Have you any news?'

'Did you hear about Sir Thomas?'

'I haven't seen anyone since you left on Monday. What about him?'

'He's dead. He shot himself.'

'The poor man,' she said, shaking her head. 'But with what he's gone through, I can't say I'm surprised.'

'No, me neither. It's a shame though, he was a decent fella.' Ben pulled up a chair next to his mother's, and asked, 'Now that's he's gone, do you know who'll take over the Burnside estate?'

'Let me think,' said Lizzie, putting her hands on the chair arms to lift herself up. 'I'll just put the kettle on. You'll want a cup of tea after walking all the way from Eastgate in this weather.'

'Sit there, Mother. Let me do it.'

Ben picked up the empty kettle from the fireplace and went outside to fill it, and as he stood at the tap, he looked around the smallholding and, despite the covering of snow, he could see how neglected it was. He knew his mother was finding it hard to manage the house and take care of herself, never mind see to the land and stock as well. Even though he came home to help out every weekend, there was still too much work for her during the week. He sighed loudly — it was difficult seeing his mother crippled with pains and unable to cope, especially when he remembered the strong, independent woman that she'd been not so long ago; years of hard physical work and long, harsh winters had wrecked her joints.

He carried the kettle inside and put it on the hook above the fire to boil.

'Phyllis,' said Lizzie.

'What?'

'Phyllis — Sir Thomas's daughter — that's who'll get the estate. I'd almost forgotten about the lass. They sent her away to live with some relations down in Yorkshire, you know, when all that happened.'

Ben racked his brains trying to put a face to the name, but failed.

'You won't remember her,' said his mother, as though reading his mind. 'She was older than you, and quite a plain girl, really, but then any lass would look plain standing next to Connie Peart. By, she was a bonny lass! Anyway, I think Phyllis must be getting on for thirty. She's probably married with a family of her own by now.'

'Do you think she'll keep me on?' Ben asked. 'I don't know what I'd do if she finished me.'

'The lass will need a shepherd, just like her father did, and you know the job.'

While Ben spooned the tea leaves into the pot and

poured boiling water onto them, he chewed over what his mother had told him. He hadn't known that Sir Thomas had a daughter. He hoped she was like her father, and nothing like her monster of a brother, Henry. Just the name was enough to rile him, stirring up all the hatred and anger buried deep inside. Feeling his body tense, he knew he had to get out.

His hand shook and the cup rattled in its saucer as he passed his mother her tea, and he avoided looking her in the eye when he said, 'I won't be long.'

Ben darted for the door and slammed it shut behind him, and shivering, he ran towards the byre where he picked up a shovel that was propped up against the outbuilding. Like a madman, he cleared the paths of snow, metal scraping stone, his chest heaving, his breath visible in the late afternoon light. When he'd finished, he returned the shovel to its resting place and opened the byre door.

The warm air inside smelled sweetly of hay, and Martha, their shorthorn cow, looked at him with large, soft eyes, and mooed gently. He felt the tension in his muscles slipping away. Seeing that her udder was full, he moved a small stool to her side and placed a bucket underneath her, and then he sat with his face against her belly and milked her, talking to her all the while.

Lizzie sat and watched the steam rise from the full cup of tea that Ben had left on the table and wondered where he'd gone, and what he was doing. She worried about him; she'd done nothing but worry about him for years, ever since she'd told him that his sister was dead; that she'd been murdered. She'd seen the look in his eyes when he went out, and it troubled her that he was still hurting so much after all this time.

With a groan, she lifted her frail body up from the chair, and hobbled over to a sack that stood in the corner of the kitchen, and carried a couple of potatoes back to the table. Taking a knife, she peeled and sliced them to make tatie cake for tea — Ben's favourite. She knew he'd come back in an hour or so, completely exhausted, with an appetite like a horse, and feeling a bit better. It was his way of coping.

The following Tuesday, Ben attended the funeral of Sir Thomas Forster at St Andrew's Church, Westgate. He lifted his head to see who else was there, and instantly regretted it as icy particles blew into his face. Apart from the estate workers and household staff from Burnside Hall, few mourners had turned out, but he wasn't surprised by that, considering the family's fall from grace. The words of Reverend Richards' final prayer swirled around the people wrapped in woollen coats and shawls. He examined the faces, some tear-stained, some with red-rimmed eyes, and some almost as white as the snow that surrounded them, but not one of them was Sir

Thomas's daughter.

Ben wondered what kind of woman wouldn't go to her father's funeral. He'd still been a boy when his own father had been killed in the mine, but he'd gone to the funeral with his mother and sister, Kate, to pay his respects. And Kate's funeral — he'd gone to that too. A lump formed in his throat as he remembered how hard it had been to stand at his mother's side that day, but he believed it was right to give your loved ones a proper send-off.

And then he wondered if perhaps Phyllis Forster's absence meant that she wasn't coming back to Burnside Hall, and that the estate would be sold. Maybe he wouldn't have to work for Henry's sister after all. Ben was clenching his fists tightly in his pockets, and he stretched out his hands to relieve the tension. He'd only known about her existence for a few days, and already the wait to find out what she was like was torturing him.

Chapter 2

Eastgate, Weardale
February, 1881

The carriage, pulled by a pair of black horses, didn't slow down as it passed through Stanhope. Inside, a young woman was dressed in black from head to toe. She looked out of the window at the row of snow-covered shops lining the street, and at the market place with its stone cross and medieval church. Nothing had changed much in the years since she'd last been there — seven years in fact — since her parents had sent her away.

Her journey was almost at an end. Burnside Hall was just a few miles away, and the knowledge that there would be no father, or mother, or brother, to greet her when she returned to her family home weighed heavily on her mind. There had been enough suffering, and she was determined that there would be no more. From this day forward, she vowed to take control of her life. She was the only Forster left now, and she was ready to take her rightful place as mistress of Burnside Hall.

The carriage jolted as a wheel hit a pothole in the road, releasing Phyllis from her thoughts, and she glanced out of the window. There was a man walking through the snow with a collie dog at his heels in a field that belonged to her, and she wondered for a moment what he was doing there, but then she realised that he must be the shepherd her father had hired shortly after she'd left. She watched him enviously as he strolled through the snow, looking as though he didn't have a care in the world, and then suddenly he stopped and turned to watch the carriage as it travelled up the road. He took off his cap and ran a hand through his thick, dark hair.

When Ben heard hoofbeats and the jingling of harnesses, he'd turned to watch a carriage travelling up the dale road. Inside it, a woman wearing mourning dress was looking directly at him, but she turned away quickly when she realised that he'd seen her. That brought a smile to his face. She looked far too grand to pay attention to a common man like him.

He knelt down next to Bess, his faithful dog, and said ruefully, 'Aye, they don't know how well off they are, do they, lass? With all that free time and plenty of money, they can do whatever they want with their lives. Not like the rest of us that have to work for a living, until the day comes when we cannot work anymore.'

And then a thought struck him like a bolt of lightning — the lady in the carriage was Phyllis Forster, his new boss, and with that realisation came a feeling of dread.

By the time the carriage stopped, the front door of the Hall was already open and a butler in a black suit stepped out onto the driveway. Phyllis remained seated until he opened the carriage door and held out his hand to help her down.

'Good afternoon, Miss Forster. Welcome home!'

'Thank you, Todd. Please pay the coachman for his services, and have my luggage taken to my room.'

Her voice was steady and clear; it didn't betray any of the emotions that she felt at coming back to her childhood home. She climbed the steps and entered the hallway, and looking about her, she realised that the house was just as she remembered it — but without her family. She went to the music room and was relieved to see that the grand piano was still there. Lifting the lid, she pressed a few keys.

'Oh, there you are, Miss,' said the housekeeper. 'Can I bring you anything?'

'Tea, please, Mrs Gibson,' Phyllis replied, 'and a bite to eat.'

'It won't be long, Miss. I hope you don't mind me saying, but it's good to have you back.'

'Thank you.'

Mrs Gibson left the room, and Phyllis sighed. She was the lady of the house now and she had to act the part, even though being back at the Hall made her feel like a child again. When her parents had first sent her away, she'd missed her father and mother terribly. 'But it's for the best,' they'd said. Phyllis hadn't been convinced by their words then, and she still didn't believe it had been the right thing to do. No matter what the family had been going through, she should have been at home with them. Harrogate was less than one hundred miles away, but it may as well have been half way around the world because she had never seen any of her family again.

The housekeeper returned with a tea tray, which she set on a small circular table by the window. 'Now, Miss, I've brought you a pot of tea, some ham and bread, and a piece of gingerbread. Gingerbread was always your favourite!'

'Thank you,' said Phyllis, although she hadn't been partial to gingerbread for years; it reminded her too much of home. 'Please prepare a bath in my room and I'll retire early tonight. It was a long journey from Harrogate.'

'Yes, Miss.'

As Phyllis ate her meal, she watched large snowflakes floating slowly to the ground. She couldn't wait for winter to end. This winter had been by far the worst she'd known; snow had been falling for months now, and she was sick of it. On her way home, several coachmen had refused to go out onto the highways because of the treacherous driving conditions, and that had prolonged her journey by days, too many days; she'd arrived home too late for her father's funeral.

The following morning, Phyllis rose early, and when Mrs Gibson came into her room to open the curtains, she found her mistress fully dressed and attempting to fix her hair.

'Let me.' The older woman took the brush from Phyllis's hand and soon had her hair tied up in a neat bun.

Phyllis looked at her reflection. The dark circles under her eyes were evidence of a poor night's sleep, but the eyes themselves looked steely and determined.

After breakfast, she went to her father's study, where she sat at the desk looking through the account books for the estate, which comprised the Hall, the farm, the shooting moors and a limestone quarry. It took Phyllis several hours to take in all of the information, neatly presented in large ledgers, and to comprehend the estate's financial situation. When she'd finished, she closed the last book and summoned Todd.

'I'd like to meet the staff. Please arrange for them to be available this afternoon at two o'clock. We'll start with the household staff, then the outdoor staff, and I'll expect you to make the introductions.'

'Yes, Miss. Shall I bring them into the Hall?'

'I'll see the indoor servants in the hallway. It would be better to meet the estate staff outside, in front of the house; there's no need to trail wet boots in here.'

'What about Mr Maddison?'

'I'll ride up to the quarry and speak with him there. I'd like to see the progress they've made since I left.'

'As you wish, Miss. Although it might be wise to steer clear of the mines this week. I heard there's going to be trouble.'

'What do you mean?'

'The lead miners are on strike again and there's a rumour going around that the bosses are bringing blacklegs in on Monday and, as you can imagine, the locals aren't happy about it.'

'I see. I'll bear that in mind.'

After a light lunch, Phyllis went to her room, and checked her clothes and hair in the mirror. Did she look like the lady of the house? She watched her reflection as she tried out several smiles, but none of them appeared genuine. Smiling was not something she'd done much of for a while, so the staff would have to take her as they found her.

When she descended the stairs, they were lined up in the hallway and Todd was standing at the bottom of the stairs, waiting for her to join them.

'Todd,' she said.

'Miss, as you know, this is Mrs Gibson, the housekeeper.'

Mrs Gibson had been the housekeeper for as long as Phyllis could remember. The elderly lady dipped her knee, and smiled brightly at her new mistress. Phyllis tried to return the smile with warmth to reflect the affection she held for her.

'And this is Miss Wilson, the cook.'

The cook was not at all what Phyllis had expected; she'd always thought of cooks as middle-aged, plump women who were very homely-looking. The fair-haired woman standing in front of her was a little younger than herself, with a boyish build and a stern set to her face. Her only redeeming features were her large eyes with long lashes that made her look like a startled deer, yet she was not so graceful, and it took all of Phyllis's resolve not to laugh when Miss Wilson attempted a curtsey.

'And these two young ladies are our housemaids — Hannah and Betty.'

'Good afternoon, girls.'

Shyly, the girls said, 'Hello.' They looked so alike that they had to be sisters, and she knew that she would never remember which one was which.

'That's it, you can all get back to work now,' said Todd and, after he had dismissed the staff, he turned to Phyllis. 'I suppose you'll want a lady's maid? I'll make enquiries.'

'No, that's not necessary. I've managed without one so far, I don't need one now. Are the outdoor staff ready for me?'

'Yes, Miss.' He followed her to the door. 'Don't you want a coat on? It's cold out there.'

'This will only take a few minutes,' she said, annoyed that he was treating her like a child.

Phyllis was introduced to two gardeners, the groom, the woodsman, the dairyman and the gamekeeper.

When she reached the end of the line, she asked, 'Isn't there someone missing?'

'Yes, Miss.'

Just then, Ben ran around the corner of the house, followed by his dog and a boy of about twelve years of age. Ben took off his cap and joined the line, and the boy stood next to him breathing heavily.

Todd said, 'This is Ben Featherstone, the shepherd, and Harry Richardson, the errand boy.'

'Why are they late?' she asked her butler.

Ben interrupted, 'We're late because I was feeding the sheep on the top of the fell. Harry ran all that way to fetch me, and we got here as soon as we could.'

'I wasn't speaking to you, Featherstone, I was speaking to Todd. It was his responsibility to ensure that you were ready to meet me at two o'clock.'

At the reprimand, Todd looked down at his shiny shoes. 'I'm sorry, Miss.'

Ben said, 'It wasn't his fault. It wasn't possible for me to get here any faster unless I sprouted wings.'

Phyllis heard the other workers chuckle; she'd been quite amused by his comment herself, and impressed by his defence of Todd, but she kept her face straight; she couldn't let the shepherd show her up on her first day in charge, so she said, 'Make sure it doesn't happen again or your pay will be docked.' She turned away and walked briskly back into the house, thinking that Todd had been right; it was freezing outside. When she stepped inside, she heard Featherstone's voice loud and clear.

'I'm sorry you got into trouble, Mr Todd. The lad ran as fast as he could.'

'It's alright, Ben. I can look out for myself.'

Phyllis returned to her study and sat in her father's leather chair by the desk, and it wasn't long before she heard footsteps approach and a light tap at the door. Todd entered, and said, 'I hope you don't mind me saying, Miss, but I think you were a bit harsh on the lads back there.'

'I do mind you saying, Todd. They work for me, and they'll do as I ask from now on. And so will you. My father ran this estate well, but he was a tolerant man — too tolerant, perhaps. The profits for an estate this size should be better, and I can see ways that savings could be made as well as production increased. There are going to be some changes around here.'

The next morning, Phyllis left the house early and made her way to the stable block across the yard, where she found the groom checking the hoof of a large shire horse.

'Thompson, I need to go to the quarry. Please show me the horses that are suitable for riding.'

'There's not much choice these days, Miss.' He walked over to a big grey stallion. 'Samson's the best horse we've got. He was your father's hunter. He takes a bit of handling 'cos he's a strong 'un, mind.'

Samson pawed at the straw on the ground and snorted loudly.

'He looks like he could do with a run out,' she said.

'Aye, he's not had much exercise since...' Thompson

looked down at the floor, and said, 'I'm sorry, Miss.'

'Please saddle him up for me,' she said hastily, and left the stable to wait outside in the yard. A few minutes later, he led Samson out of the stables and stood him beside the mounting block. Phyllis stepped up and climbed on board. It was a long time since she'd ridden a horse and it felt strange to be back in the saddle. She took the reins, thanked the groom, and then set off for the quarry.

The yard had been cleared of snow, but there was still a good covering on the road, so she took her time and walked Samson steadily for the mile or so to Scarside quarry.

She directed Samson onto a narrow track that led to the quarry and, as she approached it, she could hear men shouting. They must have set a charge at the rock face. She wasn't sure whether or not to turn back, but she kept going slowly up the slope. There was a loud bang, and then a low rumble as rock fell to the quarry floor. Phyllis was relieved when Samson reacted with no more than a swish of his tail, and she realised that, even though she had forgotten the sound of blasting, the stallion would be accustomed to it.

'Good boy,' she said, as she leaned forward and patted his neck, and then she laughed when the horse whinnied in reply.

When she arrived at the quarry, a stout man with a dark bushy beard came over to her.

'Morning, I'm Abel Maddison. You must be Miss

Forster? I've been expecting you.'

'Good morning. Yes, I am.' She dismounted, and then shook his hand firmly. 'I've come to see how the quarry is doing, and to have a chat about expected output for this year.'

'You don't beat about the bush,' Mr Maddison said, with a laugh.

She ignored the comment, and said, 'I understand you have twelve men working here, the same as last year. Is that correct?'

'Aye, it is. They're all good workers,' he said defensively.

'Don't worry, Mr Maddison. I've no intention of finishing anyone — I just want to understand the business, that's all.' She smiled what she thought was a reassuring smile, and then said, 'And you're still working the same face as last year?'

'Aye, we are.'

A young lad approached them, and said, 'We'll be blasting in five minutes, Mr Maddison. You and the lady had better find some cover.'

'Thanks, lad.'

The boy rubbed his chapped hands together, and blew on them to warm them, before running back to the workmen who were huddled together, waiting to find out who the visitor was.

Oblivious to the workmen's scrutiny, Phyllis continued, 'Good. So, the output this year should be roughly the same as last year. That's what I expected. Is there anything that I should know about? Or anything you need here?'

'We have everything we need, thank you, Miss. Although you might be interested to know that we've broken into another cave.'

'Another cave?' she asked in surprise, as she wasn't aware of any caves being discovered at Scarside quarry.

'The last one was years ago — you'd just have been a baby back then. It had a pool full of white fish that were as blind as bats!'

'I had no idea that fish could live in caves,' she replied.

'You don't come across them very often but, if we find any in this one, I'll let you know, so you can come up and see them for yourself. Oh, by the way, the word's already out that we've hit the cave. I suspect Green over there,' he said, pointing at a short, lean man, 'might have said something in the pub.'

'Just look out for anyone snooping around, and make sure the place is clear when you're blasting. If there's anything you need, anything at all, my door is always open.'

He shook her hand firmly, and then she climbed back onto her horse. She was pleased with how her meeting with the quarry manager had gone, and with the revenue that the quarry should produce for the estate.

On the ride home, Phyllis wondered about the Weardale caves, which she knew as fairy holes, and the strange white fish that dwelt inside them. Was it fanciful to think that whoever had named them 'fairy holes' had seen the white fish and believed them to be magical spirits?

Large snowflakes began to fall around her, and normally she would have thought that they were pretty, but she was sick and tired of winter. After visiting the quarry, she'd intended to take Samson into a field and put him through his paces, but with the weather turning again, she thought it would be wiser to head straight home.

Chapter 3

Westgate, Weardale
March, 1881

'Are you comin' down to the mine this mornin'?' Davey
Bell asked his wife, as he sat down on a chair and tied his
boot laces.

'Try 'n' stop me!' replied Martha, who was hurriedly
clearing up after breakfast, their three children still
sitting at the table watching their parents with interest.
'Everyone'll be there. It'll be a proper protest. I still can't
believe they've brought in miners from Cumberland to do
your jobs, while you lot are out on strike. It's disgraceful!'

'Aye, it is. It makes you wonder what the Beaumonts
are paying them, for them to come over here and put up
with the grief that they're goin' to get.'

'Grief!' scoffed Martha, 'That's one word for it. They're
goin' to regret coming to Weardale and doin' our men's
work, that's for sure.' Turning to their eldest boy, she
said, 'Make sure you get your brother and sister to school
before the bell goes. I'm going out with your father.'

She threw a shawl over her shoulders, picked up a pan and a rolling pin, and said, 'Right, Davey, are you ready?'

Davey fastened his coat, and he and his wife left their small cottage, stepping onto the main road that ran through the village, and they joined a crowd of people who were marching towards Low Rigg mine, intent on their purpose. The men looked weary and defeated, but the women, all carrying pots and pans, looked ready to do battle.

At the mine entrance, Davey said, 'Are you sure about this? It might get nasty.'

'Of course, I'm sure. I wouldn't be anywhere else.'

Davey had never seen his wife so riled up about anything before, but then things had never been so bad before. The new pay system meant that not just him, but all of the miners, had been taking home less money and most of them were struggling to pay their bills. The agents had been no use; they'd listened to the miners' complaints but had done nothing to help. So, the miners had gone out on strike in the hope that the old pay system would be restored, but the owners had instead brought in blacklegs to keep the mines working.

A crowd of local men and women stood around the mine entrance, waiting for the strike breakers to show up for work; they were getting more and more restless in the cold morning air.

Davey watched men, walking in pairs, come into view and approach the mine. The womenfolk began to beat their rolling pins on their pots and pans, and the noise was deafening. He joined in the shouting and jeering, and names such as 'Scab' and 'Blackleg' could be heard above the din. Just for a second, the chain of men paused when they saw the formidable resistance up ahead, but then they put down their heads and moved towards the mine, jostling through the mob to reach the adit, and safety.

The women saw their moment's hesitation and played on it, threatening the miners that they'd be there every day that they went to work in place of their men. The husbands and sons were more withdrawn, and Davey wondered if they were thinking the same as him — that maybe striking had been a bad move, because if the mines were still working, the only ones hurt by the strike were the strikers themselves. They would get no pay.

When the last of the miners disappeared underground, the women continued with their banging and clashing, knowing the sound would echo through the mine and annoy the blacklegs. But after a while, people began to drift away, promising to be back later, when the miners finished their shift.

'Come on, Martha, we should get home,' said Davey, rubbing his hands together. 'Are you not cold?'

'Aye, a bit. But it'll not stop me from comin' back tonight.'

As they walked back towards the village, Davey said, 'The way you and the lasses were goin' on, I thought you were goin' to follow them into the mine and torment them all day!'

'Don't give us any ideas,' laughed Martha, and then she said seriously, 'Someone has to stand up to them. We'll make their lives hell until they go back to where they came from.'

'Well, give them hell then, because we don't need them interfering in our business. The sooner we're back to work, the better.'

'You can count on us lasses.'

He had always been able to count on his Martha, and he knew that marrying her was the best thing he'd ever done; he thought the world of her and their bairns.

Chapter 4

Yet more flakes of snow floated in the air, and there was a thick blanket of it on the ground.

'Look at this, Bess!'

Ben brushed the dusting of snow off the large sandstone boulder with his hand, revealing swirling patterns on its face. He traced the strange circles with his finger.

'I wonder who carved this, all the way up here? It's beautiful, isn't it, lass?'

The black and white sheepdog, standing by his side, looked up at her master and wagged her tail; he gently stroked her head.

Ben prided himself on his knowledge of the fell, and he was surprised that he'd never seen this carving before. Perhaps it was the dusting of snow that had highlighted the markings and made them catch his eye.

He noticed that the ancient stone had been weathered

by years of exposure to the northern wind and rain, sun and snow, and he wondered how many generations of ancestors he would have to count back in time to find the artist who'd created this masterpiece, and whether or not it was the same 'old man' who had dug the early mines in the valley, in search of metal ores.

Ben surveyed the landscape around him. Standing there, at the top of Eastgate Fell, he could see for miles in all directions, and it felt as though he was on top of the world. As he wondered who may have stood in this same spot and admired the same view all those years ago, he felt a shiver run down his spine.

'Come on, lass, we'd better get back to work.'

Ben followed the flock of sheep through the fell gate, and turned to close it behind them. Bess stayed close by his side, only darting out to keep the sheep moving in the right direction, then running back to him. The ewes walked slowly down the hillside, their bellies hanging low to the ground. The first lambs would be born in a few weeks and Ben hoped that it would be warmer by then.

The gate to a field in the valley bottom was wide open, ready to receive its new occupants. Bess knew instinctively where to take them; she herded the sheep through the gateway and waited for Ben to come and close the wooden gate behind them.

'Good lass,' he said, as he rubbed behind her ear. 'Let's go and get some dinner now.'

As they walked home, Ben heard the sound of

hoofbeats. He looked around, and saw Phyllis Forster coming towards him, riding Sir Thomas's horse, steam rising from its nostrils. Phyllis passed by without seeming to notice him, cantered across the field, leapt over a small stream before slowing to a trot, and then she disappeared into Parson's Wood.

Phyllis had been at Burnside Hall for three days and this was the first time he'd seen her since they'd been introduced, and the fact that she hadn't summoned him to the house since then, he hoped, meant that she wanted him to stay on as shepherd for the estate. Anyway, until he heard otherwise, he would carry on doing the job that he knew inside out; he didn't need a master or mistress to tell him what to do.

Ben walked back to Shepherd's Cottage, a stone-built house on the southern bank of the River Wear, where he lived during the week. There was no garden or yard; the door opened directly onto a path that ran along the river's edge. He lifted the latch and the door swung open on its squeaky hinge. Ben ducked down to avoid hitting his head on the lintel as he entered the small, dark room, which had a fireplace, with a pan and a kettle on the hearth, and an oak table and chair in front of a small sash window. A wooden ladder led to the room upstairs, which had a tiny fireplace that had never been used in all the time that Ben had lived there, and an iron-framed bed with a straw mattress. A rickety chest of drawers held the few things that he owned.

Bess went to her bed, an old proddy mat by the door, and she circled a few times before curling up on it. Ben poked the fire, which he'd banked up before he'd gone out, and it sprang back to life, the orange flames warming the room. Standing at the table, Ben cut a thick slice of bread from a loaf, and spread a thin layer of butter and a bit of his mother's bramble jam on it, and ate it in large bites. Then he poured himself a mug of milk from a jug and gulped it down. On such a cold day, he thought it would have been nice to have something warm for dinner, but that was all he had.

Phyllis had forgotten how beautiful Weardale was. She'd been out for several hours and had ridden a circular route around by Stanhope and Westgate before returning to the Hall before dark. The cold air had brought roses to her cheeks, and blood rushed through her veins; she felt alive, and she smiled to herself. This was only her second ride on Samson, and already she knew that the two of them would get on splendidly. The stallion had been frisky at first, but he'd soon settled down and did exactly what she asked of him.

As she passed the place where she'd seen Featherstone when she'd rode out, Phyllis remembered how she'd envied his carefree life, but no more, because when she'd been out on Samson that day, she too had felt happy, a feeling she hadn't experienced in years. Riding, she thought, could be her escape from the real world, and from the past; it felt wonderful to forget, even if only for a short time. The gates of the Hall loomed up ahead and, all too soon, she'd be back to reality.

Chapter 5

The Moss, Lanehead, Weardale
March, 1881

Ben made slow progress walking up the dale through the well-trodden snow. The roads were slippery and he fell several times, to the amusement of the bairns who were playing in the villages. He passed two men going down the dale on skis, making good progress, and he thought that perhaps he should make some for himself. If the winter lasted for much longer, skis would make the weekly journeys to visit his mother much quicker and easier. As he began to climb up the hill towards The Moss, he noticed fox tracks in the snow, and he hoped that it hadn't found its way into his mother's hen house.

When he eventually reached the smallholding, it was almost dark. He opened the door and was surprised that the inside of the house was in darkness too. The room was cold and he saw that the fire had gone out, and his mother was not in her chair. Panic began to set in.

'Mother!' he shouted, but there was no reply. He picked

up the candlestick from the mantelshelf, lit the tallow candle, and rushed through the house to search for her, but there was no sign of her inside, so he placed the candle in a crudely-made miner's lamp and ran outside. 'Mother!' he called, 'Where are you?'

'Ben?'

'Yes, where are you?'

'Beside the woodshed.'

He ran over to his mother, who was lying prostrate on the frozen ground.

'What happened?'

'I slipped on some ice and I fell. I couldn't get meself up.'

He put his arm around her and lifted her gently onto her feet.

'I can manage now,' she said, but as she stepped forward, she groaned.

Ben picked her up and carried her into the house and placed her carefully in her chair. He noticed that there was no weight to her body and worried that she'd not been eating well. Her chin was dothering with the cold; he grabbed the quilt from her bed and wrapped it around her, and then he lit the fire. Once it was burning well, he filled the kettle with water and put it on to boil.

'How long were you out there?' he asked gently.

'I don't know, a few hours, mebbe? I went out about dinner time, I think.'

'Have you had anythin' to eat today?'

'Aye, I had a bit of bread for me breakfast this morning.'

'I've brought some food from the Hall. Miss Wilson gave me a meat pie. Would you like some of that?'

'Aye, lad. That would be grand.'

As he cut the pie into slices, he said, 'Miss Wilson's very generous with me rations. She gives me a lot more than Mrs Grieves ever did. There's plenty for me and Bess, and some to spare. She even slips me a bottle of ale now and again.'

When there was no witty retort from his mother, he knew she was lost in her thoughts. He handed her the plate and he watched her eat the pie slowly, savouring each mouthful, while he made a pot of tea.

He wondered what would have happened if his mother had fallen earlier in the week when he was away, but he knew the answer — she wouldn't have been found until he'd come home at the weekend. She would have perished out there in the cold, all alone. The thought of her frozen body lying undiscovered for days out in the yard was sobering, and he came to the conclusion that as much as she loved her home, and her independence, she couldn't stay at The Moss, not by herself. She needed someone to keep an eye on her.

The next morning, Lizzie limped to the table and sat down slowly. Ben filled two bowls with steaming porridge and placed a jug of milk and a bowl of sugar between them. Over breakfast, Ben said, 'I know you'll not like what I'm about to say, but I don't think you should be up here on your own.'

'You're right, I don't want to hear it. But at the same time, I know that you're right. What happened yesterday scared me, Ben. I couldn't get meself up off the ground, and I didn't have the strength to drag meself back to the house. I shouted for help, but nobody came. You know, when you were bairns, I used to like living in a house that was out of the way, not overlooked by anybody, and I never saw the danger before. But if you hadn't come home when you did, I'd be up there meeting me Maker now.'

'Don't talk like that.'

'But it's true. It's bad enough that me hip's black and blue, but it could have been a lot worse.'

'Aye, I know,' said Ben. 'I think you should come and live with me at Eastgate. I can put a bed in the kitchen for you.'

'I appreciate the offer, but from what you've said about your cottage, it's not big enough to swing a cat. We'd be falling over each other.'

'You've done enough falling over,' said Ben with a smirk. Now that he knew she wasn't seriously hurt, he dared to joke about it.

'Very funny,' said Lizzie sarcastically, 'but I've got a better idea.'

'What's that?'

'I'm sure our Mary would take me in.'

Ben thought for a moment. He wanted his mother where he could keep an eye on her, and his cousin Mary Milburn and family lived near Westgate, just a few miles up the dale from his cottage. If she stayed there, he'd be able to check on her more often.

'Aye, I suppose there's no harm in asking, but if she's not keen, you'll come and stay at my place, alright?'

'Aye, alright.'

Ben saw her face drop, and asked, 'What's wrong?'

'What'll happen here?' she asked sadly.

'We'll have to give notice to the agent. You know, I'm still surprised he let you stay on here when I stopped working at the mine.'

'That was just because nobody else wanted to take the place on. There aren't the jobs in the mines that there used to be, and there's any amount of houses standing empty, especially since all those folks sailed off to New Zealand a few years back. I suppose the company thought it better to have someone in the property, and get a bit of rent for it, than leave it empty. But that's not what I meant, Ben. What'll happen to Mabel, and the sheep, and the hens, and the geese?'

'I'm sure Tom and Mary would take the animals down to their farm. And there's not much left in the garden, just a few turnips, it'll not take me long to pull them up.'

'You're a good lad, Ben. You'll make someone a good husband one day.'

'Aye, well, we'll see about that.'

Ben hoped that the Milburns would take his mother's animals because he knew it would break her heart if they had to go to the market. She was very fond of them, especially Mabel, the small cow that she'd owned for the last ten years.

To take his mother down to High House Farm, Ben borrowed a horse and trap from a friend he used to work with at the mine. He helped her into the trap and then wrapped her in a thick woollen blanket to shield her from the bitterly cold wind. Ben noticed tears in her eyes as she turned back to look at the house that she'd lived in for over thirty years, and he rested his hand on hers as they set off slowly down the icy road towards Westgate. He was pleased that it wasn't snowing, so that they could admire the beautiful snow-covered hills as they made their way down the dale, a welcome distraction from their mission.

When Ben pulled up the horse in the farmyard, Mary rushed out of the farmhouse and hugged them both. 'It's good to see you, Aunt Lizzie,' said Mary. 'It must be getting on for a year since I was up at The Moss.'

'Aye, it's been a while.'

'Come on in and tell us what's been going on.'

Ben helped Lizzie down from the cart and they followed Mary into the kitchen. Jane Milburn, her mother-in-law, and Mary's three bairns turned towards the door to see who was visiting, and Jane said to Mary, 'I'll make the tea, lass.'

They all sat around the large kitchen table. 'By, you lot have grown,' Lizzie said, looking at the children. 'You're not going to be little 'uns for much longer if you keep growing like that.'

They giggled.

'Where's that thimble? Go and fetch it, and we'll play a game,' she said.

'What game?' asked Josie, the eldest at seven years old.

'Hunt the thimble, of course!'

They went scurrying off to fetch the thimble from their mother's sewing box, and while Lizzie kept the children occupied, Ben whispered to Mary, 'Can I have a word?' He pointed towards the parlour door so that she knew he meant in private.

Nodding, she led the way to the parlour and they went in together without being noticed. Ben asked, 'Is Tom about?'

'No, my husband spends more time out in the fields than he does in the house. We only see him at mealtimes!' Mary laughed.

'I was hoping to speak with both of you. Mother had a fall yesterday. I found her when I got home last night. She'd been lying outside for most of the day. Her hip's bruised and she was freezing cold, but I think she'll be alright.'

'That's awful. Poor Aunt Lizzie. Look, you don't need

to say any more — she can stay with us if that's what she wants.'

Ben let out a sigh, and said, 'Aye, it is. Thank you. But don't you want to talk to Tom about it before you agree to take her in?'

'He won't mind. Aunt Lizzie was good to me when I had nowhere else to turn, and we're both grateful to her for that. So, taking her in now, when she needs help, well, it's the least we can do.'

'I don't think she's been eating enough. She's as light as a feather.'

'Don't worry about that, she'll be well-fed here. Me and Jane both love cooking, we fight over the oven most days!' Mary laughed.

'And there's one more thing,' said Ben. 'You know how fond she is of her animals? She'd hate to see them end up at the market. Do you think Tom could bring them down here?'

'Of course he will.'

'Thank you, Mary. There's no hurry because me mate, the one I borrowed the cart off, he's happy to see to things up there for now, in return for fresh milk and a few eggs.'

Mary smiled, and said, 'Let's go and tell her the good news.'

Chapter 6

Burnside Hall
March, 1881

Phyllis went outside and crossed the yard, to where the carriage, pulled by two bay horses, was waiting to take her to St Andrew's Church at Westgate. Beyond it, the old coach was harnessed to the shire horses, and she noticed that the housemaids were already inside. Thompson, dressed in his Sunday best, ran over and opened the door for her and she thanked him as she climbed in. Mrs Gibson came over and handed her a woollen rug, saying, 'Pop this over your knees, it'll keep you warm.'

Phyllis rolled her eyes and placed it on the seat next to her. Did she look like a child who needed to be cared for? When the rest of the servants had embarked, they began the short journey to the village of Westgate. Phyllis looked out of the window miserably; she couldn't wait for the snow to melt and for spring to arrive, and for everything to be green again. She noticed a trap heading down the track from High House Farm, and she was sure it was Featherstone who held the reins. An older woman sat next to him – his mother, perhaps – and another cart with a large family followed them. She recognised Tom and Mary Milburn, and Tom's mother, and there were at least three children with them. It struck her how happy they all looked. She wondered why Featherstone was there — were they friends, or family? Once again, she found that she was jealous of him. He obviously didn't have a worry in the world, and he was surrounded by people who cared about him; she hoped he knew how fortunate he was.

She watched both the trap and cart pass by and was surprised to see Featherstone tip his cap at her. Phyllis guessed that they would be going to the Methodist chapel, which was a little further up the road.

The coach pulled up in front of St Andrew's and Phyllis stepped out onto the verge. She was very aware that she had not yet visited her parents' graves, and she'd intended to keep her eyes looking straight ahead as she walked up the path to the church, but she couldn't stop herself from scanning the ground for a newly dug grave. Her father, Sir Thomas Forster, had been buried next to his old friend, Mr Peart. He would have liked that, she thought, and that gave her some comfort. She wondered how her childhood friend, Connie Peart, was doing, and remembered that she was Connie Milburn now. She'd married Joe Milburn shortly before Phyllis had been sent to Harrogate.

On entering the church, she made her way to the front and sat in the family pew, alone, for the first time. Phyllis heard murmurs from people sitting behind her, and felt their eyes on her back. She looked straight ahead, pretending not to hear the commotion that her arrival had caused. Of course, she'd realised that her return to Weardale would cause a stir, and that she'd most probably be the subject of gossip for a while, but she was confident that it would settle down in time.

Reverend Richards, whom she remembered well, stood by the altar with a young sandy-haired man, with a freckled complexion. When everyone was seated, the congregation fell silent, and Reverend Richards stepped into the pulpit. 'Ladies and gentlemen, I have an important announcement to make. I have been the vicar here at Westgate since the church opened, and it has been a pleasure to serve you all. However, I have decided that it's time for me to retire and move on to pastures new. This week I will leave Westgate and I will travel to Devon, where I shall stay with my sister and her family.'

Phyllis could tell that the news had come as a surprise to the villagers, who mumbled to each other in the pews. When the noise died down, Reverend Richards continued, 'I am leaving you in the very capable hands of my colleague, Reverend Dagnall, who has come here from Oxford. He's very keen to start his work here, and he will begin this very day by presiding over this morning's service.'

Reverend Richards stepped down from the pulpit and Reverend Dagnall took his place, thanking the older man for his kind words, before turning his attention to the congregation and his first sermon.

Phyllis thought he looked young to be a vicar; he was about her age, certainly not much more, and he had a boyish face with large blue eyes, which sparkled with enthusiasm throughout the service. During the hymns, his beautiful tenor voice stood out above the rest, and Phyllis admired his passion and his faith.

When the sermon ended, he and Reverend Richards walked to the back of the church and opened the door, where they could speak with the parishioners as they left the church. Phyllis rose from her seat and led the way down the aisle, as her family had always done, aware that every eye in the church was fixed on her.

'Good morning, Miss Forster,' said Reverend Richards brightly when she reached the door. 'It's good to see you again. May I introduce Reverend Timothy Dagnall?'

'Good morning,' she said.

He took her hand and, looking into her eyes, he said, 'Good morning, Miss Forster. It's a pleasure to meet you. If I can ever be of any assistance to you, or your family, please don't hesitate to seek me out.'

Reverend Richards shuffled uncomfortably at the mention of family and Phyllis's smile slipped for a second.

'Have I said something amiss? I'm ever so sorry if I've

upset you.'

She quickly composed herself, and said, 'I'm fine, thank you. I can tell by your accent that you're not from this area. May I ask why you chose to come to Westgate?'

'When I was at Oxford, I heard about the Heathery Burn Cave at Stanhope, and the bronze-age finds that were discovered there. They fuelled my imagination about the people who lived there all those years ago, and my intention is to find out more about them and write a book someday. When there was a vacancy in the very same valley, I knew it was meant for me.'

'From what I understand, they found things there over a number of years as the quarry cut further and further into the cave.'

'Yes, that's right, and who's to say that there isn't more to be found?'

'I'm sorry to disappoint you, but the cave was totally consumed by the quarry several years ago. There's nothing left of it now.' She inclined her head slightly as she said, 'It was good to meet you.'

Then turning to Reverend Richards, she said, 'Thank you for everything you've done here, and I sincerely hope you enjoy your retirement.'

'Thank you, Miss Forster.'

She shook his hand warmly before walking up the path and, when she glanced back, she saw the old vicar pointing towards her father's grave and a look of horror cross the young man's face, but it was quickly replaced by one of sympathy as he looked in her direction. She continued to the roadside, feeling rather upset; sympathy was something that she couldn't bear.

As she was about to climb into the coach, she heard someone shout, and recognising Connie's voice, she turned to see her friend rushing down the path towards her, with her mother, Mrs Peart, and her husband, Joe Milburn, trailing behind. It was Joe's brother, Tom, and his family she'd seen earlier with Ben, and she thought it strange how people swapped between church and chapel after they were married.

'Phyllis! I didn't know you were back,' said Connie.

'Hello! It's good to see you.'

They hugged each other, unaware that they were being watched by people leaving the church.

'I was sorry to hear about your father,' said Connie. 'He was such a lovely man.'

'Thank you. I didn't get home until after his funeral — because of the snow.'

'That's a shame,' she said sadly. 'Everyone will be gone soon, if you'd like a moment at his graveside?'

'Not today, perhaps another time.'

'Oh Phyllis, it's good to have you back. We must go for a ride together — like the old days,' she said grinning. 'Shall I come around tomorrow morning?'

'Yes, please. That would be lovely. How about ten o'clock?'

'Perfect. See you tomorrow.'

Joe and Mrs Peart caught up to them and they greeted Phyllis heartily after her long absence from the dale. Phyllis was grateful to see some friendly faces and she got into the coach feeling happy for the second time since she'd returned home.

The next morning, Phyllis ordered Samson to be saddled for her and, as soon as she'd eaten breakfast, she went out into the yard. Connie arrived a little early, but Phyllis was ready; they were both eager to go out together. They rode side by side up the drive, along the road, and then onto a track that led up to the moors. Phyllis realised that Connie was taking her on one of their favourite routes, which would take them back down through the woods and along the riverside.

Phyllis and Connie had been close friends and it wasn't long before they were chatting away like old times. After discussing their current horses, Connie asked, 'So what was Harrogate like?'

'The town itself is very impressive, and there are some nice shops and parks.'

'What about the people you stayed with? Were they good to you?'

'Yes, they were,' she said flatly.

'Come on, it's me you're talking to. Was it that miserable?'

'I know I should be grateful to them, but to be honest, I was bored there. I was stuck in a town house most of the time with my aunt and uncle, who felt sorry for me. They took me out to social events occasionally, but I soon tired of men wanting to dance with me just so they could ask about my brother. You see, I couldn't escape him even there. So, in the end, I stopped going out altogether.'

'Oh Phyllis, that must have been dreadful. What did you do?'

'I played the piano. Aunt Phoebe is an excellent pianist and she taught me to play well. I can get lost in music and forget who I am, and where I am — it's the same when I'm riding.'

Connie gave her a rueful smile.

'So, what's been happening here while I've been away?' asked Phyllis.

Connie told her about everything that had happened in Weardale during her absence: about the recent miners' strikes and mine closures, about the farm rents going up so much that tenant farmers were unable to pay and had been forced to leave their farms, and about the mass emigration of Weardale people who'd sailed to New Zealand to seek a better life. And then she filled her in with all the gossip about people she knew.

As they approached the wood, Connie turned to her and said, 'Now for the fun part! I'll go first in case you can't remember where the jumps are.'

Connie urged her horse to canter and went on ahead. Phyllis pulled Samson back and followed at the same pace. They jumped all of the fallen trees that lay in the wood, and by the time they emerged at the other end, they were both laughing.

'That was great!' said Phyllis. 'I missed riding so much when I was in Harrogate.'

'I'm so pleased you've come home at last. I've missed you!'

'Shall we go out again next week?' asked Phyllis.

'Yes, we must.'

'I'll come over to your place on Monday morning.'

'I can't wait!' said Connie, and then she rode away, turning back to wave before she was out of sight.

Phyllis rode back to the yard, dismounted and led Samson back to the stables. She thought it strange that Connie had talked a lot about other people but that she hadn't said anything about herself, or Joe, or their marriage. She hoped that they were happy together and made a mental note to ask Connie if everything was alright.

Phyllis had thoroughly enjoyed her morning out in the fresh air and she'd worked up quite an appetite; she hoped Miss Wilson had prepared something tasty for lunch.

Chapter 7

The lead miners were back at work, for now at least, and The Half Moon public house filled up quickly as they finished their shift and called in for a quick one on their way home. The air was so full of smoke that it was almost impossible to see from one side of the room to the other, and steam and stench rose from the men's work clothes as they dried out in the heat of the open fire.

Standing at the bar, Davey Bell lifted a beer tankard to his lips and took a loud slurp, leaving a white moustache of froth on his upper lip. The man next to him picked up his tankard and drank the pint down in one long gulp.

'Impressive, Jack, but you're a Methodist now, you shouldn't even be in here, never mind downing pints like that,' Davey said to his younger brother. He looked at Jack's face, and couldn't help the rush of jealousy that ran through him. If it wasn't for Jack's slightly cross-eyed gaze, he could have been called handsome, with his dark hair, pale blue eyes and a complexion that most women would envy. The only thing the two men had in common was their dark hair; his own eyes were hazel, and smallpox had scarred his face when he was just ten years old.

'Stuff that. It's our Beth that's the Methodist, not me.'

'You converted so you could marry the lass.'

Davey knew this because he'd done the same thing to marry his Martha. He sat through the services with her every Sunday, but he wasn't really one for religion. When he was in the chapel, his thoughts were on his family and his work, not the Bible.

'Aye, I know,' Jack said, smiling for the first time since he'd walked into the pub, 'and she was worth converting for.'

Jack ordered another drink and leaned on the bar, resting his head in his hands. 'But Davey, how can I go home and tell her that I've lost me job?'

Davey let out a sharp breath and shook his head, but said nothing. The blacklegs had tired of the hassle and abuse every morning and had packed up and gone home, which is what they'd wanted to happen, but the agents still refused to bring back the old pay system.

Bitterly, Jack continued, 'Temporary closure, they called it, but they don't know when the mine's goin' to start up again. Why did this have to happen just after she's had the bairn? How's that for timing?'

'You've got responsibilities now, Jack. You're goin' to

have to find somethin' else to do until the mine's working again.'

'Aye, I know.' Taking the second pint from the barman, Jack took a long drink.

'I hope Low Rigg stays open,' said Davey. 'With a wife and three bairns to feed, I cannot afford to be out of work.'

A man stepped over to them, and said, 'Forgive my intrusion, gentlemen. I couldn't help but overhear your conversation. I'm Walter, and I'm very pleased to make your acquaintance.'

Davey looked the man up and down and couldn't quite fathom him out. The clothes he wore were high quality, but he looked a bit scruffy, like someone down on his luck. His voice was educated, aristocratic even, and seemed very out of place in a village pub in Weardale. Nevertheless, he held out his hand and said, 'Davey Bell, and this is me brother, Jack.'

'Could I get you another drink?' He nodded to the barman. 'And you can tell me how being out of work will affect you and your families.'

'Don't get me started!' said Jack.

'But I'd really like to know.'

When their tankards had been refilled, Walter said, 'Please, come and sit with me.'

They followed him to the small table near the bar, from where he'd overheard their conversation, and they sat down together.

'Please go on, I'm listening,' said Walter, as he sat back in his chair and took a beautiful ornate pipe from his coat pocket and attempted to light the tobacco in the bowl.

Davey had never seen a pipe anything like it, with its silver and amber stem, and a wooden bowl carved in the shape of a gentleman's head. If he'd seen anyone else with it, he'd think it was stolen, but somehow it seemed appropriate for this gentleman to have it. A look passed between the brothers, and Davey knew Jack was thinking the same thing.

As he sucked on his pipe, Walter's head bobbed up and down, his eyes pleading with Jack to talk, impatient to hear what he had to say.

'My wife's just had a bairn — she's a bonny, little lass. Anyway, without me wages coming in, I'll not be able to pay our rent or put food on the table. With this new pay system, I'm already in debt to the landlord, and the shopkeeper, and Mr Spark who runs this place. The old system worked well enough. I don't know why Mr Cain had to change it. Do you know Mr Cain? He's one of the mine agents.'

Walter said stiffly, 'Yes, I know the man.'

Looking directly at Walter, Jack asked, 'In the last year, do you know how many months I've gone home with no pay? Four months! That's how many. How's a man supposed to live when his pay packet's empty at the end of the month?'

Walter's eyes narrowed, and he looked as though he

was trying to work something out, but he didn't comment; he simply nodded for Jack to continue.

Warming to his subject, Jack said, 'God knows, we're used to tough times and makin' do, but none of us could see an end to the troubles this time. So, there was nothin' else for it — we had to go on strike. We had to show Beaumont and his agents that they can't treat us this way. But did they change back to the old system? Did they heck! They brought in some fellas from over Cumberland to come here and do our jobs. It was hard for us to stand back and watch that happen, but the womenfolk gave them a hard time.' He chuckled to himself. 'They were standing at the mine, clattering their pans and rolling pins like mad, and threatening to use the rolling pins on the miners. The lads had a good right to look afeared, the womenfolk were a terrifyin' sight. But things got worse after that, and they started to close down the mines, one by one, and nobody knows why it's happening or when it will end.'

When Jack stopped long enough for someone else to get a word in, Davey said to Walter, 'Good men have had to take their families to the workhouse because they couldn't pay their dues. It just isn't right.'

Walter nodded wildly, as puffs of aromatic smoke rose like clouds above his head, adding to the haziness of the room.

Jack took a drink and licked his lips, and then he said solemnly, 'I would rather die than take Beth and our Lucy to the workhouse.'

'I'm deeply sorry for your troubles,' said Walter, his eyes blazing with anger. 'The situation is dire, very dire indeed.'

'And what has this got to do with you?' asked Davey.

'Please allow me to introduce myself properly. I'm Walter Beaumont, brother of your employer.'

Jack glared at him, and said, 'Wentworth Beaumont's your brother? Did he send you to spy on us?'

He was about to rise, but Walter put a surprisingly strong hand on his arm to stop him, and said, 'What my brother is doing to the miners of Weardale is disgraceful. Believe me when I say that I will do anything in my power to help you and your colleagues to return to work, with a decent remuneration. In the meantime, please accept this small gift for your wife and child.'

He reached into his pocket and held out a handful of coins, amounting to five shillings and sixpence. 'It's all I have right now, but take it. Your need is greater than mine.' And with a flourish, Walter Beaumont inclined his hat to the brothers and walked out of the public house.

'Well, what do you make of that?' asked Jack.

Davey had watched the whole episode in amazement. 'Dunno. He sounds on the level, but it's hard to believe that Beaumont's own brother would speak out against him, especially to people who work for him.'

Jack looked at the coins in his hand and smiled. 'At least I've got something to give our lass when I get home.

Mebbe she won't take the news quite so badly now.'

'Let's go fishing when the weather picks up,' suggested Davey, out of the blue. 'I bet your Beth would like a nice bit of trout for tea.'

'Aye, she would.'

'And Jack, don't worry too much. You'll get by, somehow.' He gave his brother a pat on the shoulder, and they went their separate ways. On the walk home, he couldn't help thinking about how unfair it was that Jack, who'd worked hard every day of his life since leaving school, should be struggling to make ends meet. Life wasn't fair.

Chapter 8

High House Farm, Westgate
March, 1881

As Ben waded through the snow towards High House Farm, he wished that it was gone. It was March now, and the sheep would be lambing soon. If he'd been a religious man, he would have prayed that the snow would be gone before the lambs started to arrive. Lambing time was hard work in any weather, but the lambs were much less likely to survive if they were born in snowy or icy conditions. The field dykes didn't give them the shelter that they needed.

Ben knocked at the farmhouse door, and when it opened, he was hit by the most wonderful smell of dinner cooking on the stove.

'Come on in, Ben,' said Mary. 'We thought you might turn up tonight. We've set a place for you.'

'Thank you. That's very kind of you.'

Ben looked at the kitchen table, with its place settings for eight, and he felt a bit strange; he'd never sat at a table with so many people before, and it reminded him of when he'd first started work at the Hall. Sir Thomas had said that with him being a single man, with no wife to take care of him, he should take his meals with the servants in the kitchen. But Ben hadn't wanted to do that because he preferred to keep his own company, even if that meant eating bread and jam instead of meat and potatoes, and when he'd said as much, Sir Thomas had ordered Mrs Grieves to prepare a daily ration for Ben to collect from the house. That had worked well enough, but he'd been thankful when Mrs Grieves retired last year and Miss Wilson had taken her place; the food had improved and she was more generous with the helpings. It had crossed his mind that Miss Wilson might have her eye on him, as she always smiled at him when he went into the kitchen, but he wasn't sure. Maybe she was just being friendly.

'It's beef stew tonight,' said Mary.

The lovely smell of food was making Ben's mouth water, and he realised that he'd had nothing to eat except bread, cheese and jam all week, which was unusual. Realising that Miss Wilson hadn't been as generous with the portions, or the variety of food, that she'd left out for him lately, he wondered if he'd done something to upset her.

'Ben, I thought I heard your voice.' Lizzie came over to him and gave him a quick hug.

'How are you?' he asked his mother.

'I'm fine.' The smile on her face was reflected in her

eyes and he could tell that she was genuinely happy there. That was a relief because, although he would gladly have taken her to his cottage, there really wasn't enough space for two people to live there.

'That's good,' he said. 'Are they keeping you busy?'

'She's great with the bairns,' said Mary. 'I don't know how we managed without her.'

Ben didn't know if Mary was just humouring his mother, but he didn't care, because she looked contented in her new home. With more rest and plenty to eat, she looked better than she had done for months.

Mary and Jane placed large plates of beef stew, with dumplings and creamy mashed potatoes, in front of everyone. As Ben picked up his fork to dig in, his mother put a hand on his to stop him. She whispered, 'They say grace here.'

Ben's stomach growled, but he put down the fork and waited for Tom to say a short prayer in thanks for their food.

While they ate, Tom asked, 'So, what's it like at the Hall now, with Phyllis in charge?'

Ben replied, 'She's strict with the staff and they say she's tighter with the purse strings than Sir Thomas ever was. She's made a few changes, which not everyone's happy about.' It dawned on him that the changes to his food rations may be down to Phyllis, and said, 'The only thing I can complain about is that I'm getting less food than I was. There's barely enough for me and Bess.'

'Sorry to hear that, lad. If you need anything, you're always welcome to join us here for tea, and we can spare a bit of bread and a few pies. You'd think me mother and Mary had an army to feed, the amount of baking that they do between them!'

Mary piped up, 'You'd be the first to complain if there wasn't any food on the table, Tom.'

'Aye, well, when a man works hard, he needs feeding.' Tom smiled lovingly at his wife.

Throughout the meal, the three children sat very quietly and they made no effort to hide the fact that they were watching Ben, a stranger to them, and hanging on his every word.

The food was better than Ben had imagined and, to his delight, it was followed by treacle sponge pudding and custard. He hadn't eaten so much in ages. After dessert, the women began to clear the dishes, and Tom said, 'Care for a drop of ale before you head home?'

The men sat by the fire and supped their beer.

'It's been a long, hard winter,' said Tom, 'and there's no sign of it letting up yet.'

'Aye, it has. I'm pleased we had plenty of hay to see us through.'

'Yes, we had plenty an' all. I feel for old Johnson up at Wearhead. He ran out of hay a few weeks back, and nobody would sell him any 'cos there was none to spare. He sold most of his flock to John Peart for a pittance, and the rest went to the butcher. It's such a shame. If I'd known sooner, I'd have taken some of them off his hands.'

'The poor fella,' said Ben, thinking how horrible it would have been if the estate had run out of fodder and he'd had to part with his sheep. He knew them all individually, and he'd have been loath to pick out ones for slaughter. He felt sick at the thought of it.

Tom reminisced about winters past, and although he'd lived through some bad ones, he was certain in his own mind that this one had been the worst, and that it wasn't over yet.

When Ben finished his ale, he excused himself and said goodbye to his mother. Mary had made up a bundle of food for him to take away with him, for which he thanked her, and then he walked home once more through the snow. Ben wasn't used to company, but even so, he had enjoyed his evening at the Milburns. They'd made him feel very welcome and he was pleased that his mother was staying with such kind people.

After work the next day, Ben went to collect his food from the kitchen and found Miss Wilson alone, kneading bread dough on the table. She lifted her head and smiled at him. He thought this might be a good opportunity to talk to her.

'I wanted to say thank you for leaving food out for me every day,' he said.

'You're welcome, but I'm just doing my job.'

'I was just wondering, have I done something to upset you?'

Blushing slightly, the cook said, 'No, you've not done anything to upset me. Why do you ask?'

'It's just I've noticed you've not been giving me as much as you used to. It's hardly enough for me and Bess — me dog.'

'I'm sorry, but that's not down to me. Miss Forster's been looking at how much we spend in the kitchen, and she's cut the budget for food. We're all eating less than we were.' Imitating Phyllis, she said, 'We need to save money. We need to buy less and waste less.' And then in her normal voice, she said, 'I daren't put any less on her plate though.'

Ben smiled, and said, 'Never mind, we'll get by.'

Phyllis appeared as if out of nowhere, and said, 'Is everything alright in here?'

'Yes, Miss,' replied the cook.

'Featherstone?'

'I was asking Miss Wilson about my food rations, and why she's giving me less than she used to.'

'It's because she was giving you enough to feed two, and I believe you live alone. Isn't that correct?'

'I live with Bess, my dog, and she needs to eat as well.'

'Ah, the sheepdog. Well, I suppose she's an estate worker too.'

Turning to Miss Wilson, she said, 'Make sure Featherstone has something to give his dog.'

And then her attention was firmly back on Ben, and she said frostily, 'I trust you'll let Miss Wilson get on with her work now.'

'Aye, I will.'

Feeling like he'd received a scolding, he took his food and left.

Chapter 9

Springbank Farm, Westgate
March, 1881

A week later, on a cool but clear morning, Phyllis rode up to Springbank Farm to meet Connie and, as she entered the yard, she was greeted very warmly by Connie's mother, Mrs Peart.

'It's good to see you, Phyllis. We don't get many visitors up here, and I don't get down to the village very often these days. Come in, won't you, and have a cup of tea?'

'No, thank you. I've just come to meet Connie. We arranged to go riding this morning.'

Mrs Peart's eyes lost their shine, but the smile didn't leave her lips. Phyllis knew that she'd upset the old lady by refusing her offer of hospitality, and she was annoyed with herself because she should have known better. Since when had she become so impolite and unsociable?

'On second thoughts,' Phyllis said, 'I would love a cup of tea. It's rather chilly this morning.' She dismounted and tethered Samson in the yard, and then followed

Mrs Peart into the farmhouse kitchen, rubbing her hands together as if to warm them.

'We'll take tea in the parlour,' Mrs Peart said to a small girl who was scrubbing dishes in the kitchen, and she led Phyllis though to a room that was almost as grand as those at Burnside Hall, although on a somewhat smaller scale.

They sat in armchairs, on either side of a round table that supported a large, shiny Aspidistra potted in a green-glazed bowl.

'Now, tell me. Was coming back to Weardale the right thing to do, do you think?' asked Mrs Peart, looking at her earnestly.

'I – I think so,' she stammered, the question taking her by surprise. 'When I received a letter informing me of my father's death, my aunt encouraged me to come home for the funeral. I packed up all of my belongings and left Harrogate, and I never had any intention of going back.'

'It's a shame that you didn't make his funeral. It was a lovely service.'

'It was the dreadful weather. I was held up at Darlington for days.'

'You could have sold the place, and lived anywhere you wanted.' Mrs Peart looked lost in her thoughts for a moment, and then added, 'It's not too late. If things don't work out for you here, promise me you'll sell up and move away.'

'Why shouldn't it work out?' asked Phyllis. She had no

doubt in her own mind that she was capable of running the estate, and she was enjoying the challenge.

'Phyllis, dear, there's still a lot of bad feeling towards your family, and people around here have long memories.'

'You're referring to Henry, aren't you?'

'Yes, I am. If there's any trouble, any trouble at all, you have the means to get away from here. That's all. Promise me you'll remember what I've said.'

Mrs Peart waited for an answer.

'Yes, of course I will. I promise,' said Phyllis, still a little perplexed by the older woman's words. Was it true that wisdom came with age, or was Mrs Peart's mind starting to wander? Was she imagining trouble where there was none?

The ladies chatted about Harrogate as they drank their tea, until they were interrupted by Connie bursting into the room.

'There you are!' she said, looking at Phyllis. 'I saw Samson outside, and I've been looking all over for you. Are you ready to go?'

Phyllis finished her tea and set the cup back on its saucer. 'Thank you, Mrs Peart. I hope to see you again soon.'

'Bye, lass. Take good care of yourself.'

Connie gave Phyllis a puzzled look as they left the room. As they walked through the house, she whispered, 'What was that about?'

'I'm not sure,' replied Phyllis. 'She seems to think there may be trouble coming my way.'

'Surely not!'

'Is she alright? I mean, she doesn't imagine things, does she?'

'Are you asking if my mother is losing her mind?' Connie laughed out loud. 'She's as sharp as she's ever been.'

Connie's strong denial that there was anything wrong with Mrs Peart's state of mind concerned Phyllis, because it meant that she should heed the warning. She wondered what could possibly happen to make her want to leave Weardale, the place she'd missed so much when she'd been forced to flee from it and seek sanctuary with her aunt.

Connie and Phyllis took their horses up to Westgate Fell, where they walked slowly over the snow-covered heather and rushes. When they came to a long flat area, they knew they had reached the usually grassy track they'd called 'the racetrack'. They looked at each other and laughed, knowing that the same thought had crossed their minds, and they urged their horses forward. As soon as their powerful mounts were given their heads, they galloped along with their tails held high, their hooves kicking up snow and dirt, leaving a mucky trail in their wake. Phyllis's hair came loose and flowed behind her. She felt the wind on her face, the blood rushing through her veins and she smiled broadly once again; she hadn't felt so good and so wonderfully free in years.

'Look!' shouted Connie.

Phyllis looked to the side where three wild deer were running alongside them, their white backsides bobbing in the air as they leapt over the moorland terrain. She grinned. Roe deer were such timid creatures and rarely seen, never mind at such close quarters. They stayed with the horses for almost half a mile before they veered off and ran to higher ground.

The women slowed their horses to a walk before they reached the end of the track, and looked back at the deer that had come to a stop further up the hill, where they stood alert, watching and listening for predators.

'Can you believe that?' asked Phyllis, still smiling.

'They must have thought the horses were running from danger, and that they should follow suit,' said Connie, bemused.

'I don't think they realised we were here or they wouldn't have come so close. They're beautiful creatures, aren't they?' And as she said it, she thought of Miss Wilson looking at Featherstone with her doe-like eyes, and the memory soured her mood.

'Yes, they are,' replied Connie. Looking down the hillside, she said, 'I think we should go down the track today. The fields have some deep drifts in them, and the horses might struggle to get through.'

Phyllis let Connie lead the way and, in the silence that followed, she remembered that she'd intended to ask

Connie about her husband and her marriage. She'd also been thinking about her own marriage prospects, or lack thereof, and wondered what she would be missing out on if she spent her life as a spinster.

Coyly, she asked, 'What's it like being married?'

Connie raised her eyebrows a little, and hesitated slightly before saying, 'Some people seem to like it, but I can't say that I do very much.'

'Oh!' exclaimed Phyllis, surprised by her friend's candid comment. 'Why not?'

'Joe's a good man, and I've grown quite fond of him really. It's just...' Connie's voice trailed off.

Phyllis saw an expression on her face that she'd never seen before — a look of incredible sadness.

'What is it?' Phyllis asked.

'I'm not sure, but I — I think Joe hates me.'

'No! You must be mistaken.'

'Oh, I don't know. We argue a lot, we always have! But Joe is so desperate for a son and I haven't been able to give him one. I don't think I ever will.'

'Don't say that. It could still happen.'

'You don't understand. I get with child easily enough, but I've lost them all before they've even started to show. There's been so many now that I've almost lost count. It's heart-breaking, and each time it happens Joe gets more and more distant. It's like he blames me for it.'

'Oh, Connie, I'm so sorry.'

'I wish Joe would just accept that it's not going to

happen, and stop coming to my room at night. He should just leave me alone.'

'You don't sleep in the same room?' asked Phyllis.

'We did when we lived at High House Farm with his mother, but not since we moved into Springbank Farm. There are plenty of rooms in the house, so we might as well have one each.'

Phyllis found it hard to believe that a young, married couple didn't share a bedroom. Certainly, her parents had always shared the same room, and her aunt and uncle had too, so she'd assumed that all husbands and wives did.

If Joe had been her husband, she was certain that she'd have wanted him to share her room. He was an attractive man, with his dark hair and large brown eyes. At one time she'd had a crush on him, but she'd known her father would never have agreed to the match, so it had remained her secret, and she was glad that she'd never told Connie about her feelings for Joe.

'Don't you like...sharing a bed with him?' Phyllis asked bashfully. She expected Connie to tell her not to be nosey, as she used to when they were children, but she didn't seem to mind the question.

'You're still a virgin, aren't you?' Connie replied.

'Of course, I am!' said Phyllis, surprised that Connie might have thought otherwise, and then bitterly she added, 'And it looks like I'll stay that way. Miss Phyllis Forster, the spinster.'

'There's plenty of time for you,' said Connie, in an obvious attempt to reassure her. 'You're not even thirty yet.'

Phyllis let out a sigh, but remained silent.

'To answer your question,' said Connie, raising her eyebrows, 'the first night I spent with Joe was awful, but it did get better, and sometimes it was very...enjoyable,' Connie smiled briefly, and then said, 'but I don't enjoy it anymore because I worry too much about getting pregnant again, and losing another baby.'

For the first time since Phyllis had given up hope of marriage, she thought that perhaps she wouldn't be missing out on too much after all. What Connie had been through must have been terrible for her and had obviously affected her marriage. She reasoned that if she didn't marry, she would never suffer the heartbreak of losing an unborn baby or a child, or have a husband treat her like a brood mare, giving her a child year after year.

But on the other hand, she was physically attracted to men — quite often men that she shouldn't be attracted to — and it was clear that Connie's dislike of the marital bed was not because of the act itself, but the fear of suffering more miscarriages. So, despite Connie's awful revelation, Phyllis hoped that there might still be time for her to find a partner, after all.

When they reached the valley bottom, the women agreed to meet again the following week.

Riding back to the Hall, Phyllis saw Ben Featherstone

climbing over a wall, from the field onto the road up ahead, and he stood still, waiting for her to pass.

'Good morning,' she called out to him.

'Mornin'! It's a lovely day.'

She pulled up her horse alongside him. 'Yes. Yes, it is,' she said brightly. 'How are the sheep doing?'

'Not bad considering the winter we've had. Luckily there was plenty of hay in the barns to keep them fed.'

'That's good to hear. When are they due to start lambing?'

'Early April.'

'Thank you, Featherstone. I won't trouble you any longer, I'm sure you have a lot to do.'

'It's no trouble,' he said, as he tipped his cap at her and smiled.

She urged Samson into a trot and, as she rode home, her thoughts remained on Featherstone. He looked young — younger than her by a few years, she guessed — which would put him in his early twenties, but he had a maturity about him that she found surprising for someone of his age. She hadn't seen him mixing with the estate workers, and she wondered why he didn't come to the house to eat with the rest of the staff. He spent a lot of time with animals, and she'd noticed how gently he handled the sheep, how he calmed them with his voice, and it was obvious how much he loved his dog. For some reason she couldn't explain, she'd been curious about him ever since she'd first seen him.

She liked that he'd passed the time of day with her; few people in the dale had shown her the same courtesy since her return. Mrs Peart's words of warning came back to her, but she pushed them to the back of her mind.

Chapter 10

Burnside Hall
March, 1881

On Monday morning, Phyllis was eating breakfast in the dining room, when Mrs Gibson came in and handed her a letter on a silver tray. Phyllis glanced at the envelope and instantly recognised the handwriting as Connie's. She reached out and took the envelope, thanked Mrs Gibson and waited until the older woman had left the room before removing the hand-written note and reading it.

My Dearest Friend

I am very sorry to inform you that I shall be unable to go out riding today as we had planned. I suspect that I am with child again. Joe has forbidden me to ride because he fears it may affect my pregnancy. The doctor has advised me to rest in the house or garden, and to avoid travel, exercise and excitement. How dull that will be for me!

I do hope that you will visit me during my

confinement as I would dearly love to see you. I have enjoyed your company very much since you returned to Weardale.

Your friend always

Mrs Connie Milburn

Phyllis purposefully put the notepaper onto the fire, and watched as it was quickly engulfed by flames. She couldn't risk leaving it where servants might see it and then spread word of her friend's condition.

She intended to have Samson saddled that morning so that she could visit Connie, but before she could give the order to Todd, she was interrupted once more by Mrs Gibson.

'Mr Maddison is here. He said he'd like to see you.'

'Show him into the study. Tell him I'll be there in two minutes.'

'Right you are, Miss.'

Phyllis finished her cup of tea, and then made her way to the study, wondering why the quarry manager was visiting again so soon.

Mr Maddison got to his feet when Phyllis entered the room, and sat down again once she was seated in the large office chair. He ran his fingers over his beard in a futile attempt to tame it.

'Good morning, Mr Maddison. What can I do for you?'

He shifted on his chair and raised one eyebrow slightly, as he said, 'I thought you should know that the men have found some stuff in that cave.'

'White fish?' she asked expectantly.

'No.'

'Then what kind of 'stuff' have they found?'

'Just some old broken tools and such like. Jimmy Gowland says they look like the things that came out of the cave at Heathery Burn. He used to work there. And...'

'And what?' she asked impatiently.

'I think...I think there might be gold up there.'

Phyllis couldn't hide her surprise. She leaned forward in her chair and asked, 'Gold? Are you sure?'

'Well, I think I'm sure,' he said, with uncertainty in his voice. 'I'll tell you what happened, should I?'

'Yes, please go on.'

'I saw one of the men showing something to the others after they'd finished their shift last night, and then put it in his pocket. I asked him to show me what he had, and he pulled out a small arrowhead that looked like it was made of bronze. So, I took it off him, and asked him to show me where he'd found it. He took me about thirty feet into the cave and pointed down at the floor. The bottom of the cave is covered in thick mud, but I put my hand in and felt around a bit, and I found a bead about the size of a pea. I'm sure it's gold.'

'Where is this bead now?'

Mr Maddison reached into his inside coat pocket and pulled out a small bead, which he carefully placed on the desk so that it wouldn't roll off. It had been roughly cleaned, and the gold that showed through the remaining dirt was bright yellow in colour. Phyllis picked it up, and was surprised by its weight, considering its small size.

'What do you think we should do?' asked Mr Maddison.

'I think we should keep quiet about this.' She looked up and saw that he was nodding in agreement. 'When the story about the discoveries at Heathery Burn was published in the papers, it attracted a lot of attention — and not all of it good. We don't want any treasure hunters at the quarry. Have you told anyone else about this?'

'No. Just Martindale knows. He's the one who showed me where he'd found the arrowhead. He's friendly with Green though, the little fella you saw at the quarry.'

Phyllis frowned slightly as she recalled the man. 'Wasn't he the one you suspected of telling everyone that you'd broken into a cave in the first place?'

Mr Maddison said, 'Aye. That's him. He's not a bad fella, really, but some people don't know how to keep their mouths shut, and he's one of them.'

Phyllis thought for a moment, and then said, 'So there's a good chance that the news will get out. Why don't you tell Martindale that the bead looked like gold but that it wasn't, that it was actually made from gilt bronze. That sounds plausible, doesn't it?'

'I'm not sure he'd believe it; the men up there have worked with rocks and minerals all their lives and they know what's what, but it's worth a try.'

'We'll have to take that chance. To be on the safe side,

hire someone to watch the quarry. He can see off any unwelcome visitors when you're not there. If there's any trouble whatsoever, let me know.' Phyllis paused for a second, and then said emphatically, 'I can't abide stealing!'

'Alright, Miss. I'll do that.'

'Other than that, continue working as before, and if you find anything else, please bring it to me.'

'Yes, Miss.' Mr Maddison stood up and, as he left, he said, 'Thank you.'

Phyllis looked at the bead on her desk and she wondered what it would look like if it was properly cleaned. She climbed the wide staircase, and went to her bedroom, closing the door behind her. Crossing to the wash stand, she poured some cool water from a fine porcelain jug into a matching bowl, and then with a cotton handkerchief, she carefully cleaned the surface of the bead and took a closer look. There was a small hole through the centre, which was still full of dirt, so she found a thin dressmaker's pin and gouged it out, little by little, until the pin appeared out the other side. Holding it up to the light, she could see right through it. Then she began to search for a gold chain that was fine enough to fit through the narrow hole. Eventually she found one in her late mother's jewellery box; she threaded the bead onto it and fastened it around her neck. Looking in the long mirror, a slight smile adorned her face; she was pleased with her morning's work.

But as she stared at her reflection, she realised that what she'd been doing was frivolous, the sort of thing that women and girls without any responsibilities would do. She wasn't a young girl anymore and she had work to do. With a pang of guilt, she returned to the study, sat at the desk and opened the large ledger, and she remained there for the rest of the day, reconciling the accounts. Her plan to visit Connie was forgotten.

The next morning, Phyllis came in from the garden and Todd announced that Mr Maddison was in the study, waiting to see her on an urgent matter. Phyllis smiled as she flung off her cloak and handed it to the butler, and then walked quickly to the study.

'Good morning, Mr Maddison,' she said, as she entered the room. 'I hope you haven't been waiting long.'

'No, Miss, not at all. I'm sorry to disturb you, but I just wanted to let you know that I've hired a night watchman for the quarry. He'll be there from the time the workmen finish their shift until they start again the next morning — so the cave will be safe from looters.'

'What's his name?'

'Jack Bell. He's from Westgate.'

'I don't think I know him.'

'He worked at the mine that closed a few weeks back, and he jumped at the chance of a job, even though it's working nights.'

'Thank you, Mr Maddison. Is that all?'

The quarry manager recognised the dismissal in her voice, and left with a hurried farewell. Phyllis remained in her chair and sighed deeply. She'd been pleased to hear that he'd employed a night watchman, but she was disappointed that he hadn't brought news of more finds from the cave.

A distant memory of a family Christmas flashed through her mind, and the feeling of anticipation at seeing beautifully wrapped presents under the Christmas tree, and not being allowed to open them until the whole family assembled in the drawing room after dinner. Moving her hand to the bead that she wore around her neck, she realised that it had brought back the thrill of expectation that she hadn't felt for a long time, and she was thankful for it. She had something to look forward to again.

Chapter 11

Burnside Hall
March, 1881

Phyllis stood at the window and sighed. She'd intended to ride over to Springbank Farm to visit Connie, but it was not a day to be outdoors. Incessant rain ran down the window panes, streams ran down the fields that were devoid of snow for the first time in months, and she wondered how so much snow could have thawed so quickly.

After lunch, she went into the study to update the account book and, when she was finished, she decided to play the piano to pass the time, but she found it difficult to keep the tempo of the music because the rain hammered the large windows with a rhythm of its own. She gave up and spent the rest of the afternoon sitting by the window, looking out at the dismal view.

Todd knocked at the door, bringing her ennui to an end, and he said, 'Richardson's just got back from Stanhope. He says the river's flooding badly, and, would you believe it? One of the bridges has been washed away!'

'Really!'

'Yes. He said he saw trees and pigs, and even a cart, being carried away by the river. It's broken its banks in a few places, and some of the houses in Stanhope have been flooded. The Hall should be alright though, it's above the flood plain.'

'That's good to hear,' said Phyllis. 'And thankfully there's no stock in the lower fields at the moment.'

'The only building at risk of flooding is Shepherd's Cottage as that's right on the riverside.'

'Isn't that where Featherstone lives?'

'Yes, Miss.'

She thought for a moment, and then said, 'Send Richardson down, and tell him to bring Featherstone up here for the night. And ask Mrs Gibson to prepare one of the spare rooms in the servant's wing.'

'Yes, Miss.'

She sat and watched the rain pelting the windows. A little while later, Mrs Gibson came in and lit the oil lamps, and then closed the curtains, which much to Phyllis's relief, dampened the incessant sound of the heavy rain.

'Dinner's ready. Would you like to eat in the dining room, or in here, Miss?'

'I'll eat in the dining room tonight, thank you.'

Sitting at the large table, Phyllis looked at the empty chairs and she could picture her father seated at the head of the table, with her mother at the other end. Phyllis had always sat facing the windows that looked out towards the river, and Henry had sat opposite her, facing the family portraits hanging on the wall. She missed them all and, by the time she had finished her meal, she felt desperately downhearted.

Anxious for news, Phyllis went in search of Todd, and she found him in the hallway talking to Richardson, who was speaking in a raised voice and making animated gestures. Whatever was the matter? She saw Todd pat him on the shoulder and walk him to the door. When he turned and saw her, he quickly came over, and said, 'I'm afraid it's not good news, Miss. The cottage is flooded already and the lad didn't dare go into the water to look inside, it was flowing far too fast, and he was worried he'd be washed away. But he said he'd shouted for Featherstone and there was no reply. Now, I know Featherstone had finished work and gone home because Miss Wilson said he'd collected his rations from the kitchen. It's possible he might have drowned, Miss.'

'I see,' she said calmly, masking her inner turmoil. 'Keep me informed of any developments.'

'Yes, Miss.'

Phyllis returned to the music room and closed the door behind her. Never before had she felt the weight of responsibility that came with being the owner of Burnside estate as she did at that moment. She was liable for the safety of everyone who worked for her, and, if Featherstone died, she would be held accountable for his death. Although she hadn't known him long, he had stood out amongst the workers, and she had a soft spot for him. If he'd perished, she realised that she would miss him.

She went to the piano and started to play a piece from a concerto by Beethoven, which reflected her sombre mood, and then she sat by the fire, deep in thought until bedtime. Before she went to sleep, she said a short prayer for her shepherd's safe return and that he would have the strength to survive whatever challenges were sent his way that night.

The next morning, Todd informed Phyllis that nobody had seen Featherstone that morning, and she began to fear the worst. She ate little of her breakfast, which earned her a disapproving look from Mrs Gibson when she came in to clear the plates away. Her mind was on the missing man. She had hardly slept, but when she'd finally drifted off, she'd dreamt of being swept away by a wall of water, tumbling and turning, reaching out in desperation for branches and debris that floated just out of reach. If Featherstone had perished in the river, he would be the first fatality on the estate since the quarry accident, twenty-three years ago. She remembered it well, even though she had just been a small child at the time. Two workmen had been crushed by falling rocks, and she had seen how their deaths had haunted her father afterwards. Unconsciously, she put her hands together as she asked God if there was any chance that Featherstone could have survived the flood.

A couple of hours later, Todd came to give her an update and told her that both gardeners had gone down to the cottage that morning, but the water had been too high for them to get inside. They'd shouted for Featherstone but there'd been no reply; there'd been no smoke coming from the chimney, and there were no other signs of life.

'It's a bad flood,' he said. 'As well as the bridge that was washed away yesterday, half of the railway bridge at Stanhope disappeared last night, and the gas main was severed as well! Can you imagine the force of water it would take to damage a gas pipe?' he said, shaking his head in disbelief. 'They'll be no gas in Stanhope until they get it repaired.'

'There's nothing we can do until the water level drops. Is that right?' Phyllis asked.

'Yes, that's about it.'

'Thank you, that will be all for now.'

Todd left the room, and Phyllis sat in the chair by the fire, wishing that her father was with her. Sir Thomas wasn't the sort of man who would sit around and wait for the water to go down, he would have done something. But what would he have done? She racked her brains to think of an answer.

Phyllis stood up quickly and ran to the door, calling for Todd. He appeared instantly, and she said, 'Get the men, and some ropes, and come down to Shepherd's Cottage.'

She grabbed a winter cloak, put on a stout pair of boots and left the Hall. She walked towards the river; the fields were sodden and her feet squelched in the mud, leaving a trail of watery footprints behind her. As she approached the river, the sound of the rushing water was overwhelming. She had never seen the river so high, nor flowing so fast, and there were all sorts of objects being hurled downstream in the turbulent current: she spotted a fence post, a doll, a shawl and a dead sheep. Watching the fast-flowing water was almost hypnotic and she felt herself sway towards the river. Quickly, she turned her eyes away and concentrated on the cottage. Seeing it for herself, she could understand the boy's reluctance to look inside. The door on the front of the house, which usually overlooked the river, now stood in it. The riverside path was submerged and there was water flowing around the back of the house, she guessed to a height of about two feet. Phyllis was worried about the strength of the current when the river was flowing so fast, but she told herself that she had to do something, she had to know if he was in there — dead or alive.

The two gardeners, the groom and the errand boy arrived with Todd, carrying the ropes that she'd asked for, their faces serious, evidently concerned about what their mistress had in mind.

'Bowman, take the rope and loop it around that tree trunk,' she said to the older gardener, pointing to a large elm tree that stood behind the cottage.

'Thompson, tie the ropes together to make one long one,' she said to the groom, whom she expected would know how to tie strong knots in his line of work.

'Yes, Miss,' he said.

'Hogarth, I know you're one of the youngest here, but you're tall and you're strong. I need you to go into the water, and check inside the cottage to see if Featherstone is in there. Do you understand?'

'I can't swim, Miss,' he said, his eyes wide with fear.

'You won't need to swim. You'll have this rope tied around your middle. The men will hold it, and pull you back if you lose your footing. It's tied to the tree as a safeguard so you'll be fine.'

The young man allowed Thompson to tie the rope around his waist and then he set off as directed, edging his way carefully into the fast-flowing water. He reached the back corner of the cottage and grabbed the wall, his fingers splayed to get a better hold. He steadied himself and took a deep breath before walking around the side of the house. At the point where the currents from the front and back of the house collided, Hogarth looked as though he was about to fall. Phyllis's heart skipped a beat, but he regained his balance and reached the far corner. He was only a few feet from the door, but the water was moving much faster at the front of the house, and he stepped back; the look he directed at Phyllis was full of fear. With words of encouragement from his workmates, he reached around the corner and grabbed the door frame, and managed to pull himself into the cottage.

'I'm in!' he shouted triumphantly.

'What can you see?' asked Todd.

'The water's up to the top of me legs, and it's filthy. I cannot see the floor. There's sticks and peat floating around. There's nothing on the table.'

'Look upstairs,' Phyllis shouted.

There was silence for a moment while the young man climbed the ladder and checked the upstairs room. He shouted, 'He's not here.'

'Thank you, God,' said Phyllis under her breath.

'Just 'cos he's not in the house, doesn't mean he's not been washed away, Miss,' said Bowman.

'We know he didn't drown in his house,' she replied. 'That's a good start. Perhaps he went to his family at Westgate and spent the night there. Richardson, go to High House Farm, and ask if they've seen him.'

The boy set off at a run, and as she watched him disappear from view, she realised that if Featherstone had been safely tucked up at Westgate the previous night, he would have shown up for work that morning. Her heart sank once again.

'Can I come out now?' Hogarth begged.

'Yes, we have the rope ready,' said Thompson. 'Just take it slowly, lad.'

When Hogarth was safely back on dry land, Phyllis urged him to rush home to change his clothes, and she went back to the Hall to wait for news.

It was an exactly an hour and a half later when Richardson returned to Burnside Hall. Phyllis heard the boy talking to Todd, and then Todd's footsteps approach her study. He knocked quietly before opening the door.

'Miss, the lad spoke to Featherstone's mother. She said she hasn't seen him since Sunday, when he was last there for a visit, but she said that we shouldn't worry because Ben isn't stupid enough to get caught out by a flood.'

'Thank you,' she said. 'I hope she's right. So, what do we do now?'

'Perhaps we should inform the police that he's missing?' suggested Todd.

'Yes, of course. Would you do that? Get Thompson to drive you down in the carriage.'

'Yes, Miss. Have you heard that two men drowned at Barnard Castle yesterday? Apparently, a watchmaker and a gamekeeper got washed away with a bridge, in front of a crowd of people from the town. Grown men really should have known better than to stand on a bridge when the river was so high.'

'How terrible!'

Todd left the room, and Phyllis leaned back in her father's leather office chair, sighing loudly. She had done everything she could think of, and now all she could do was wait for news — good or bad. She recalled the brief encounters that she'd had with Featherstone since her return, and she thought, based on what she'd seen, that he'd at least had a happy life, albeit too short.

Phyllis was shocked out of her reverie by Miss Wilson, who unceremoniously barged into the study, with a handful of herbs, and soil all over her apron. She shouted, 'He's alive!'

Ben heard Phyllis ask, 'Where is he?' as he stepped into the room and saw her moving towards him, and then she paused and said, 'That will be all, Miss Wilson.'

Her eyes fixed on Ben and she could hardly contain the relief she felt at seeing him again, alive and well. She had a sudden urge to hug him, but she simply stood there and stared.

'Miss Wilson said you thought I might have drowned. As you can see, I'm fine. It'll take more than a river to get rid of me,' he said, smiling at her.

'That's exactly what your mother said.'

'You spoke to me mother?'

'No, I sent Richardson to see if you were staying with her.'

'I'm sorry for all the hassle I've caused, Miss Forster,' he said, shaking his head. 'I didn't think for one minute that anyone would miss me.'

'Please take a seat. I'll ask Miss Wilson to make us some tea, and then I'd like you to tell me why you disappeared and where you've been all this time.' She left the room.

Ben sat in the chair that she'd indicated and waited patiently until she returned with the cook, who brought in a tea tray and set it on the desk. Phyllis sat opposite him, poured the brew and placed a cup and saucer in front of him.

'Please, tell me what happened yesterday,' she said, leaning back in her chair.

'Well, yesterday morning, the first thing I noticed was that it felt warmer outside than it had done for months, and that was really nice after having so much ice and snow. It felt good to be warm again.'

He noticed her nodding, so he continued his tale, 'It was a beautiful sunrise, the birds were singing, and it felt like spring had finally come. Water was dripping off the trees and I noticed that the snow was melting. I looked down into the river and saw the level was higher than usual, and it was flowing quite fast. Anyway, me and Bess went up to the fell. The track was really slippery, hard-packed snow, with a layer of water on top, but we made it up, eventually.'

Ben laughed, as he said, 'There were little patches of grass where the snow had gone, and the ewes were pushing each other out of the way to grab a mouthful. I suppose it's not surprising that they were fighting over it after eating hay for so long. I walked around and checked on them, and then it started to rain, just drizzle at first, but it wasn't long before it got heavier, and started to pelt the ground, so I set off back down. I went to the kitchen and Miss Wilson wasn't there, but she'd left a bottle of ale and some bread and cheese on the table for me, so I put them under me coat to try and keep them dry. When I went back to my place, I was soaked to the skin so it didn't really help much. As I walked towards the cottage, I could hear the roar of water and went to the edge to have a look, and was shocked to see how high the water was. It was almost up to the riverbank. By then, I knew that with the heavy rain, and the melting snow, it would overflow its banks and flood my place, and it was then that I saw a couple of rats running away from the river. I said to Bess that it was time for us to go as well. So, I changed into some dry clothes, grabbed a bag of supplies, and we got out of there.'

'But where did you go?'

'Up in the pasture, there's a ruined building that the sheep sometimes use as a shelter. It must have been an old farm at one time, and there's enough of it still standing to give us a bit of shelter for the night. I sat up there and watched the rain come down, and wondered who'd decided to build a shepherd's house down by the river, instead of up on the hillside where I spend most of me time!

'Anyway, from up there I could see the Hall in the valley bottom, and all the way down to Stanhope — I could see the gas lights glowing and then they went out, leaving the place in darkness. I don't know how that happened.'

'The gas pipe was severed where it crosses the river.'

'Really?'

'Yes, I believe so.'

'I spent the night up there and woke early the next morning, and as we were on the edge of the fell already, I decided to go straight up there to check on the sheep rather than go home to see how the cottage had fared in the storm. There was no doubt in me mind that it would be flooded and, if that was the case, there was nothing I could do until the water went down, so I thought I might as well get on with me job. When we'd finished, we walked back down. The track was like a river, with water flowing down off the hillside. Most of the snow had thawed by then, leaving the ground sodden. I got back to the Hall and went to the kitchen, which was empty, but there was no food left for me this time, so I took off me dirty boots and went to find Miss Wilson. She was in the greenhouse. I must have startled her because, when she saw me, she jumped back and knocked a pot off the table behind her. It smashed and made quite a mess — that's why she was covered in soil. She told me that you'd all been worried about me because I was missing, and then she dragged me in here to see you,' Ben took a deep breath. 'I'm sorry, I didn't think anyone would miss me.'

'We were worried about you,' said Phyllis. 'And all that time you were up on the fell, safe and sound.'

'Aye, I was.' He didn't know what else to say. He was still reeling from the fact that she'd noticed he was missing and had been worried about him. Nobody except his mother had ever worried about him before.

'Well, I'm pleased that you've turned up safe and well.

Obviously, the cottage is still flooded, and it'll need a good clean before you can move back in. You should move into one of the servant's rooms until it's habitable again.'

'I'm sorry, but I can't.'

'Why ever not? It makes perfect sense.'

'It's not that. It's me dog. She's always stayed with me. I couldn't leave her outside on her own.'

'I've nothing against dogs, Featherstone. My father always kept dogs in the house. Just make sure she's clean before you bring her inside.'

'You mean she can stay, as well?'

'Yes, by all means.'

'Thank you, that's very good of you. In that case, I'd be pleased to take up your offer.'

Phyllis called for Mrs Gibson, who arrived promptly.

'Please show Ben to the largest room in the servant's wing,' Phyllis said.

The look of surprise on Mrs Gibson's face was evident to them both.

'Yes, Miss,' she snapped, and quickly turned away from her mistress.

Ben followed the housekeeper up the back staircase and into the servant's wing, which was a dark corridor with doors arranged opposite each other on either side. He'd never concerned himself with the household, but he realised that there must have been a lot more servants living there at one time. Now, there was just Mr Todd, Mrs Gibson, Miss Wilson, Harry Richardson and the two maids living in. Bill Thompson had a room above the stables, and the other estate workers lived nearby. Ben counted the doors quickly — there were twelve — and so half of the rooms were empty.

He heard Mrs Gibson mutter under her breath, 'The largest one,' as she tried to fathom out why Ben was deserving of the largest room. She took him to the end of the corridor and opened the last door. Ben followed her inside and turned a full circle, taking in the double bed, four large windows, the thick curtains, the ornate fireplace, and the table with two chairs pushed underneath and an oil lamp placed in the centre.

'This is the largest one. In fact, it's the best room in this wing. It was reserved for married couples and it's not been used since the last butler left.'

'It's nice, thank you, but I won't be staying long. I'll move back to the cottage as soon as it's fixed up.'

'I suppose you'll be eating with us in the kitchen while you're living in. I'll tell the lasses to set another place tonight.'

Ben could tell that Mrs Gibson didn't approve of him, a lowly shepherd, staying in the best room. Even amongst the servants there was a hierarchy, with the butler and housekeeper at the top, the indoor servants in the middle, and the outdoor servants at the bottom, and he knew that moving in here would stir up trouble. The largest room had been Phyllis's suggestion, not his. He guessed she wanted the dog to have plenty of space. If he'd turned down this room, he wouldn't have had many options — he could have stayed with the Milburns, but their house was already full, or he could have slept rough again, like he had last night, but the thought of doing that for another week or more wasn't appealing. The bed looked better than any he'd ever seen before, and he was looking forward to a good night's sleep. He went downstairs to fetch Bess.

Chapter 12

Burnside Hall
March, 1881

Ben woke and stretched out in the large, comfortable bed. It took a moment for him to remember where he was, and he looked around the room and smiled to himself. The curtains were so thick that he couldn't see if it was light outside yet, so he got up and opened them to see a beautiful golden sunrise. He guessed that it must be almost seven o'clock and was surprised by that because he was usually awake well before daybreak. He quickly washed his face and hands in the wash bowl in his room, and then went down to the kitchen for breakfast.

He sat at the long table with the indoor servants while Miss Wilson served out their breakfast — a plate of bacon and eggs, with buttered bread — and he was shocked to see how well they ate. For once he'd be going out to work on a full stomach.

That afternoon, he washed and changed when he came

down off the fell, and was looking forward to his dinner. He made his way to the kitchen and as soon as he sat down, a plate was put in front of him, filled with pork sausages, mashed potatoes, carrots, cabbage and gravy. He'd been working at the Hall for nearly five years, and he wondered if he'd been stupid not to take Sir Thomas up on his offer to take his meals at the Hall.

'Do you mind if I call you Ben?' asked Miss Wilson.

He nodded. Ben or Featherstone, he didn't feel strongly either way.

'So, Ben, where do you come from?'

'Lanehead,' he said, between mouthfuls.

'Do you have any family?'

'Just me mother now.'

'You must have a girlfriend, a handsome lad like you?'

Why would anyone think he had a girlfriend? Was she teasing him? She must be. He saw that the others were trying to stifle their smiles; they were enjoying his discomfort. Miss Wilson waited patiently for an answer.

'No, I haven't.'

'You don't say much, do you?'

Ben shrugged. Idle conversation wasn't something that came easily to him. Reserved by nature, he found her attempts at friendship, if that's what they were, intrusive. He didn't like people being nosey, prying into his family and his background; they didn't need to know any of that. He'd come to the estate to do a job, and he did it the best he could, that's all he'd agreed to do. Living in and putting up with personal questions hadn't been part of the bargain. He quickly finished his plate and, getting to his feet, he said, 'Thanks for dinner, but I'll be off now.'

'Don't you want pudding?' asked Mrs Gibson.

'Pudding?'

'I've made a ginger sponge and white sauce,' said Miss Wilson, smiling at him. 'I'll be offended if you don't stay and try some.'

'Alright, I will.'

He sat back down at the table reluctantly but, when he tasted the pudding, he was pleased that he had stayed; it was delicious. His bowl was the first to be emptied, and when he looked up, he saw Miss Wilson's grin of satisfaction.

'Thank you. That was nice,' said Ben.

'You're welcome, Ben,' Miss Wilson replied. 'And if you want, you can call me Amy.'

Ben nodded.

Mrs Gibson said, 'That's enough. I'll not have any flirting at the table. Featherstone, you'll refer to Cook as Miss Wilson when you're in company. Do you understand?'

Ben looked around the table. The maids were both looking into their bowls. Todd cleared his throat and gave Ben a sympathetic shrug, and Miss Wilson blushed slightly.

Ben said, 'I wasn't flirting, Mrs Gibson.'

'Come with me,' she said, taking hold of his arm and

leading him out of the kitchen into the hallway, where they wouldn't be overheard. 'It's not you I was referring to. I don't think you even realise it, but that lass has a fancy for you. If you have feelings for her, then so be it, you can go ahead and court her with my blessing. But I'll not have anything untoward going on between the servants, is that clear?'

'Yes, I understand what you're saying. But are you sure she likes me?' he asked uncertainly.

'Yes, take it from me, she likes you.' Mrs Gibson left him standing there in shock.

When he went upstairs, he tiptoed along the corridor for fear of disturbing the other servants in their rooms. With his room being right at the end, he had to pass all of the others, and he didn't know which were occupied, or if anyone would be trying to sleep. He opened his door and Bess came over to greet him, with a little nudge of her nose.

'Hello, Bess,' he said, stroking her head. 'I wish I understood people the way I understand animals.'

He sat on the mat in front of the fire, and Bess snuggled up next to him. He rested his hand on her back and, staring into the flames, he asked himself what he thought of Miss Wilson. When she'd first started working there, he had a feeling that she might like him. He saw her almost every day when he collected his food from the kitchen, and she always looked happy to see him, but she never said much. He wondered if she'd had a little swig of sherry while she'd been cooking that evening because she seemed more chatty than usual.

Even though they were a similar age, he'd never found her particularly attractive. He couldn't put his finger on what it was exactly, but he couldn't see the two of them together. If Mrs Gibson hadn't told him that Miss Wilson liked him, he wouldn't have been thinking about her at all. Who would he have been thinking about? Probably someone like Phyllis Forster, although she was so far out of his reach, he may as well have his eye on one of the royal princesses.

The more he saw of Phyllis, the more he'd come to realise that she was very much like her father, Sir Thomas, who had been his friend and confidant, and he was thankful that he couldn't see any similarity between her and her late brother.

As the embers dimmed, Ben undressed and climbed into bed, naked. Bess stood at the side, and whined.

'No, lass. You can sleep on the floor.'

Bess lay down beside the bed, with her head between her front paws, and Ben laughed because he knew she was sulking. He pulled the covers up and laid his head on the feather pillow. He was getting ideas above his station, staying in this beautiful room, sleeping in a bed fit for a king, with a full belly, and harbouring thoughts of Phyllis Forster. He closed his eyes and drifted off to sleep.

Ben woke with a start and sat upright in his bed. There

was somebody in the room; he could sense it. The fire had gone out and it was completely dark. Bess was growling deep in her throat, sounding a warning to the intruder not to come any closer.

'Who's there?' Ben asked.

'It's just me — Amy.' Her voice came from near the door. 'Does your dog bite?'

'No. What are you doing in here?' he hissed.

'Do you really have to ask?'

He heard her footsteps, softened by the carpeted floor, coming towards him. He didn't want her in his bed. He didn't like her in that way. But what could he say without causing offence?

'Please, leave.'

'What?'

'I want you to go...please.'

'Are you serious? Do you not want me?'

'No. I'm sorry, but I don't want this.'

'What's wrong with you?'

'Nothin'. He wished she would just go. If he'd had clothes on, he would have got out of bed and taken her out of the room himself.

'Do you not like girls?' she sniggered.

'Get out!'

Bess growled loudly.

'Alright, I'll go. But you'll not get another chance with me, Ben Featherstone.'

He heard the door click shut and listened for any

disturbance in the corridor, but all was quiet. Hopefully she hadn't been seen anywhere near his door — he didn't want any trouble. When he was sure she was back in her own room, he got up and turned the key in the lock. That was something he'd never done at The Moss, or at his cottage; there'd never been a need.

After that night, Ben spent as little time in the kitchen as he could, and when he was there, Miss Wilson seemed to avoid him as much as possible. The situation was very awkward, and he was anxious to leave the Hall and get back to his cottage as soon as he could. He couldn't wait until it was just him and Bess again.

It was three days later before the river receded to its normal level and, as soon as it did, Ben went down to the cottage to assess the damage. He was pleased to see that the building had survived the flood, and that the windows and door were still intact. Looking inside, he turned up his nose; the floor was covered in thick brown mud, which smelled vile, and about four feet from the floor, there was a horizontal line on the lime-washed wall that clearly showed the highest point the flood water had reached.

He'd taken a shovel and wheelbarrow with him, and he got straight to work. He shovelled up the slime, slowly filling the barrow and then wheeling it to the riverbank where he tipped the mud into the steady flow of water, immediately turning it brown. He removed almost twenty barrow loads before he finished for the night.

The next evening after work, he returned, and set about washing the kitchen's stone-flagged floor, sweeping it thoroughly with a large broom and swilling it out with buckets of water. Once he was satisfied that it was clean, he took the table and chair outside and washed them down, before carrying them back into the house. He climbed the ladder to his bedroom and found that everything was as it should be, and he opened the upstairs window to clear the stench rising from the lower floor. As he left, he decided to leave the door open, thinking the flow of air would help to dry the house.

A week to the day after the flood, Ben picked up his few belongings from his room at the Hall and looked around, sadly. If it hadn't been for Miss Wilson's nocturnal visit, and being expected to chat with the staff at mealtimes, he could have stayed longer. But in truth, as small and basic as it was, he couldn't wait to get back to his cottage. He closed the door behind him, ran down the stairs, and went home with Bess.

Chapter 13

Westgate
April, 1881

'Afternoon, Jack,' said Davey.

'How do? It's nice to see a bit of blue sky, isn't it?'

'Aye, it's a canny day — at last.'

The brothers walked side by side towards the river, heading towards a deep pool in the River Wear, where they'd regularly caught trout, and occasionally salmon, in their youth.

Davey said, 'It's still a bit cold for fishing, but beggars can't be choosers.'

'Heh! That's not funny, Davey. We're not far off being beggars.'

'I'm sorry, Jack. I should have been more careful with me words. I didn't mean owt by it.'

'Aye, I know. It's just that it's been a long winter. I'm glad that we have a bit of decent weather so we don't need to worry about lightin' the fire anymore. I've been out almost every day, collectin' bits of wood that's lyin' around, but there's hardly any left. The woods have been picked clean. I noticed a few good trees have been cut down as well, for firewood, no doubt. People are gettin' desperate, Davey. What were the bloody mine owners thinkin' when they closed the mines, eh?'

'God only knows,' said Davey. 'How's Beth?'

'Not good. She's not sleepin' well with me being out at night, and she's cryin' more than the bairn does. She's worried we'll end up at Stanhope.'

'In the workhouse! It'll not come to that. The job at the quarry's going alright, isn't it?'

'It doesn't pay very well, 'cos it's not proper work really. I don't have to do anythin'; I just have to be there.'

'You know, I'll help you out if you need it.'

'I know, Davey. But you've got your own family to worry about. Who knows how long your place will stay open?'

'Aye, you've got a point there. Me hours have been cut this week and I'm on half time now.'

They reached the river and Jack stepped down carefully into the water, making no sound and hardly a ripple, and then he slowly lowered himself down into the water until he was on his knees. He felt under the rocks for the familiar feel of a fish. Davey lay down on the riverbank, leaning over the edge, with his hands under the bank. A startled water vole brushed his fingers as it swam out from its hiding place and headed downstream. Knowing that there would be no fish hiding where the vole had been, he got up to move upstream, but he stopped to watch his brother who was slowly tickling the belly of a large trout. A moment later, he ducked as Jack grabbed the fish with both hands and threw it up in the air, shouting, 'I got one.' The fish landed on the grass behind Davey.

'A big one an' all,' said Davey, suitably impressed. He killed it quickly, wrapped it in newspaper and put it in his pocket.

Davey held out his hand to help Jack out of the water.

'By, it's cold in there. Me fingers are frozen. It reminds me of when I worked on the washing floor.'

'Thank God, we don't have to do that anymore!' said Davey, resuming his position on the river's edge. After ferreting around for a while, he got up and dried his hands on his trousers. 'I think we'd better stick with the one. Me hands are numb. Beth needs some good food inside her, with her feedin' the bairn, so you take it back with you.'

He took the fish out of his pocket and handed it to Jack.

'Are you sure?'

'I want you to have it.'

'Thank you. She loves a bit of fish, so that'll put a smile back on her face.'

They walked briskly to the village and, as they were about to split up, Jack asked, 'D'you know what we should do?'

Davey shrugged.

'The fells are full of grouse. We should go and help ourselves to some.'

'But that's poachin',' said Davey. 'And anyway, we haven't got a gun.'

'We could borrow one. A mate of mine has one.'

'I don't know about that, Jack. What about the gamekeepers? They'll shoot us on sight if they see us.'

'But there's not much chance of that, is there? There's a lot of fell up there, and not many gamekeepers...'

Jack looked at him expectantly.

Davey had reservations about his brother's idea — lots of reservations in fact. Aye, they'd gone fishing a few times in the river, which was wrong as well, but everybody did it. Poaching was a different matter altogether. Davey knew that his brother would never have contemplated doing something so reckless if he'd still been working at the mine, but times were desperate now and his family needed to eat.

Davey had never been able to say 'no' to his younger brother. His mother used to laugh about it when they were little, and she'd said that it wasn't just him that couldn't say 'no' to Jack either. He'd been such a cute little boy, and he'd perfected a pleading look with his big blue eyes that made everyone do just what he wanted.

Growing up had been much harder for Davey, with his pock-marked face; he'd always struggled to get what he wanted. Regarded with suspicion by strangers, and scorned by the lasses, he was thankful that he'd found his

Martha. She seemed to be the only one who could see through his damaged skin to the man he was inside. Pushing his misgivings aside, he heard himself say, 'Aye, alright then.'

As he approached his terraced cottage, Davey regretted that he was going home empty-handed, and that they hadn't stayed longer to catch another fish, but he couldn't feel his hands or feet. He hoped Martha would have a good fire burning in the grate when he got home, unlike at his brother's house. He knew Jack and Beth were more in need than he was and that he'd done the right thing in giving the fish to them.

When he got home, Davey was met at the door by his five-year-old daughter, Lottie.

'Did you catch one?' she asked with wide eyes, looking to see if he was hiding a fish in his coat, or behind his back.

'I'm sorry, pet. Not today.'

'Aw, don't be sad. Maybe you'll catch one next time.'

He smiled wistfully as he picked her up and hugged her tightly.

Martha was standing beside the kitchen table and he shook his head at her. He noticed a fleeting look of disappointment when she turned to the sack of potatoes and took out a handful, placing them on the table.

He lowered Lottie to the floor, and she ran to the kitchen to tell her mother.

'He didn't catch one, but he will next time,' she said.

'Never mind, it's just as well we like taties, isn't it?' said Martha. 'How should we have them tonight? Should we mash them up with a bit of milk?'

'That's my favourite!' she squealed, and danced around the room.

Davey watched her, as he took off his coat and hung it up on the back of the door and then sat in his chair by the fire. He wished he could be as enthusiastic about having mashed potatoes for tea again. He wished he was bringing more money home so he could feed his family better, as well. What he wouldn't do for a plate of fresh vegetables and a bit of meat and gravy!

His earlier doubts about poaching soon subsided as he thought about how long it had been since his family had eaten a proper meal. He was sick of having no money and hardly anything to eat, and he vowed that he would go up onto the fell with Jack, and he'd do his best to fetch the bairns back something for their tea — hare, rabbit, or maybe even grouse.

Chapter 14

Burnside Hall Estate
April, 1881

On the third day of April, Ben was almost finished for the day when he decided to do a final check on the sheep that were due to lamb soon. He stood at the gate and looked over the flock; they all appeared calm.

'There's nothing happening yet, lass,' he said to Bess, who was sitting by his side.

He was about to turn away when he heard the weak bleat of a lamb.

'Looks like I spoke too soon. We'd better see what's going on.'

Ben opened the gate, went through and closed it behind him. He walked between the resting sheep, towards the far end of the field where he thought the sound had come from. A small, white lamb was lying on the ground, hardly moving. Its mother was nudging it with her nose, encouraging it to get onto its feet.

Ben picked up the lamb and rubbed it to help it to

breathe; he then placed it under his jacket and sat down, with his back against the wall. The ewe circled him, calling loudly for her baby. Ben's body heat warmed the lamb, and before long, it began moving against him and bleated. It was time to give her back to her mother.

'There you go,' he said, as he put the lamb under the ewe. The lamb nudged the ewe's belly until she found what she was looking for, and then suckled contentedly. 'You'll be fine now.'

As he made his way back to the gate, he recalled that Sir Thomas had always wanted to know when the first lamb was born, and he decided to take a detour to the Hall to tell Phyllis about the new arrival.

Ben stood at the large front door and rang the bell. Todd opened it almost immediately, and Ben asked to see Miss Forster. As the butler went to find her, Ben heard the sound of piano music — beautiful, soft music — coming from somewhere inside the house, and he was disappointed when it stopped. Todd returned to the door and showed Ben into the study.

'Good evening, Featherstone. What can I do for you?' greeted Phyllis.

'I thought you'd like to know that the first lamb has just been born. A pretty little gimmer. It needed a bit of help, but it'll be fine now.'

'Oh! Thank you. That is good news. I suppose you'll have a few busy weeks ahead of you now.'

'Aye, I will.'

'You've worked here for some time, I believe.'

'Since I was sixteen.'

'Then you know what's involved. That's reassuring because this is all new to me.'

'Don't worry, Miss Forster. I'll take care of the sheep.' He smiled at her, and then he heard himself say, 'Was that you playing the piano when I came to the door?'

'Yes, it was.'

'It was beautiful. You're a very accomplished player.'

He noticed that her cheeks turned red at his compliment.

'Thank you. It was a sonata by Mozart, it's actually one of my favourite pieces.'

'Well, it was lovely. Anyway, I'd better go and get a good night's sleep,' said Ben. 'There might be more lambs by the mornin'.'

Phyllis walked him to the door but, before they reached it, they heard a loud knock. Todd strode past them and opened the door, and then turned to Phyllis, and said, 'It's the census enumerator, Miss. Shall I have Mrs Gibson see to him?'

'The census enumerator,' she repeated. 'I read about that in the paper. Yes, Mrs Gibson will be able to give him the information that he needs. Take him through to the kitchen. Oh, do you know if he's been to Shepherd's Cottage yet?'

Todd went back to the door and returned a moment

later, and said, 'The gentleman called there on his way here but there was no answer at the door.

'You'd better speak to him first, Featherstone,' she said. 'Go to the kitchen with them, and I'll see you tomorrow. Goodnight, and thank you again.'

'Goodnight, Miss Forster.'

Ben followed Todd and the enumerator into the kitchen, and sat at the table, watching the gentleman open a large book and set out his pen and ink.

'Your address is Shepherd's Cottage, Burnside Estate, Eastgate,' stated the gentleman.

Ben nodded.

'What's your full name?'

'Benjamin Featherstone.'

He wrote that in his book before asking, 'How old are you?'

'Twenty-one. I'll be twenty-two at the end of the month.'

'Are you married?'

'No.'

'Your occupation, I assume, is a shepherd?'

'Aye, that's right.'

'And where were you born?'

'Up at Lanehead.'

Ben saw that he wrote 'Stanhope, County Durham' in very neat writing in the last column of the book.

'And you live alone?'

'Yes. Yes, I do. Unless you count me dog?' Ben said,

with a laugh.

'No, that's quite alright. Thank you.'

Ben stood up to collect his food from Miss Wilson and Mrs Gibson took his place at the table. He didn't envy her having to answer all those questions for everyone living under the roof at Burnside Hall.

The enumerator said, 'Right, could we start with the owner of the house?'

As Ben left, he heard Mrs Gibson say, 'That would be Miss Forster — Miss Phyllis Margaret Forster, is her full name, and she's 28 years old.'

Ben walked slowly back to the cottage with a smile on his face. He was pleased with the way the day had turned out; the first lamb born that season had survived, and when he'd told Phyllis about it, he'd surprised himself when he'd asked her about the piano music, but she didn't seem to mind talking to him. When they'd first met, he'd thought Phyllis was severe but, since then, he'd noticed that her harsh exterior was gradually crumbling away, and tonight he had seen a different side to her altogether — a softer side. And she wasn't all that much older than him, really.

Chapter 15

Burnside Hall Estate
April, 1881

Ben swung the axe at a large log with such strength that it split in two, the pieces landing several yards apart. He'd dreamt about his sister, Kate, again last night, and she'd seemed so real, until he'd reached out to touch her and she had disappeared into thin air. He'd woken with such a start, covered in sweat, and feeling angry that their Kate had been taken from them. She'd been so young — younger than he was now. The anger was overwhelming and he'd had to get outside and take out his rage on something. That had been over an hour ago.

He picked up another log and swung the axe once more. As he collected the pieces, he heard hoofbeats coming along the path towards him. He put down the axe and took a deep breath; it wouldn't do to be seen in the state he was in. As he watched the water in the river flow slowly downstream, he began to feel calmer, and he wondered who would be out riding this early in the morning. The sun had only risen about half an hour ago and it was still low in the sky.

Samson appeared on the path and trotted towards him, without a rider. Ben quickly took in that the horse was saddled and bridled, which meant Phyllis must have fallen. When the horse got close enough, he reached out and grabbed the reins, pulling him to a stop. Ben quickly loosened the girth and removed the side saddle, placing it inside his cottage for safe-keeping, then leapt onto Samson's back and turned him back down the path to search for Phyllis. He hoped she was alright.

Ben followed the tracks left by Samson's muddy hooves, which led him into the woods. The horse carefully stepped over small branches lying on the ground, and Ben leaned low over his neck, to avoid hitting his head on low hanging branches as he wound his way through the trees.

'Miss Forster!' Ben shouted, and listened carefully for a reply, but there was none. He kept following the tracks, making slow progress through the dense undergrowth. After a while, they reached a woodland track, and Samson whinnied and pulled at his bit. Ben let him increase his stride to a canter, now that it seemed safe to do so, but it wasn't long before they slowed down again as a large tree trunk came into view. It had fallen across the track, completely blocking their path. Samson adjusted his stride and prepared to jump, but Ben pulled him up sharply.

'No, you don't lad,' he said, as the hunter stopped with a snort. 'She might be able to take you over that, but not me.'

He found a way around the obstacle, and they continued on their way. A little further on, he saw another tree trunk lying across the track, and slowed Samson to a walk.

'Miss Forster!' he called again.

'Featherstone? Is that you?'

He jumped off the horse and climbed over the fallen tree. Phyllis was sitting on the ground, with her back against the mossy trunk.

'What's wrong?' he asked, as he went to her side.

'I've hurt my leg. I can't put any weight on it.'

He looked down at her legs, covered by her long skirts.

'Is it broken?' he asked.

'I don't think so. How could I tell?'

She looked up at him, her eyes pleading with him to help her. Had she been a friend or family member, he would have run his capable hands over the injured leg to feel for a break, but his cheeks coloured at the thought of running his hands over Phyllis's leg.

He cleared his throat, before saying, 'Sometimes you can tell by feeling it.'

He turned his head away as she felt under her skirt.

'It's my knee,' she said. 'It feels swollen, but I don't think there's anything broken. Would you check it for me?'

When Ben turned around, he saw that she had raised her skirt to just above her knee. He swallowed deeply, and then knelt on the ground next to her. He placed one hand on each side of her leg and felt the joint. She winced at his touch, and he quickly removed his hands.

'Is it broken?' she asked.

'No, I don't think so. We need to get you home so the doctor can check it out and strap it up for you. If I help you up onto the horse, do you think you could ride back?'

'No! It hurts too much. I'm not sure I could even keep my balance, never mind control a horse like Samson.'

'We're a few miles from the Hall,' said Ben, trying to work out the best way to get her home. 'I'll have to ride back with you.'

Ben lifted Phyllis up onto Samson's back, and then used the tree trunk as a mounting block so he could climb up behind her. He placed an arm around her waist to hold her still, took the reins in his other hand, and urged the horse to walk on. He felt Phyllis lean back against him with her head on his shoulder, and she relaxed in his hold. The silence felt strange, with them being so close, and he was pleased when Phyllis started to talk.

'I wasn't concentrating back there. I misjudged the jump. Somehow Samson got over it, but he landed badly, and I fell forward over his neck. Luckily, he didn't trample me.'

Ben grimaced, and involuntarily tightened his hold on Phyllis; this young woman could easily have lost her life that morning. 'Aye, that was lucky,' he said.

'I thought I would be there for hours before anyone came to find me. How did you know I'd fallen?'

'Samson came trotting past my place. I knew there was something wrong when he was saddled up and you weren't with him. So, I followed his tracks back to you.'

'Thank you. I'm very grateful.'

'You're welcome. In case you're wondering, I took the saddle off. It's at my place.'

'I've never seen a man ride side-saddle.'

Ben could feel her laugh as she leaned back against him, and he thought it felt good to have a woman in his arms. She was soft, and warm, and her hair smelt of flowers. Some protective instinct made him want to hold her, to keep her safe and secure.

He even began to wonder if his life might be better if he did find a wife, like his mother kept telling him. He smiled to himself — his mother was always right; he'd never known anyone as wise as Lizzie Featherstone.

Ben pulled Samson to a halt outside the grounds of the Hall.

'I'll get off here,' he said, 'and lead Samson into the yard. It's better that we're not seen riding together.'

Phyllis hesitated, before saying, 'Yes, that's probably a good idea. I should be able to manage.'

He didn't want to let go of her, but he loosened his grip and slid down Samson's side. As he pulled the reins over the horse's head, he looked up into her eyes. 'Hold onto his mane,' he said gently, 'I don't want you to fall.'

When they entered the yard, Todd ran out of the house towards them.

'What's wrong, Miss?'

'I fell off Samson, and Featherstone found me. He was kind enough to help me home.'

'Thank you, Featherstone,' said the butler. 'You may go now.'

'But I can't walk, Todd. I've hurt my knee. How will I get into the house?' asked Phyllis.

Looking around, Todd said, 'I don't think I can manage to get you inside on my own. Perhaps Featherstone could give me a hand?'

Ben looked up at Phyllis, and for the first time, he saw her smile. She looked years younger when she smiled. She held out her arms, so that he could help her down from her horse. He went over to her, and she put her arms around his broad shoulders. He lifted her down and carried her straight into the house, not waiting for Todd's assistance.

'Where would you like me to take you?' Ben asked, suddenly feeling a surge of embarrassment when he realised that he was carrying a woman across the threshold of her home.

'Go straight ahead along here, and then it's the door to the right — the music room. On the chair by the window, please.'

He lowered her gently into the chair, with her holding

onto him for support. When she was seated, he asked, 'Will you be alright now?'

'Yes, thank you, Featherstone. You may go,' she said with a wave of her hand.

Her voice sounded formal again, and her easy dismissal of him hurt after what he'd done for her, but then he noticed the reason for her sudden change — Todd and Mrs Gibson were standing behind him.

'We've sent Richardson to fetch the doctor, Miss. Is there anything you'd like in the meantime? A cup of tea, perhaps?' asked the housekeeper.

As Ben turned to leave, he noticed the view from the music room window. From her favourite seat, Phyllis could see the lambing fields, the meadows, and the fell, in fact all the places where Ben tended the sheep. He wondered if she sat there and watched him while he worked.

The following morning, Phyllis's knee was swollen and painful, so she sat on her chair in the music room with her feet on a cushioned stool. The doctor had confirmed that there were no bones broken and had advised her to rest it until it recovered. As much as it hurt, she could do little else. She chuckled to herself as she remembered her attempt at coming downstairs that morning, which had resulted in her sliding down the steps on her bottom. She was thankful that nobody had been around at the time to see her.

A book lay open on her lap, unread. Her mind kept drifting back to the ride home with Ben, his firm body supporting her back, his strong arm holding her tight against him, making her feel safe and secure. She'd had so little contact with people that she'd forgotten how good it felt to be held by someone, knowing that they cared. Her eyes scoured the hillside for any sign of him, the slightest movement making her heart skip a beat, but as yet, she hadn't seen him.

'Miss, there's a note for you,' Mrs Gibson, said from the doorway. She walked over to Phyllis and handed it to her.

'Thank you.'

'It's a couple of hours since you had a cold cloth on your knee. Shall I prepare another one?'

'Yes please, the doctor said it would help.'

The housekeeper left the room, and Phyllis turned her attention to the note, which she opened and read. The writing was child-like, with large letters badly formed.

I saw you with him.
£10 to keep me quiet.
Hide it under the white stile.
Don't tell the police or you'll be sorry.

Phyllis read the words over and over again. It took a while for her to realise that someone must have seen her with Ben when they were riding Samson, and they were trying to blackmail her. Was it a joke? If so, it wasn't very funny. But if it was a genuine threat, she wondered who could do such a thing?

Thinking back, they must have been seen very early in the morning, and there was rarely anyone in the woods at that time. The fields that they'd ridden across could possibly be seen from the road, and also from the Hall, and both sides of the valley looked down onto them. Could they have been recognised from that distance? She thought it was ironic that Ben had dismounted before they'd reached the yard, the busiest part of the property, so that they wouldn't be seen riding together.

Although a little unsettled by the note, Phyllis wasn't unduly worried at first. There'd been a good reason for Ben and her riding together — a member of her staff had merely helped her home after she'd been injured. If the blackmailer spread gossip, she asked herself, what harm could it do?

She told herself that it could ruin her reputation and make marriage even less likely than it already was, and it could damage her family's reputation still further. Also, Ben's name being linked with hers could be detrimental to him, and he didn't deserve that after he'd come to her rescue.

While her knee was so sore, there was nothing she could do, but she decided that as soon as it was healed, she would go to the stile and leave ten pounds for the blackmailer, providing that the gossip had not already been spread by then.

As Mrs Gibson returned with a towel, soaked in cold

water, Phyllis placed the note inside her book and closed it, then lifted her skirt so Mrs Gibson could place the compress on her damaged knee. Mrs Gibson went to fetch her some dinner and Phyllis resumed her watch over the hillside.

Chapter 16

Eastgate Fell, Weardale
May, 1881

The vastness of open fell always surprised Davey, who spent most of his days underground in constricted mine tunnels. He stood and surveyed the landscape around him in wonder. There were valleys and ridges as far as the eye could see and he wondered if the furthest hills might even be in Scotland, they were so far away.

'Don't just stand there,' said Jack, who carried a shotgun in his right hand. 'You should be looking out for grouse an' hares an' stuff.'

They made their way across the deserted moorland, and Davey thought to himself that maybe Jack had been right. There was only one gamekeeper on the Burnside estate, so the chances of running into him were slim, especially on a Sunday afternoon; it was more than likely his day off.

A movement caught Davey's eye.

'Over there!' he whispered to Jack.

Jack walked stealthily towards the disturbance and stopped sharp when he saw something in a clearing up ahead. Davey caught up with him. Just a few yards ahead, four male black grouse squared up to each other, and ran at each other time and time again, hissing what sounded to Davey like the words, 'How? Why? How? Why?'

The blue-black feathers of the birds shone in the sunlight, the red patches on their faces looked like devilish eyes, and their white tails were fanned out behind them. These magnificent creatures, so intent on impressing the greyhens, were oblivious to the immediate threat posed by the two men who watched the lek in silence.

Jack raised the shotgun and pointed it towards the largest cock bird, and placed his finger on the trigger, ready to squeeze. Davey looked at the beautiful birds with regret, but then he remembered that he had a family to feed. He looked away and closed his eyes, and then he heard a loud bang and smelled gunpowder.

When he looked into the clearing, all of the grouse had disappeared into the cover of bracken and heather, and there were no dead birds lying on the ground.

'Did you miss it?' he asked.

'No. I saw a hare and went for that instead. I've never been keen on grouse anyway. The lords and ladies are welcome to them,' Jack scoffed. 'Come on — it's over here.'

Davey followed his brother across the slope, picked up

the dead hare and slung it over his shoulder. They continued in search of another.

It seemed to Davey that they'd walked for hours without seeing any more game of any sort, and wondered if the sound of the gunshot had made all the wildlife for miles around go to ground. 'We're wasting our time up here,' he said. 'Let's head back.'

They were quietly making their way down the hillside when they heard a gunshot. They looked around and saw the silhouette of a man standing on the horizon behind them, aiming a shotgun in their direction. They fled as quickly as they could down the rough slope, heading for the woodland that bordered a small burn. Although the trees would slow their pace, they'd also give them cover.

The brothers walked as quickly as they could downstream to the valley bottom, and then followed the river back up to Westgate, all the while staying out of sight as much as possible. They were fairly certain that the gamekeeper was no longer following them, but they were careful just in case. Davey was startled by a wood pigeon flying clumsily out of a tree, and he dropped the hare. This, under normal circumstances, would have had Jack in fits of laughter, but he just said, 'Hurry up, Davey, man.'

Jack called in at a small cottage and dropped off the shotgun he'd borrowed from a drinking mate, and then the brothers took the hare back to Davey's house. The smile on Lottie's face melted Davey's heart. His wife took the hare to prepare for the oven, and he removed his jacket and cap and hung them on a hook beside the front door.

As Davey walked his brother out, he said, 'Bring Beth and the bairn over tonight.'

'Are you sure?'

'Yes, you're more than welcome to join us for tea.'

They heard a horse on the road approaching at speed, and it slowed to a trot as it got closer. They both turned to look. It was the gamekeeper from the Burnside estate, and he had a shotgun attached to his saddle.

'Stay calm,' said Davey to his brother.

The man looked at them suspiciously as he passed.

'How do?' said Davey. 'What's the rush?'

'You haven't seen two men pass here, have you? One carrying a gun.'

'No. I'd remember seeing someone with a gun. You didn't pass anyone on the way over here, did you Jack?'

'No. I've just come through the village and I didn't see anyone.'

'Bugger! They must have gone down Stanhope way.' He turned his horse and cantered away in the direction from which he'd just come.

'Thank God, he didn't recognise us!' said Jack.

'Aye, that was a close one, but it'll be worth it tonight when we have some meat on our plates.'

'You're making me mouth water just thinking about it! I can't remember the last time I had meat for me tea.'

'Never mind, we'll eat like kings tonight.' Davey patted his brother's shoulder, and then watched him walk up the street to his house, whistling to himself.

Chapter 17

Burnside Hall
May, 1881

As the sun shone through the large windows directly onto the breakfast table, Phyllis decided that she must go out today, it was too nice a day to stay indoors, but she wasn't sure whether she should spend the day visiting Connie or taking Samson up onto the fell for a long ride. Although it hadn't been a serious injury, it had taken several weeks for her knee to recover from the fall, and it had been almost a month since her horse had been exercised properly; he was growing restless in the stable. As a compromise, she decided that she would go onto the fell first and then call at Springbank Farm on the way home, as a visit was well overdue. Whenever she thought about Connie being cooped up in the farmhouse, she pictured a wild animal pacing backwards and forwards in a cage, getting more and more frustrated by its captivity. And there was something else that she needed to do too.

Phyllis asked Todd to make sure Samson was ready for

her to leave at ten o'clock and, when she went out into the yard, the groom was walking the horse out of the stable, fully tacked up. She used the mounting block to get onto the large hunter, and thanked Thompson before riding out of the yard.

She made a slight detour to the riverside path and stopped by a large white stile that straddled a dry-stone wall. Sliding off Samson, she went to the wall and saw that there was a loose stone behind the stile, and she lifted it out. There was a piece of paper in the gap, with the words 'Thank you' written on it. She deposited the money in the hole and replaced the stone, looking in both directions to check if she was being watched, but she couldn't see anybody. She used the steps of the stile to help her mount her horse and then headed off towards the fell.

It really was a beautiful morning — the sky was blue, with just a few high clouds floating ever so slowly over the hills. The sunlight made the natural colours vibrant — the green of the grass interspersed with yellow buttercups and small white daisies; the new leaves freshly opened on the trees; the sandstone of the dry-stone walls with patches of pale lichen that looked like splotches of paint. The slow-flowing water in the burn reflected the light like a mirror, making it impossible to see beneath the surface.

Phyllis smiled when she noticed the cows grazing contentedly in their fields, while calves pranced around them in play. There was a slight breeze, but no dampness in the air, as there so often was in Weardale. It felt good to be back in the saddle and out in the fresh air.

The fell looked greener than usual because so much rain had fallen in the spring, and there were dark patches of burnt ground on the hillside where the gamekeeper had set fire to old woody heather so that new shoots could grow to provide food for the grouse chicks that would be hatching soon.

Phyllis spotted Ben and his dog walking down from the highest peak, and she guessed that their paths would cross in a few minutes. She considered turning back, or taking another route, but decided that she really should thank him for helping her after her fall, so she continued on her way, not sure why she felt awkward about meeting him again.

'Morning, Miss Forster. It's a grand day!' said Ben.

'Good morning, Featherstone. It's lovely, isn't it?'

'I'm pleased to see you out riding again. Your knee must be better now?' he asked, looking towards her leg that was covered by her thick velvet skirt.

'Yes, thank you. I've missed going out these last few weeks. By the way, I must thank you for searching for me that day, and for being kind enough to help me home.' She blushed slightly as she remembered sitting so close to him on her horse, and feeling the heat and strength of his body against her back.

'I had to find you. I couldn't have left you out there, not

knowing if you were hurt...or worse,' he said, and then looked away quickly.

She noticed the sudden change in his voice and saw the sadness in his eyes, and wondered what she'd said to upset him.

'Well, I'm very grateful to you,' she replied.

'You're welcome.' His gaze was still directed to the hillside just above the track. He turned back to her, and said, 'You must have spent a lot of time up here when you were younger. Have you noticed that strange stone up there?'

'No, I don't think so. There are quite a lot of boulders lying around.'

'This one's different. It has carvings on it.'

'No, I don't recall seeing it.'

'It's just up here, if you'd like to have a look.'

Phyllis nodded her head, dismounted and, leading Samson by the reins, she followed Ben up the hillside until they reached what she would call a small boulder that protruded from the bank top.

She watched in wonder as Ben pushed back the heather and revealed the ancient circular markings and grooves, carved in stone.

'It's wonderful! Did you engrave it?' she asked.

'No, not me. If the cuts were new, the edges would be crisp and sharp, but look.' He ran his fingers over the pattern on the rock, and she did the same. 'They're weathered and smooth, showing its age.'

'Then who did carve it?' she asked.

'The men that lived here long ago — maybe the ones that lived in the caves, or the ones that dug the first mines. I don't suppose we'll ever know for sure.'

She looked more closely at the young man standing by her side, and wondered at how perceptive he was for his years; he was so in tune with his surroundings: the hills; the weather; and the animals. He wasn't like any man she had ever met before, and she found him intriguing.

Realising that she was staring, she looked away, and said hastily, 'I'm going to visit Connie Milburn this morning, so I'd better be on my way.'

Ben was still looking at the intricate patterns, but her voice broke the spell, and he suddenly blurted out, 'You're nothing like Henry.'

Phyllis stepped back and the colour drained from her face. Nobody had mentioned Henry to her since she had returned home — nobody — and now Ben had dared to speak her brother's name out loud.

'Whatever made you say that?' she asked abruptly.

'You mentioned Connie Milburn. What your brother did affected so many of us — your family, the Pearts, my family...'

'Your family? How, may I ask, did Henry affect your family?'

'You don't know, do you?' He looked at her and waited for a response, but when she remained silent, he continued. 'The girl that worked in your house, the one that was found dead in the mine, she was me sister. Your brother murdered our Kate.'

Phyllis recoiled in horror but her eyes remained fixed on Ben. She had tried so hard to forget what her brother had done, but how could she when horrific scenes haunted her dreams night after night?

'I'm so sorry,' she said weakly.

'It's not your fault. You're not your brother. You're not to blame for what he did.'

She looked away for a moment, and when she turned back to him, there were tears in her eyes, and she said, 'The way people look at me sometimes, I think they hate me for what he did.'

'Don't take any notice of them. That's all in the past now, and there's nothing we can do to change what happened. We have to move on — although, God knows, it's hard.'

Phyllis could see that Ben was suffering too, and knew that she had found a kindred spirit, someone who understood how she felt. She smiled at him, as she led her horse back to the track.

'Would you like a hand up?' Ben asked.

'Yes, please.

Ben helped Phyllis back onto her horse, and then she looked down at him and said, 'The gamekeeper told me he saw two men poaching up here. They had a shotgun. Would you keep a look out for them?'

'Aye, I will,' he said, but he didn't mean it. Although he

knew that people shouldn't take what wasn't rightfully theirs, the miners in the villages were getting desperate, and their families were close to starving. And he'd done the same thing as a boy; he'd gone out hunting with his lurcher and had often brought back a rabbit or a hare for tea. He was sympathetic to the miners' plight, and he wondered if Phyllis, or any landowner, would really miss a bit of game.

Ben watched as she rode into the distance, and lifted a hand in farewell as she turned back to look at him.

Half an hour later, Phyllis entered the yard at Springbank Farm and spotted Joe by the barn door, talking to one of the twins that worked for him. Joe shouted, 'Hello, Phyllis! Connie will be pleased to see you. She's bored out of her mind in there.'

Phyllis dismounted, and was about to tether Samson, but Joe took the reins from her, and said, 'I'll see to him. You go on in.'

'Thanks, Joe.'

Phyllis walked quickly to the door, eager to see her friend, and when she went in, she found Connie sat at the kitchen table with a newspaper spread out in front of her. Connie stood up and hugged her friend.

'Thank God, you've come at last. I know you haven't been home long, but I've missed you all the same.'

'I meant to come sooner, but I took a tumble off Samson about a month ago and hurt my knee. Today's the first day I've been out since.'

'Yes, I got your note. It's good to see you back on your feet. We make a right pair, don't we?' laughed Connie.

A maid appeared in the doorway, and looked uncomfortable when she saw that her mistress had a visitor.

'Don't just stand there with your mouth open, girl, put the kettle on and make a pot of tea.' Turning to Phyllis, she rolled her eyes and said, 'She's new, and she has so much to learn.'

Phyllis noticed the maid's cheeks turn red at Connie's harsh words, and she couldn't understand why Connie hadn't waited until the girl had left the room before commenting on her inadequacies. Perhaps her lack of judgement was due to her pregnancy? Although she couldn't remember Connie being polite to the maids at Springbank Farm in all the time that she'd known her.

'Come and sit in the parlour, and we can catch up on everything that's happened. How on earth did you fall off Samson? He has a back like an armchair!'

Phyllis followed Connie into the parlour, and the young girl brought in a tea tray. Phyllis told her about the accident, and mentioned that Ben had found her, but didn't tell Connie about riding back in his arms. She thought her friend would be shocked that she'd enjoyed being held by a humble shepherd, but then again, Joe had been a tenant farmer before he'd married Connie. Was that much different to a shepherd? Anyway, she didn't tell Connie about it because she wanted to keep the memories of that day to herself.

'So, how are you, Connie, really?'

'Honestly? I'm bored to tears. I've never enjoyed doing any of the things that women are supposed to do indoors — reading, embroidery, and such like. All I've ever wanted to do is ride horses.'

'But you have to think of the baby.'

'I know.' Connie put her hand on her abdomen and felt the small curve of her belly. 'I'm four months gone,' she said with a smile. 'That's longer than any of the others...'

'That's good!' said Phyllis, not wanting Connie to dwell on the babies she'd lost.

'Joe's grinning like a madman half the time, and fussing around me like a mother hen the rest of the time.' Connie laughed, and then turning serious, she said, 'I just hope I can give him the son he wants this time.'

'I hope so, too,' Phyllis said sincerely.

'And what about you? Any luck finding a man yet?'

'No.'

'You liar,' Connie chuckled. 'You're blushing. Spill the beans!'

'Unfortunately, you're mistaken. There isn't anyone.'

'I don't believe that. You've never been good at telling lies, Phyllis. Why won't you tell me about him? Is he married?'

'No, he's not married!' said Phyllis indignantly.

'Ah, so I was right. There is someone.'

Connie had always been good at wheedling out information from people, and Phyllis was no match for her, but she couldn't possibly tell Connie about the man who was on her mind — she could hardly admit it to herself. Not only was there a difference in their classes, but there was also a significant difference in age — she must be almost ten years his senior. And after his revelation that morning, she knew that he had every reason to hate her.

'Please Phyllis, tell me who he is, and how you met. I've had nothing to occupy my mind for ages. An exciting love story is exactly what I need to hear.'

'Let's just say that he's somebody I can never have, even though he's not married, so I must put him out of my mind.'

'This is getting more intriguing by the minute.' Connie was beaming. 'But I'm pleased somebody's caught your eye at last.'

Phyllis started to clear the tea things, but Connie realised that she was creating a diversion. 'Put those down. The girl can do that. Please explain what's going on. You never know, I might be able to help.'

Phyllis sat back in the winged armchair and looked up at the ornate ceiling, and whispered, 'If only you could.'

'Try me.'

Phyllis looked at Connie. This woman had been her only friend in all the years she'd spent in Weardale. If she couldn't confide in her, who could she confide in? What harm could it do? So long as she didn't mention his name.

'There's an age difference.'

'Oh! By how much?'

'I'm not sure. Somewhere between five and ten years, I'd guess.'

'That's nothing! I've heard of men over fifty marrying girls still in their teens.'

'Me too, but it's different when the woman is older than the man, don't you think?'

'He's younger than you!' Connie could hardly contain her excitement at that titbit.

Phyllis nodded, and said, 'And that's not all. He's a working-class man.'

Connie sat back in her chair, speechless.

'I told you it could never work, so let's not talk about it anymore, please.'

'Phyllis, I'm so sorry. You know you must find someone else, don't you? It couldn't possibly work out for the two of you.'

Looking away sadly, Phyllis said, 'Yes, I know.'

As Phyllis left the farmhouse, she promised to call again soon. Joe stood by his wife in the doorway, with one arm around her thickening waist, looking so proud. Phyllis was envious of the couple. They had everything that anyone could ever want — a nice house, land, plenty of money, each other, and a baby on the way. Phyllis wondered if she would ever find a partner with whom she could be as happy.

Chapter 18

Burnside Hall
May, 1881

Phyllis was sitting in the office with the account ledger open in front of her, recording the monthly expenditure for the estate, when she was interrupted by a knock at the door. Todd came in, and announced, 'Reverend Dagnall is here to see you, Miss.'

'Oh! I wasn't expecting him today. Show him into the drawing room, and ask Mrs Gibson to take in a tray of tea and biscuits. I'll be there in a moment.'

He nodded and closed the door on his way out. She listened to them moving through the hallway, chatting politely. She finished the entry that she was writing up and blotted the ink before receiving her visitor.

'Good morning,' she said, as she entered the room.

The vicar stood up and offered her his hand, which she shook firmly. 'Good morning. Thank you for seeing me when I've called unannounced.'

'It's my pleasure.'

'With being new in Weardale, I thought it would be nice to get to know my parishioners better. It would be useful to glean an understanding of the area, the people, their way of life, et cetera.'

'That's very considerate of you.'

'I must say, I'm sorry if I upset you when we met at the church. I wasn't aware that you'd just lost your father, and I rather put my foot in it, didn't I?'

'There's no way you could have known.'

'I felt so dreadful when I found out.'

She desperately wanted to change the subject because she still found it difficult to talk about her father, and she suspected that that was where the conversation was heading. The vicar's interest in the cave at Heathery Burn sprang to mind, and gave her the perfect opportunity to divert his attention from her loss.

'There is something that I would like to confide in you, but you must promise me that you'll keep it a secret.'

'That sounds most interesting! And if you can't trust a man of the cloth, who can you trust?' he said, with a chuckle.

'You'll be aware that caves form in limestone, and that there is a lot of limestone around here. We actually have a limestone quarry here on the estate, and the quarrymen have just come across a cave in it.'

She noticed his eyes widen, so she continued. 'And the most exciting part is that a bead was found on the cave floor, so it appears that it was inhabited at one time.'

'That is exciting! Do you think I could I see it?'

'Of course. Wait here, and I'll bring it down.'

Phyllis went to her bedroom and retrieved the bead from a drawer in her dressing table. The vicar was on his feet when she returned to the drawing room, and he crossed the room with long strides to meet her in the doorway. She held out the bead, which he took, and he then returned to the window and held it up to the light, closed an eye, and examined it closely. He made a few appreciative noises, before saying, 'Well, this is very surprising. Over two hundred items were discovered in the cave at Stanhope, but only two of them were gold.' Handing the bead back to her, he said, 'I can't wait to see what else will be discovered in this cave. Perhaps there'll be more gold!'

'I did wonder that myself, and that's why I want this to be kept quiet. I don't want any treasure hunters snooping around the place.'

'My friends from Oxford, the archaeology group I told you about, are coming to Weardale for the summer. They'd love to see this,' he said, holding up the bead, 'and the cave where it was found. Perhaps they could even do a dig there.'

'A dig?'

'Yes, they search for ancient artefacts underground.'

'Oh, I see. That would be wonderful.'

'In terms of archaeology, is there anything else in Weardale that my friends might like to see while they're here?'

She thought for a moment and nothing obvious came to mind, and then she remembered the stone on the fell that Ben had shown her.

'Well, actually there is something. On the fell above Eastgate, there's a rock that's carved with strange circles. I was told that it must be very old.'

'Really! You must tell me where it is so I can take a look myself.'

Mrs Gibson came in with the tray, and poured two cups of tea.

'Would you like a biscuit?' asked Phyllis.

'I am rather hungry, and they do look delicious.'

Mrs Gibson placed two biscuits on a plate and handed it to the vicar.

'Thank you.'

'And for you, Miss?'

'No, thank you.'

When Mrs Gibson left, Phyllis said, 'After you've finished your tea, if you can spare the time, why don't we take a walk and I'll show you the stone?'

Reverend Dagnall looked at her in surprise, and said, 'Why! That would be delightful.'

As they walked up the hillside, the vicar asked a lot of questions about Weardale, and Phyllis was pleased to answer them. As the stone came into view, she pointed it out to him. He knelt on the ground next to it, pushed the vegetation to one side with his hand, and sat and stared at it.

'What do you think?' asked Phyllis. 'Is it old?'

'It's truly magnificent. Several of these have been found on the moors in Northumberland and Yorkshire. It's believed they were carved by the pagans before Christianity came to this country, so yes, it's very old indeed.'

'I think it's beautiful.'

'I wonder what purpose it served?' he asked, more to himself than Phyllis. 'I must come back to sketch it. Would you mind?'

'No, of course not.'

'Thank you.'

They made their way back down to the valley bottom, where they went their separate ways — the vicar went up the road to Westgate, and Phyllis down the road to Burnside Hall.

Chapter 19

Davey Bell stood in the shadows between the miners' cottages. He'd been waiting nearly an hour for his brother to show up, and his patience was wearing thin. He could have been tucked up in bed with Martha, but instead he'd agreed to go to the quarry with Jack, who was desperate to have a look inside the cave to see if there was any treasure in there.

Damn the mine owners! If it hadn't been for them closing the mines, Jack would never have considered doing this. Since he'd got the job at the quarry, the family were coping better than before, but Jack knew the job was just temporary and that he'd be unemployed again soon.

With Jack being the only night watchman on the site, there was little risk of them getting caught, but Davey was well aware that what they were going to do was wrong. At the very least it was trespass and, if they took anything of value, it would be theft; their parents had brought them up better than that. He hoped that there was nothing there for them to find and that they'd return home empty-handed.

He heard footsteps approaching, and slunk back against the house wall until he could make sure that it was his brother walking across the road towards him.

'Are you there, Davey?' Jack whispered.

'Aye, I've been waiting ages. Where've you been?'

'Sorry, I lost track of the time. Come on, we'd better get a move on.'

They crept through the village and set off up the hill, seeing nobody on their way. When they arrived at the quarry, the craggy rock face glowed eerily in the moonlight, and Davey had a strong urge to turn back.

Jack pointed to a patch of blackness about twenty feet above the ground. 'That's the cave,' he said. He took Davey's arm and led him to the workmen's hut, where several ladders were lying flat on the ground. Together, they picked up a long wooden ladder and carried it to the quarry face, where they stood it upright and wedged it in place with large rocks so it wouldn't fall, and then they climbed up in silence, Jack leading the way. When they got to the cave entrance, they stepped onto the ledge and lit a candle before going into the pitch-black hole. The cave walls were surprisingly smooth and the floor was covered with brown muddy silt. Davey thought it wasn't unlike mine workings in some respects, but in others, it was very different. Mines were built by engineers, and the tunnels were dug on a slight incline so that ground water drained out, whereas caves were created by running water that exploited weaknesses in the rock on its race to return to the water level. Davey and Jack were hardened miners, but they were cautious in this unfamiliar subterranean environment. Locally, caves were known as fairy holes, and superstitions abounded about them. Who knew what you might stumble across if you went inside?

About ten yards from the entrance, Jack pointed out an area where the silt had been disturbed, and said, 'Let's have a look here.'

Jack took out a small fire shovel from his coat pocket and scraped away the sediment, layer by layer, while Davey held the tallow candle above his head. The initial excitement slowly ebbed away until they were almost on the point of leaving, but then Jack spotted something glinting in the flickering light. He took a handful of earth and ran it through his fingers until he found what he was looking for — a small gold bead.

The brothers looked at each other in surprise, and Jack laughed out loud. He said, 'I knew they'd found somethin' up here when they took on a night watchman, but I never thought that it'd be gold.' He put the bead in his pocket.

Davey stood back and leaned against the damp wall. He could understand why his brother was so happy to find a piece of gold, even a small piece, because he could sell it with no questions asked. But he was also aware that they had crossed a line; stealing was a serious crime.

He watched Jack digging in the sludge, hoping to find more, and after what he guessed was about quarter of an hour, the iron shovel made a dull noise when it came into contact with something solid.

'I've found something!' Jack exclaimed.

Not wanting to damage whatever it was that lay hidden under the silt, Jack slowed down and dug more carefully, scraping away the dirt with his hands until he felt something hard and round that was set firmly into the ground.

'Show us a light over here. I can't see what it is.'

Davey moved closer and held the candle right above the hole in the ground, and looked down. Both men jumped back in fright, and Jack shrieked. In the hole was a human skull, with large empty eye sockets staring right back at them, unseeing.

Jack quickly got to his feet and ran for the ladder, with Davey right on his heels, and they slid down the ladder without using the rungs to get to the bottom as fast as they could, and then they ran out of the quarry and onto the track.

'Great idea that was!' said Davey sarcastically, as he walked quickly down the hill. 'We go looking for treasure and end up disturbing the bloody dead!'

'The dead can't hurt you.'

'I'm not so sure about that. We'll be cursed for what we just did,' said Davey, his eyes wide with fear, 'you mark my words!'

'Don't be so daft.'

'They'll know someone's been in the cave because we left the ladder there, and we didn't cover that... that thing back up.'

'You worry too much.'

'They'll know it was you, Jack, because you're supposed to be guarding the site. You should go back and cover our tracks.'

'Huh! I'm not going anywhere near that place. Anyway, if I'm on duty, how can I explain that somebody got into the cave? I'll just have to make up an excuse — I'll say I was called back home because the baby was poorly, or something. If I wasn't there, anyone could have gone in.'

'I hate all this lying,' said Davey. 'I wish I'd never agreed to go with you in the first place.'

'Well, it's too late for that. Anyway, I'll split the money with you.'

'I don't want it. I want nothing more to do with it,' said Davey, shaking his head.

Davey had never felt as uneasy about anything in all his life, not even on the morning of his wedding, or during the births of his children. He thought he might throw up. He wanted to get home and climb into bed and hold his wife, and pretend that none of this had happened. A shiver ran down his spine. Looking down at the track, he noticed that the cobbles were sparkling in the moonlight.

'Look at that! It's almost summer and there's a frost! That must be a sign of somethin'?' said Davey.

'Don't start with all that superstitious nonsense. We're not cursed!'

At Westgate, the men separated and when Davey got home, he locked the door behind him, something he rarely did. Tonight though, he felt unsettled and knew he wouldn't sleep if the door was unlocked, although he didn't know if a door was enough to keep out spirits. He wished they'd had a garden next to the house, with room to plant a rowan tree, like his parents used to have. His mother had told him that they protected houses from evil spirits. He went to bed and drifted into a restless sleep, and dreamed of dead bodies coming back to life, and being chased by ghosts.

The next morning, Davey woke to the sound of songbirds outside the bedroom window; the shrill notes seemed to pierce his head. His head hurt. He hadn't had a drink last night, had he? No, he remembered that he'd gone to the quarry with Jack. So why did his head hurt so much?

He reached across the bed, but it was empty, and he thought Martha must have got up early. He tried to get out of bed, but he fell back down. What was wrong with him? He felt as weak as a kitten and his nightshirt was soaked with sweat.

He tried to call for Martha, but the sound came out as a croak because his throat was dry and sore. He would just have to lie in bed and wait until someone came into the bedroom. He dozed for a while and woke when he heard his wife open the door.

'Are you not up yet? You're goin' to be late for work.'

When there was no reply, she went to the bed and sat on the edge, looking down at Davey's face. His cheeks were red and beads of sweat covered his brow.

'Are you alright?' she asked.

He made a sound that was not decipherable.

'Davey, you're scaring me. Do you need the doctor?'

He inclined his head ever so slightly, and she ran from the room. He heard her shout at the bairns, 'Don't go in our room. Your father's not well. I'm going for the doctor.' And then the door slammed shut.

The next thing that he was aware of was the doctor standing over him, looking into his throat, and feeling his neck and brow.

'He has the 'flu, Mrs Bell, and his temperature's very high,' said Dr Rutherford. 'He doesn't need this thick quilt. Strip the bed to just one sheet, and open the window to let some fresh air in.'

Martha did as he said.

'And keep the children away from him,' the doctor added in a firm voice. 'We don't want them to catch it.'

'He will be alright, won't he?' she asked.

'I hope so. He's a strong fellow so he has every chance.'

As soon as the doctor left, he heard Martha say to one of the children, 'Go to the mine and tell the foreman your father's taken bad. He won't be in work for a few days.

Hurry up!' She came back into the bedroom and stood next to the bed, stroking his hair back from his clammy brow. He opened his eyes and saw the concern in hers. He managed a weak smile to try to reassure her, but he felt far from well.

The next few days passed in a blur — his wife, the doctor, children's hushed voices, and pain — lots of pain — in his head, his muscles, his belly. Pain so bad that he thought he might die.

But on the fourth day, when he woke up, he was relieved that the pounding headache had gone. His throat was parched and he needed water. He saw there was a jug on the washstand, so he sat up on the edge of his bed and tried to stand up, but his legs buckled beneath him and he fell to the floor with a loud thud. The noise must have alerted his wife. He heard Martha running up the stairs and she barged through the door, and then she knelt next to him on the floor.

'Davey, are you alright?'

'Help us up, hinny,' he groaned.

His wife was stronger than she looked, and she managed to pull him to his feet and help him back to bed, and then she pulled the sheet over his body.

'What were you trying to do?' she asked.

'Water,' he replied, in a croaky voice.

She rushed downstairs and brought him a mug full of water, which he gulped down greedily.

'Are you hungry?' she asked. 'I made vegetable soup

this morning.'

His empty stomach growled at the mention of food; he hadn't eaten in days. With an effort, he nodded. He couldn't believe how weak and tired he felt.

Before Martha had chance to return with his food, he'd closed his eyes and drifted into a sound sleep.

When Davey woke, he was unaware that several days had passed. All he knew was that his head was clear and he was ravenous, but rather than try to get up like the last time, he waited patiently until Martha came in to check on him. As soon as she walked through the doorway, he noticed the dark circles under her eyes, but her face lit up when she saw he was awake.

'Thank God, Davey. I thought we'd lost you.'

She took him into her arms and placed her head on his chest. He felt the dampness of her tears through his nightshirt. After a few minutes, she got up and wiped her eyes on her sleeve.

'Are you alright, pet?' he asked.

'Aye, I'm so glad you're better.'

'Can I see the bairns?'

Without looking at him, she said, 'Later. You should have something to eat first.'

She went downstairs to prepare some food, and a short while later she brought him a bowl of soup, but he could only manage a few mouthfuls.

'You've got an appetite like a sparrow,' she said. 'You're

looking thin, but it's good to see that you're on the mend.'

'Is everything alright?'

Before she had time to answer, there was a shout from the door, 'Daddy, Daddy! You're alive.'

Two dark-haired children ran up to the bed and hugged him. He took his sons into his arms and held them to his chest.

'Where's Lottie?' he asked.

'In heaven,' said his youngest son. 'We thought you were going with her, but you got better so you can stay with us.'

His wife's look of horror confirmed that what his son had said was true. She ushered the boys out of the door, and turned her attention back to Davey. He was sat up in bed with his eyes shut and his hands together, mumbling. She could hear enough to know that he was saying a prayer for his family and asking God for forgiveness.

When he'd finished, Martha took his hands in hers and looked him in the eye. 'It's not your fault. She wasn't the only one that didn't make it. The doctor said there's been quite a few people had it, and it's taken a few of the bairns. I did me best for her.'

With tears in his eyes, he said, 'But our Lottie! Why couldn't it have been me?'

'Don't talk like that. God works in mysterious ways and it's what he wanted, Davey. There was nothing we could do.'

Davey wished with all his heart that he had died during

his illness so that he wouldn't have to feel the terrible pain in his chest, and live the rest of his life without his beautiful daughter. Martha was there for him, and she held him tightly, and this time he was the one to cry.

Chapter 20

The Half Moon, Westgate
May, 1881

After visiting his mother, Ben decided to call at The Half Moon for a quick pint. He went to the bar and the landlord handed him a tankard of beer. Bess sat quietly at his feet.

The pub was quieter than usual, with most of the tables unoccupied. Ben took a long sup from his tankard, and then placed it back on the bar and looked around the room to see if there was anyone he knew. He recognised a few of the men, but he didn't know them well, so he leaned back against the bar and took another sip of his drink; he didn't plan on staying long anyway.

There were four men at the table by the window and their furtive behaviour caught his eye. He saw one of them take something out of his pocket and hold it in the palm of his hand to show the others. He was only about eight feet away and Ben could clearly see that the man held a small piece of gold. He recognised him; he'd seen him regularly walking the track to Scarside quarry. Ben turned his back on the group; he didn't want them to know he'd seen them. Men like that didn't have gold in their possession unless it was stolen, and he felt as though he should do something about it but he couldn't apprehend four men on his own, so he decided that he'd mention it at the next meeting of the Weardale Association for the Prosecution of Felons and Other Offenders. Ben had been a member of the group for years.

Ben finished his drink, bade the publican goodnight, and left the pub.

It was still light outside as Ben made his way back to his cottage and, when he was almost home, he thought he should check on the sheep before retiring for the night. There were still a few ewes that hadn't lambed, and as he'd been away for most of the day, he wanted to see if any of them had given birth. When he got to the lambing field, he was surprised to see Phyllis leaning against the wooden gate.

'Featherstone! Thank God you're back,' she said, with obvious relief. 'That sheep over there looks to be in distress, and I don't know what to do to help her.'

'Don't worry. I'll see to her.'

Expecting her to leave, Ben went through the gate and started to close it behind him, but Phyllis followed him and squeezed past him to get into the field. They walked over to the sheep that was lying down on the grass, breathing heavily.

'How long has she been like this?' he asked, as he lifted the ewe up onto her feet.

'I noticed something was wrong with her a few hours ago. I went to your cottage, but you weren't there.'

'I've been out — visiting me mother,' he said, as he examined the ewe. 'The lamb's coming backwards.'

'Can you help it?'

'Aye, I can, but it's tricky when they're facing the wrong way. I need to get hold of its legs and bring them forward so she can push it out.'

The ewe started to move away from them.

'Can you keep her still?' he asked. When Phyllis looked at him blankly, he added, 'Stand by her head and hold her horns.'

Without question, Phyllis held the ewe's head while Ben concentrated on manoeuvring the lamb into position, and when he was done, he stood back and waited. Phyllis moved to stand by his side and several minutes later they watched a large lamb come into the world.

Ben looked across at Phyllis and smiled.

The ewe was exhausted and didn't take much interest in the lamb, so Ben cleared the lamb's airways and helped it onto its feet so that it could suckle.

'You've got another gimmer.'

'Thank you,' she said, with tears in her eyes.

'You're welcome. They'll be fine now.'

'Would you like to come in for a drink?' asked Phyllis.

At Ben's hesitation, Phyllis' face fell slightly and she looked away, and Ben realised that she wasn't asking out of politeness, she really did want him to go back to the house with her.

'Yes, if you like,' he heard himself reply, although he couldn't help thinking how inappropriate it was. As friendly as Sir Thomas had been with Ben, he'd never invited him into the Hall for a drink. Over the years, Ben had often regarded Sir Thomas as a friend, but there'd always been a barrier between them — class.

Ben took off his boots at the door and told Bess to stay, as he followed Phyllis into the hallway.

'Good evening, Miss,' said Todd. 'Will you be using the study?'

'No, we'll be in the drawing room. Please bring in a tray with scotch and sherry.'

Ben saw the surprise on Todd's usually impassive face as he answered, 'Yes, Miss.'

'This way,' said Phyllis, ushering Ben through a wide doorway into a beautiful reception room full of sofas, armchairs and oak furniture. A red patterned carpet covered the floor and the matching floor-length curtains were closed, shutting out the moonlit night. He thought that it was even grander than the music room where he'd taken her after her accident.

'Please, take a seat.' She smiled at him warmly.

As Ben sat in a comfortable armchair, Todd brought in the drinks and poured them each a glass. Phyllis took a delicate sherry glass from the tray he offered, and Ben was handed a tumbler of scotch with a warning glance that Phyllis couldn't see from where she stood.

After Todd left the room, she sat in the armchair next to Ben. There was a small table between the two of them, and after taking a small sip of sherry, she rested her glass on it, and turned towards him. Seeing the necklace that she was wearing, Ben raised his eyebrows slightly, but enough that Phyllis noticed.

'What is it?' she asked.

'I was looking at your necklace. It's very pretty.'

She moved her hand to her neck and touched the bead.

'Thank you. Apparently, the bead is ancient — like your stone.' She smiled. 'You can keep a secret, can't you?'

'Aye, you can tell me anything and it won't go any further than me dog and the sheep.'

She laughed because she knew that what he said was true; she'd heard him talk to his dog — and the sheep. She went on, 'They've come across a cave at the quarry and Mr Maddison found this bead in it.'

'Did he just find one?'

'Yes, I believe so,' she said, looking puzzled. 'Why do you ask?'

'I saw a bead identical to this just a few hours ago. A fella at Westgate had it.'

Phyllis looked astonished. 'I don't understand how

anyone could have one the same, unless they've been in the cave. But Mr Maddison keeps an eye on the place during the day and we have a night watchman.'

'Somebody's been in that cave and taken it. Maybe I should have a word with the Felons — you know, the Weardale Association for the Prosecution of Felons and Other Offenders — but that's a bit of a mouthful,' he said with a chuckle, 'so they're known as the Felons. I'm sure they'd keep watch for you. They're all trustworthy men — I can vouch for them.'

'Yes, my father used to be a member of the Felons. And Connie's father too — poor Mr Peart.'

'Aye, that was a night I'll never forget,' said Ben, shaking his head as if trying to rid himself of the memory.

'You were there? But you can't have been more than a boy?'

'Aye, I was there.' He looked up and saw compassion in Phyllis's lovely eyes, and she reached out and touched his arm. 'I'm sorry. It must have been terrible.'

He didn't feel awkward from her attention, as he thought he should, but rather he felt comforted by her words and her touch. He said softly, 'Thank you,' and after a slight pause, he added, 'I'd better be going. Thanks for the drink.'

'You're welcome,' she said brightly, 'Anytime.'

As Ben walked home with his dog, he thought about Phyllis Forster, and for the first time, he realised that, despite her privileged position and wealth, she was lonely. She had no family, and Connie Milburn was her only friend as far as he knew, and she was confined to the farm because she was expecting a baby. He understood why she had wanted company that evening after her emotions had been stirred up from witnessing the difficult lambing that, thankfully, had ended well. But that still didn't make it right. She shouldn't have invited him in; it certainly wasn't his place to spend an evening at Burnside Hall, drinking with the mistress.

The next morning, Phyllis was up bright and early. She sat at her window seat in the music room, from where she hoped to see Ben on the hillside above the Hall.

'Miss, please may I have a word?' asked Todd.

'Yes, come in.'

'Mrs Gibson and I have been talking this morning, and we both agreed that, because you don't have a parent or guardian to advise you, we should take it upon ourselves to warn you that what you did last night was inappropriate for a lady of your position.'

Phyllis got to her feet and looked directly into her butler's face.

'What exactly did I do last night?' she asked sternly.

'You invited a workman into the house for an alcoholic drink, and you sat with him unsupervised. That was — foolish. You must think of your reputation.'

'Are you calling me a fool?' she demanded.

Todd didn't reply, but looked suitably embarrassed.

'Who I invite into my home is my business, and certainly not yours. You're not my parent, so don't ever speak to me in that manner again. Do I make myself clear?'

Todd gave a slight nod to confirm that he understood.

'Now, ask the groom to saddle up Samson. I'm going out this morning.'

Phyllis was seething as she watched Todd retreat from the room. Just who did he think he was, talking to her like that? She was the mistress of Burnside Hall and he was head of her staff. He had no right to question what she did. He was her servant and he should do as he was asked and speak when he was spoken to. Another such instance and she would have to dismiss him; she would not put up with insubordination.

Phyllis rode Samson to Springbank Farm and, as she went up the track, she saw Connie wave from the front garden. In the yard, she handed her horse to one of the Rowell twins, who took him straight over to the water trough, and she went around the front of the house to where Connie sat in a chair on the lawn. Connie stood up awkwardly to greet her, and Phyllis stared at her belly in disbelief.

Connie smiled at her reaction. 'I know! I can't believe how quickly the baby's growing.'

Phyllis had never seen Connie looking so happy and

she was genuinely pleased for her. Her hair looked thick and glossy and her skin glowed. She looked even more beautiful than usual.

'You look wonderful!' said Phyllis. 'How are you feeling?'

'Like a heavy sack of potatoes!' Connie laughed. 'But really, I'm fine. I can't believe that it's going so well this time.'

'Sit down. You should be resting.'

'You're as bad as Joe,' she said, but she sat down all the same, and Phyllis sat on the grass next to her chair.

Connie told her all about her pregnancy, but didn't have much more to talk about because she hadn't been away from the farm in months. She implored Phyllis to tell her what was going on in the outside world.

Phyllis was still fuming about Todd's interference in her affairs that morning and she told Connie the full story.

'Did you really invite Ben Featherstone into the house for a drink?' asked Connie, raising her eyebrows.

'Was I wrong to? It didn't feel wrong at the time. I was so grateful to him for saving the sheep and the lamb, but that's not the only reason; I enjoy talking to him.'

Phyllis suddenly remembered the last conversation she'd had with Connie, when she'd told her about the man that she liked but couldn't have. Would Connie guess that it was Ben she'd been referring to?

'Well, I should tell you that it was improper,' said

Connie, 'but I think you already know that. You shouldn't need a servant to tell you.'

Phyllis felt as though she'd been scolded. She did know that Todd had been right and that was why she'd been so upset by what he'd said.

'You need to mix more with people of your own standing,' continued Connie. 'I know Henry made that difficult for you, but there will still be some men out there who would be interested in having you as a friend, or a wife. What about the new vicar? He's a bachelor, and he obviously comes from a good family.'

'He's visited me several times, and I did wonder if he might have a mind to court me, but he's never made his intentions clear.'

'Why don't you invite him over for dinner one evening?'

'What! I couldn't do that.'

'Yet you invited your shepherd in for a drink?' Connie laughed.

'That's different,' said Phyllis, blushing furiously.

Phyllis wondered when Connie had become so good at giving advice, and thought it might be because she'd had so much time to sit and think about things. There had been little else for her to do lately.

'Oh, I don't know,' said Phyllis. 'Perhaps I should do as you suggest and invite the vicar. It would be a pleasant change to have company at dinner.'

'There you are, then. Put the shepherd behind you and

find somebody more suitable.'

Phyllis smiled wistfully; she knew Connie was right. Her parents would have considered the vicar to be a suitable husband — being similar in both age and status, and he had a regular income from the church. He hadn't been in the area at the time of the family scandal, either, so he might be less concerned by it.

As she departed, Phyllis waved at Connie, and promised to visit again soon.

On the ride home, Phyllis thought about the conversation and how unfair life could be. As a daughter, Phyllis had inherited the estate, but not her father's baronetcy. She wondered whether or not having the title would have helped her to take her rightful place in society again, but decided that it wouldn't have. Her wealth and estate meant that she was a good marriage prospect but, nevertheless, she had received no offers, so her options appeared to be very limited indeed. Nobody wanted to be connected with the Forsters of Burnside Hall.

In the yard, she dismounted and handed Samson's reins to Thompson, who led the horse towards the stables. Phyllis went to the front door, which was opened by Todd.

'Miss, there's a note for you. I placed it on your desk in the study.'

'Thank you,' she said, as she entered the house.

She went to her study and sat at her desk to open the

note. She gasped; it was written in the same naive handwriting as before.

You were with him again — drinking together!
£25 to keep me quiet.
Hide it under the stile.
Don't tell the police or you'll be sorry.

Phyllis had put the previous demand to the back of her mind after she'd paid it, and as far as she was aware, the blackmailer had kept to their word. But now that another note had arrived, she was concerned. Her mind started to work overtime wondering who could have sent it. She didn't recognise the writing, but it appeared to be from someone with a basic education, someone who knew the letter forms but hadn't practised writing them enough for them to become fluent.

The last time, when she'd fallen from her horse, she'd had a legitimate reason for being with Ben and could have defended her actions, but this time she had no excuse whatsoever. Inviting Ben into the Hall to have a drink with her had been a serious lapse of judgement, and gossip about them drinking together in the evening, unchaperoned, would definitely harm her reputation.

Who could have known about that night? Obviously both Ben and herself. She had confided in Connie earlier that day, but she trusted her friend to keep her secret, and she was quite certain that Ben wouldn't have told anyone. Some of the servants in the Hall had seen them, and it was possible that they could have told others too.

Phyllis suspected that Miss Wilson had her eye on Ben. Could jealousy be a motive for this kind of behaviour? It was a risky thing to do, because if it was proven, she would lose her job at the very least, and possibly face conviction and a prison term. But who else could it be? Her mind was blank. She couldn't think of anyone who would want to blackmail her.

She stared out of the window at the new leaves on the trees and considered the best course of action, whether or not she should pay the money to prevent the spread of harmful gossip, but she heard her father's voice in her head telling her not to give in to cowardly demands because, once she gave in, the blackmailer would keep coming back for more. They already had, and she feared that there may be no end to it. However, she couldn't take the chance of people finding out about her friendship with Ben and her impropriety. Her decision was made; she would pay the demand immediately; after all, it had worked the last time.

Within ten minutes, she had counted out the sum of twenty-five pounds, left the house and walked hurriedly to the riverside path where the white stile, which she had once thought to be pretty, loomed threateningly up ahead.

Chapter 21

Burnside Hall
May, 1881

Postponing her letter writing, Phyllis put down her pen and walked to the drawing room to see her visitor.

'Good morning, Miss Forster,' said Reverend Dagnall. 'It's a lovely day. I couldn't resist coming out for a walk!'

'It's good to see you again,' she replied. 'I didn't expect you to call again so soon.'

'I hope I'm not imposing.'

'No, not all. Please take a seat. Mrs Gibson is preparing some tea.'

He sat by the window and, as she joined him, Mrs Gibson brought in the tea tray and placed it on a small table between their chairs.

'Would you like me to pour, Miss?'

'Yes, please.'

The housekeeper had just finished pouring the tea when Todd came to the door, and said, 'Mr Maddison is here to see you, Miss. He said it was a matter of great urgency.'

Phyllis stood up quickly and rushed for the door, wondering what was so urgent as to disturb their tea. Reverend Dagnall followed her into the hallway where Mr Maddison stood waiting.

Looking at the vicar, and then back at Phyllis, he said, 'Miss, I've got some grave news.'

'Oh!' she exclaimed, the smile slipping from her face, her mind running through all the dreadful things that could have happened, and hoping that there hadn't been an accident at the quarry. She swallowed deeply before saying, 'You'd better come in to the office and tell me what's happened.'

When they were all seated, the quarry manager spoke solemnly.

'I'm sorry to have to tell you this, but someone broke into the quarry and went in the cave.'

She looked at him in surprise, and sighed. 'That's your grave news? I thought it was something far worse.'

'I'm afraid that's not all, Miss Forster. They disturbed...'

Her relief had made her heady, and when he paused, she said with a laugh, 'The bats?'

'No, Miss. A body.'

'Oh! I'm sorry I was so flippant.'

Phyllis felt ghastly, and chastised herself for being disrespectful. Because of her silence, Reverend Dagnall said, 'Please, tell us what happened.'

'When I got to the quarry this morning, there was a ladder propped up underneath the cave, so I went up and I could see that the ground had been dug up in a few places. And then I saw it — a skull. Still in the ground. It didn't half give me a fright!' He held a quivering hand out in front of him. 'See, I'm still shaking. Somebody must have found it, and then fled.'

Phyllis didn't know what to say, and she noticed that Reverend Dagnall looked equally perplexed. He said, 'As a vicar, I should advise you that the remains must be exhumed and buried in the churchyard, but as an archaeologist, I must say I find this most exciting. The body could be very ancient indeed, and it could even be one of the primitive cave-dwellers that I'm writing about. Do you think I could take a look?'

'I think you should,' said Phyllis. 'You must supervise the exhumation, and make sure that the bones are buried appropriately.'

'The police will need to see the body, too,' said the vicar, 'to make sure that it is ancient, and rule out any foul play. I'll let the policeman know about it when I go back to Westgate.'

'Thank you,' said Phyllis. Turning to Mr Maddison, she said, 'We can't continue quarrying until the body has been removed, so make sure all this happens quickly. I want the men back to work as soon as possible.'

Reverend Dagnall stood up, and said, 'I'll go back to the quarry with Mr Maddison now. I don't suppose you'd like to accompany us?'

'No! No, that's something I would rather not see.'

'I'm sorry. I should never have asked. I forget that ladies are more delicate about such matters.'

He took her hand, and lifting it to his lips, he kissed it quickly, before following Mr Maddison out of the house.

Phyllis's day wasn't going at all how she'd planned. The interruption by the vicar was one thing, but Mr Maddison's news had unsettled her. She returned to her desk, but was unable to concentrate on her correspondence, so she asked Todd to have Samson saddled for her. She could always rely on riding to calm her troubled mind.

At the 'racetrack', Phyllis gave Samson his head and let him gallop as fast as he wanted. She loved the feeling of power, the sense of freedom, and the rush of the wind; there was nothing better. But today, she found that it didn't have the therapeutic effect it normally had. At the end of the track, she rode uphill and crossed the moors at a walk.

She couldn't help thinking about the body in the cave, and echoes of the past haunted her mind. She hoped that it was ancient, like the vicar suspected, and not... That couldn't happen again, could it?

On her way down from the fell, she came across Ben, with his faithful sheepdog by his side. He stood and waited for her, and grinned when she reached them.

'Good morning, Featherstone.'

'Morning, lovely day again.'

'Is it? I hadn't really noticed.'

'How can you not notice when you're outside?' Looking up at the sky, he said, 'The sun's shining; there's hardly a cloud in the sky, or a breath of wind. It's as good as it gets up here.'

'I'm sorry. It's just that my mind is on other things.'

Ben didn't say anything, but waited for her to continue. If she was worried about something, he was more than happy to listen.

'You know the cave I told you about at the quarry? Mr Maddison's found a body in it.'

The colour drained from Ben's face and his expression looked set in stone, and she realised what she'd said. Noticing Ben's fists were clenched, she gave no thought to her personal safety as she jumped down from her horse and stood in front of him. Instead, she was concerned about the hurt she had inflicted by dragging up awful memories from the past. Knowing exactly what this meant to him, she hurriedly said, 'Oh, I'm so sorry, Ben. I didn't think before I opened my big mouth. Are you alright?'

He didn't move and he didn't speak.

'Please, Ben,' she said, as she reached out and put her hand on his arm. 'Speak to me.'

His far-away gaze returned to her face, and the look in

his eyes filled her with dread; she saw a mixture of anger and pain, and she didn't know how he would react — whether he might strike her, or burst into tears.

'I really am sorry,' she said again.

'I know.' He bowed his head. 'It's not your fault. It's just the way I am. Sometimes it all comes rushing back to me, and it's just too much. I can't handle it.'

'I know what you mean.'

'How can you possibly know what it's like?'

Phyllis hesitated. She had been about to tell him that she was still suffering too, and that she knew exactly what it was like, but she couldn't admit that, not to Ben, not to anyone.

'I'm sorry,' she repeated sincerely, and then said, 'I should have told you that this body is most probably ancient.'

Phyllis became still and looked deep in thought, and seeing the sudden change in her, Ben asked, 'What's wrong?'

'Please, excuse me. I need to go to the quarry right away.'

'Why the sudden change of plan?'

'Mr Maddison hired a night watchman. I wonder where he was when the trespassers were in the cave?'

'He can't have been there, or he'd have seen them off. There's something very odd going on. Would you like me to go with you?'

'Would you mind?'

'Not at all. Maybe you should get the Felons involved. They might be able to help.'

'Yes, I must do that.'

They walked side by side across the hillside, Phyllis leading Samson, and Bess staying close to Ben's heels.

Ben was right, it was a lovely day. It wasn't often that she walked anywhere, usually preferring to ride, but the slower place meant that she noticed more of what was going on around her, like cotton grass growing in the bogs, tadpoles swimming in the peaty pools, and a red-billed oystercatcher dipping for worms. There were no deer to be seen, but she spotted an adder curled up in the sun, a hare speeding over the rough terrain, and curlews flying overhead.

All the sheep and lambs had been brought back up to the fell, and Phyllis noticed Ben's expert eye checking them over as they passed.

'You did a good job with the lambing. There weren't many losses this year, and the flock looks fit and healthy.'

'Aye, most of them are strong, but there's still a few I'm keeping an eye on.'

'They're lucky they've got you to take such good care of them.'

He smiled at the compliment, and Phyllis thought he looked attractive when he smiled, and wished that he had more to smile about. Her initial opinion of Ben had been so misguided; he was far from the carefree man that she'd taken him for; the loss of his sister had obviously affected him deeply.

When they got to the quarry, the vicar and Mr Maddison were descending the ladder from the cave.

'Miss Forster!' Reverend Dagnall called out. 'Did you change your mind? I'll go back up with you, if you like.'

'No. That's not why I'm here. It's Mr Maddison that I've come to see.'

They met in the middle of the yard, Phyllis facing the manager and Ben facing the vicar.

'What can I do for you, Miss?' asked Mr Maddison.

'You employed a night watchman to mind the site. Where was he when the cave was disturbed?'

'He said he'd been called home because his missus was bad.'

'It seems too much of a coincidence that somebody entered the cave on the one night he went home. Is it possible that he hasn't been doing his job?'

'That's not likely, Miss. I've come up here a few times to check on him, and he's always been around.'

'Well, could it have been him who disturbed the cave? Or could he have told somebody else that he wouldn't be here that night?'

'Either's possible, I suppose.'

'Then I must inform Police Constable Emerson about my suspicions when he comes to see the remains. Please send him to the Hall when he's finished here.' Looking at Ben, she said, 'and I'd be grateful if you would ask the

Felons for help, on my behalf.'

Ben nodded.

'In the meantime, Mr Maddison, the night watchman is not to come back here. Do you understand?'

'Yes, miss. I'll dismiss him tonight.'

'Thank you.'

Chapter 22

As Ben turned onto the track leading to High House Farm, he spotted two boys running down to meet him. When they reached him, they jumped up and down with excitement as they greeted him, and they approached the farm together, Ben at his normal pace, the boys having to run a little now and again to keep up with him.

'We've been fishing in the stream,' said Tommy.

'Did you catch anything?' asked Ben.

'Just a tiddler. It was too small for tea so we put it back in the water. Would you like to see our camp?'

'Aye, I'd like to see your camp,' said Ben.

The boys grinned at him, and through a toothless smile, Matt said, 'It's a secret camp, but you can come in if you want.'

They led Ben to the back corner of the haybarn, where they'd stacked some tools against the wall and covered them with hay, making a lean-to shelter where they could hide. Tommy crawled in on his hands and knees, followed by his brother.

'It's a good camp, lads, but I don't think there's room for me in there an' all.'

'You're too big,' said Matt. 'Would you like a biscuit?'

'You have biscuits in there?' asked Ben in surprise.

'Aye, we have biscuits. Mother left them on the table to cool down. They're cold now so we can eat them.'

'You shouldn't just take food off the table,' said Ben.

'She doesn't mind,' said Tommy. 'She makes so many, she probably wouldn't miss them, anyway.'

'Promise me that you'll ask her next time.'

'Alright,' said Matt begrudgingly.

'Eat your biscuits,' he said, winking at them, 'your secret's safe with me.'

Ben left the boys in the barn and went to the house, where he was greeted by the women — his mother, his cousin Mary, Mary's mother-in-law, Jane, and Mary's daughter, Josie — who were busy preparing dinner. Josie made him a cup of tea and brought it to the table for him.

'There's something I'd like to show you,' she said, and then ran upstairs. A few minutes later, she held out a piece of green fluorite, the cubic crystals showing signs of wear.

'What you do think?' she asked. 'I found it amongst the pebbles, at the bend in the stream.'

'It's a pretty piece of spar. Lovely colour. What do you think?' he asked the same question of her.

'I think it's beautiful. It's a bit like the pieces on the rockery in the garden, but smaller. I have some more bits if you'd like to see them?'

He smiled as he said, 'Aye, I'd like to see them,' as she skipped away to fetch them. Every time he visited, she had something new to show him — abandoned birds' nests, snail shells, or something similar; either that, or she'd sit on the chair arm and read passages to him from her books. She was very much like her mother, Mary, with her love of books and thirst for knowledge.

When Tom came in, with his two young sons trailing behind, they all sat at the table together for dinner. Tom asked, 'What's going on at the Hall, Ben? I've heard all sorts of rumours.'

Everyone at the table turned to look at Ben.

'You mean at the quarry?'

'Aye.'

'Well, they came across a cave, and the manager found something there which made Miss Forster decide to employ a night watchman — Jack Bell, from Westgate.'

Jane said, 'I know his mother. Jack's the youngest lad. The older one got smallpox as a bairn, and it left him badly scarred, the poor thing.'

'That's Davey,' said Tom. 'I worked with him in the mines for a while. He's a good lad.'

'Anyway,' continued Ben, 'Miss Forster thinks Jack went into the mine to search for gold...'

'Gold! Oh, my word!' exclaimed Jane. Everyone around

the table looked at each other in surprise.

'Aye, maybe I shouldn't have said it, but that's what was found. Anyway, I saw a man trying to sell a gold bead in the pub one night, and it looked just like the bead that Miss Forster wears around her neck. The man in the pub was Jack Bell.'

Ben was aware that his mother was watching him keenly, but she didn't say anything.

'Miss Forster asked me to approach the Felons for help on her behalf. I suggested it to her a while back. With people digging in the cave at night, and poaching on the fells during the day, it's quite unsettling for her. She needs someone she can trust to keep an eye on the place until things settle down again.'

'I didn't know the half of it,' said Tom. 'But with so many of the miners out of work, I suppose it's to be expected. I'll call a meeting of the Felons, and we'll see what we can do to help.'

'Thank you.'

'Has she spoken to the police about Jack?'

'I don't know if she has yet, but she said she would.'

After dinner, Tom and Ben sat in front of the fire with a glass of ale, and Ben told him about the body that had been found; he hadn't wanted to say anything about it in front of the children. When the conversation came to an end, Ben heard his mother say, 'Ben, come into the parlour for a minute, would you? I'd like a word.'

He wondered what he'd done to upset her. She hadn't

asked to speak to him in private since she'd moved in with Mary and Tom. He took her arm and helped her walk to the parlour, and led her to a wooden chair, the kind she liked to sit on because she found them easier to get up from.

'What is it?' he asked. 'Are you alright?'

'I'm just the same as usual, Ben. It's not me I want to talk about, it's you.'

'What have I done now?' he said with a smirk.

'You mentioned Phyllis Forster a lot when you told your story tonight. You seem to be spending a lot of time with her.'

Ben could feel the heat in his cheeks, but he remained silent.

'I see I'm right. You do have feelings for her.'

Lizzie turned to look out of the window, and talking more to herself than Ben, she said, 'Well, I suppose that was bound to happen when you hardly see any other lasses.' Then, turning back to him, she asked, 'So what's going on? Is it just a passing fancy?'

'Nothing's going on!'

'Well, that's something to be thankful for.'

'Mother, I don't know what to say.'

'Well, listen then, because I'm not going to say this again. Phyllis is gentry, she's older than you, and she's not well-liked around here. If you get involved with a woman like her, there's no going back. Your own kind will turn against you, and her kind won't accept you. It'll never work out.'

Ben bowed his head. He knew what she was saying was right, but the feelings he had for Phyllis felt right too. When they were together, it wasn't like they were landowner and shepherd, gentry and working-class, and he never noticed the age difference. Even though she called him Featherstone, rather than Ben, it seemed to him that they spoke as equals, as friends.

'There are plenty of good lasses in the dale that would be pleased to have you for a husband.'

'I'd better be going.'

'Be sensible, lad,' said Lizzie.

As he walked out of the door, he said, 'I'll see you next week.'

Lizzie stood by the window and watched her son walk away.

When Ben walked into The Half Moon later that week, the members of The Felons were already sitting around a table at the back of the room. He went straight over to them and was greeted warmly. The innkeeper brought over a drink, slopping some of the beer onto the table as he set the tankard down in front of Ben.

'Well, now that we're all here, let's get down to business, shall we?' said Tom.

Tom was chairman of the group of respected volunteers who kept law and order in the dale.

'I've received reports that unsavoury characters are

loitering around Burnside Hall and Scarside quarry, and that there's been a theft at the quarry.'

The men's faces showed surprise, and Joe Milburn asked, 'What did they take?'

'You've probably heard rumours about what's going on up there, but I'll tell you the story as I know it. When they were blasting a few weeks ago, they broke into a cave, similar to the one at Heathery Burn. The manager found a small gold bead and informed Miss Forster, who wisely wanted to keep it quiet. But somehow word got out and the cave was ransacked. We don't know what was taken exactly, but Ben saw a man with a gold bead matching the one Miss Forster has in her possession, right here in this public house.'

The men looked at Ben and muttered their approval.

'And what's more,' continued Tom, 'they disturbed a skeleton while they were at it.'

A mixture of expressions could be seen on the men's faces then — shock, sadness and surprise. One of the men said to his neighbour, 'I told you there was a body!'

'It's hard to keep things quiet around here,' said Tom. 'Anyway, the police from Stanhope said it was an ancient burial, so that's good news at least, and Reverend Dagnall has had the remains buried in the churchyard. So, that's over and done with, but Miss Forster is concerned about men hanging around the place, and she's asked us if we could keep an eye on things. If you're in agreement, I suggest we set up a nightly watch with two of us there, just in case there's any bother. That's only one night each a week. What do you think?'

The men nodded and said, 'Aye.'

'Right, the matter's settled then. Is there any other business?'

Ben said, 'Aye, some poachers were seen up on Eastgate Fell with a shotgun. The gamekeeper went after them, but didn't catch them.'

'That's nothing new,' said Joe. 'When the miners aren't getting paid, how are they supposed to feed their bairns?'

'Aye,' said Tom. 'I was a miner myself once, and I can sympathise with their predicament. If the Beaumonts keep closing the Weardale mines at this rate, there'll be none left by this time next year.'

'What should we do about the poachers?' asked Ben.

'Nothing, lad. Folks have to eat,' replied Tom. 'We'll concentrate on catching the thieves. Was there anything else?'

There was silence, so Tom said, 'Alright then, let's get another round in,' and gestured for the innkeeper to bring them more drinks. The men worked out a rota between them and, when it was finalised, Ben thanked the men; he knew Phyllis would be pleased with the arrangement.

Chapter 23

Westgate
May, 1881

Davey Bell sat on the low wall of the back yard. With a rag, he rubbed a mixture of oil and beeswax into the leather of his work boots, the same as he did every weekend without fail. When he finished, he carried them indoors and set them in front of the fire to dry out properly; he had only one pair of boots and he was determined to make them last for as long as he could.

His sons were playing out on the back lane and Martha was upstairs tidying the boys' room. Knowing dinner wouldn't be ready for a few hours yet, he decided he'd have a walk round to Jack's place; he hadn't seen his brother for a few days. He shouted up to Martha, 'I'm going to our Jack's. I won't be long.'

'Alright, see you later,' she shouted back.

Davey knocked at Jack's front door, and walked into the living room where Beth was gently rocking Lucy in her arms, trying to get her to sleep. He whispered, 'Hello, is Jack in?'

'Haven't you heard? They've taken him to Stanhope police station.'

'What! When did that happen?'

'Shush!' she said, 'Constable Emerson was here first thing this morning, asking questions about the quarry, and then he took Jack away for questioning.'

'The fool! I told him he should have gone back and covered his tracks,' said Davey, shaking his head.

Beth put her daughter into a crib in the corner of the room, and turned back to Davey, and said, 'But there's no evidence it was him. I heard him say they couldn't prove anything.'

Just then, the front door opened and Jack walked in.

'Jack! What happened?' asked Davey.

'Do you fancy a pint?'

'Aye, if you want one.'

Beth looked upset that Jack wanted to speak to his brother rather than her, but it didn't surprise Davey in the least; the brothers had always been close.

The men left the cottage and walked down the road to The Half Moon, where they ordered a couple of beers. They sat at the table in the farthest corner from the bar, where they were unlikely to be overheard.

'Right, so tell me what's been going on,' said Davey.

'Emerson and his sergeant questioned me for ages. They've charged me with stealing that piece of gold, even though they couldn't find it. I don't even have it any more,' he scoffed. 'Anyway, it looks like I'll be up before the justice at the next sessions, but until then, I'm a free man.'

'How did they know it was you?'

'They came to talk to me because somebody in this pub saw me with the gold. It could be any one of these men that informed on me.'

He looked about the room, searching for signs of who it might have been, but nobody was taking the slightest notice of them.

'They asked to see me boots, and they were the same size as one of the sets of footprints in the cave. They said that was enough to put us away.'

'Bloody hell,' said Davey under his breath. 'And what about me? Did you tell them anything?'

'Of course not, you're me brother! If I go down for this, I'll need you to see to Beth and the bairn.'

'Aye, Jack. You can depend on that.'

'Do you want another?' Jack asked, pointing at their empty tankards.

'Go on, then. Ta.'

The next morning, Davey was woken by someone banging loudly on the front door.

'Hold your horses!' he shouted. 'Let me get me trousers on.'

When he opened the door, Beth stood outside, cradling her baby in her arms. Her eyes were red and swollen, and her cheeks were wet with tears.

'It's Jack,' she sobbed. 'He's gone.'

'He won't have gone far,' said Davey, trying to reassure her. 'Come on in.'

When she was inside, he asked, 'Did you check out the back?'

'Of course, I did — I'm not stupid. He's gone. He's left us. He's taken all of his clothes.'

Martha came downstairs and she took the baby from Beth, and asked, 'What makes you think that?'

Beth perched on a chair and took the glass of water that Davey offered her, before saying, 'He was acting strangely last night. I know he'd had a few pints with you, Davey, and normally when he's had a drink, he talks a lot...and laughs a lot. But when he got back last night, he was quiet. What he said made me realise that he was thinking about me and him — about all the good things that happened to us before he lost his job. And he got all soppy when he said goodnight to the bairn. I'd swear he was crying. I thought it might be 'cos he would miss her if he was locked up, but I don't think that's what he had in mind. And when we went to bed, I dunno, he was different. It was like...it was like he knew it would be the last night we'd have together.'

Beth was crying again, and Davey put his arm around her shoulder.

'He's gone,' she said. 'I'm sure of it, and I know in my heart that he's not coming back.'

'I'm sorry, lass. He never said anything to me about leaving, and if he had, I'm not sure what I'd have said to him. It looks like the police have enough evidence against him, and God knows how long he'd be locked up in Durham. It sounds harsh, but he wasn't going to be around for you whether he went to prison or if he did a runner.'

'That doesn't help us!' exclaimed Beth, reaching to take her baby back from Martha.

'I know, lass. We're always here for you if you need us,' said Davey, as she headed for the door.

'I'm going back to me parents' place up at Wearhead. Tell Jack, will you, if you see him.'

The look of desolation as she turned away struck Davey to his very core; the contrast between this woman and the bonny bride that Jack had married less than a year ago couldn't have been starker. He closed the door behind her, leaned against it and closed his eyes. He felt for her and the bairn.

Jack had once had it all — a job, a home, a wife, a healthy child, and even a handsome face, he thought enviously — but losing his job had changed him. He'd been pushed into crime to keep his family together, but he'd failed miserably, and now he was on the run from the police. As soon as they'd disturbed the body in the cave, Davey had known that they'd be cursed and now he knew he was right. He was angry at his brother for getting into this mess, and he was livid at him for abandoning his wife and child without a word to anyone. When he opened his eyes, he wiped a tear away with the back of his hand.

'Damn you, Jack,' he said, under his breath.

Chapter 24

Burnside Hall Estate
June, 1881

After a pleasant afternoon at Springbank Farm, chatting to Connie, Phyllis rode leisurely back to the Hall. She saw Ben up ahead, walking in the same direction, and she wondered where he'd been. Curiosity getting the better of her, she pulled Samson up beside him.

'How do you do, Featherstone?'

'Good afternoon, Miss Forster.'

'It's a beautiful day for a ride.'

'Aye, it's nice now, but did you see the frost this morning? I've never known such a heavy frost at this time of the year,' he said.

'Yes, I did. The gardeners were complaining that the seedlings they were hardening off have perished, and the gamekeeper is upset about the grouse.'

'The grouse?'

'Yes, he's found a lot of dead chicks on the moors. They're not feathered up yet so they can't survive the cold.

It's such a shame.'

'Aye, I suppose it'll affect your income if there's no game to shoot.'

'Oh, I hadn't even considered that. I meant it was a shame for the moorhens. They sit on their nests for weeks, taking care of their eggs, and it must be miserable for them to lose the chicks as soon as they hatch.'

'I'm sorry,' said Ben, embarrassed that he'd mistaken her meaning.

'I've been to visit Connie Milburn at Springbank Farm. Have you been over that way as well?'

'I'm on me way back from High House Farm. I've been up to see me mother. By the way, has Tom Milburn told you about the Felons' meeting the other night?'

'No.'

'They've agreed to keep watch for you. There'll be two men here every night, patrolling between the Hall and the quarry, and they'll soon spot if there's anyone about, so you'll be able to sleep soundly again.'

She wished that she could sleep soundly. The nightmares had returned with a vengeance since moving back home; she rarely slept well.

'Are you alright?' Ben asked.

'Yes. Thank you.'

When she was a child, her father used to say, 'No matter what's going on around you, you must stand up straight, keep your chin up and don't show what you're feeling inside,' and over the years she'd become an expert at doing just that.

'If you say so, Miss Forster.'

Phyllis looked down at Ben and she was surprised to see that he seemed to be concerned about her. It was as though he could see straight through the mask she'd created, and knew that she was suffering too. She wondered if she should tell him that she never slept well. Her father would have viewed that as a sign of weakness, but her father wasn't here anymore, and there was an old saying that a problem shared was a problem halved.

'I didn't sleep soundly even before this,' she admitted quietly, and then she glanced at Ben, his silence encouraging her to continue. 'I often have nightmares.'

'I'm sorry to hear that. They can be very upsetting.'

'Yes, they seem so vivid. And I find it impossible to sleep afterwards.'

'I get up and chop wood, or take a long walk.'

'You have nightmares too?' she asked.

'Aye, ever since, you know...'

'Yes, I know. I'm sorry.'

A look of understanding passed between them, and she felt closer to him than she had done before. She actually wanted to hold him, and feel that closeness that they'd shared when they'd ridden home after her accident. A faint smile passed her lips as she realised that she couldn't, that it wasn't right; and her mask fell back into place.

Changing the subject, she asked, 'Are the lambs faring

well?'

'Aye, they're big enough to cope with the frosts now. I was hoping to shear the ewes soon, but it'll have to wait until it's warmer.'

'It was good to see you, Featherstone.' And with that, she urged Samson forward and left Ben standing in the road.

It was three weeks later when Ben brought the sheep down for shearing and, as he followed the flock, he thought that it had been a strange year weather-wise, with heavy snowfall lasting for months, rapid thaws leading to floods, late frosts and now temperatures were soaring; he'd never known it so hot. He'd set off early that morning to gather the sheep, and he was pleased he had, because by midday the heat would be unbearable. He wiped the sweat off his brow with his sleeve. Bess walked alongside him, with her tongue hanging out. He knew she was suffering with the heat too.

As soon as the sheep were penned, he went back to his cottage, which stayed relatively cool with it standing in the shade of mature trees. He turned on the tap and drank the cold water, while Bess helped herself to a drink from the river before coming back to his side. Looking at the river, which flowed languidly around large boulders protruding above the surface, he walked to the bank and climbed down to the water's edge, where he quickly stripped off his clothes and stepped into the cool water and sighed. Plodging to the deepest channel, he lay down and felt the water flow through his hair and down his body, his eyes closed against the bright sunshine. He heard Bess scramble down the bank and splash through the water until she was only a few feet from him, and then she barked loudly.

Bess didn't bark unless there was somebody nearby. He sat up swiftly and looked around, but couldn't see or hear anything. Bess was looking downstream and growling low in her throat.

'I don't know what you can see, but I think I'd better get out of here and put some clothes on.'

Self-consciously, he climbed up the bank, grabbed his pile of clothes and took them inside to dress, just in case there was someone nearby who might see him.

He rested in the cottage for a while, and when the sun was a little lower in the sky, Ben went back to the sheep pens to begin clipping. One by one, he expertly sheared the fleeces from their bodies, in one piece, and then put the shorn sheep into a neighbouring pen before wrapping the fleece into a tight bundle. He'd only done about a dozen, when Phyllis came out to watch him work. Looking at the clean ewes, she said, 'Their fleeces must be such a burden in this heat. You can see the relief in their eyes after they've been sheared.'

'Aye, they get warm under all that wool. I hope to have them all sheared tonight, and I'll take them back up to the fell first thing in the morning.'

'I'm sure they'll be thankful for it.' Moving to the pile of fleeces and running her fingers over the oily wool, she said thoughtfully, 'It's a shame fleeces aren't worth as much as they were. The price of wool has plummeted since they started importing it from New Zealand. Connie told me about all those Weardale people who sailed to New Zealand to become sheep farmers. It's ironic that they're probably responsible for lowering the wool prices back home.'

'I suppose so,' said Ben, who didn't know what else to say. He didn't know anything about wool prices or imports, but he enjoyed listening to her when she talked to him like this. It showed him that she thought of him as a friend, and not just an employee.

'The same thing happened to the lead industry,' she continued. 'They started to import lead from other countries because it was cheaper than the lead we produce here, and now the mines and smelt mills are closing because it's not economical for them to keep working. You know, I do have some sympathy for the Beaumonts.'

'The way they're going on, closing mines and reducing men's hours, I think you must be the only one in the dale that has.'

'Perhaps,' she said, 'but the situation's not entirely their fault.' Swatting a fly away from her face, she said, 'I'll leave you in peace. It's too warm for me out here today.'

Ben looked up from the ewe he was working on, and

said, 'So long.'

Chapter 25

Burnside Hall
July, 1881

It was a still day without a breath of wind and the sun shone down relentlessly. Phyllis sat out in the garden with a glass of lemonade in her hand; a wasp buzzed around the sweet liquid, but she remained perfectly still until it eventually flew away.

She had been thinking about the advice that everyone had been giving to her recently and she was coming to the conclusion that they'd been right. Perhaps she should try to mix more with people from her own class, rather than spending so much of her time with Ben, even though she did enjoy his company considerably. The vicar's friends from Oxford would be coming to Weardale soon, and she thought it would be a good idea to host a dinner party to welcome them.

Phyllis walked slowly back to the house and took off her sunhat. The high temperatures over the last few days had made her weary, and the nights had been too hot for her to sleep, even on top of the bedclothes. Inside the house, she found the cooler air refreshing, and went to her office where she wrote a letter to Reverend Dagnall, inviting him and his friends to dinner at Burnside Hall at seven o'clock on Thursday, the seventh day of July.

There was a knock at the door, and Todd poked his head into the room.

'Hello, Miss. I'm going down to Stanhope this afternoon. Is there anything you need before I go?'

'No, I'm fine. But could you post this letter for me?'

She held out the letter to him and he took it.

'Of course, Miss. Is there anything else?'

'Please could you send in Mrs Gibson? We have a dinner party to plan,' she said with a smile, and she realised that she was actually looking forward to entertaining guests at the Hall.

'Very well, Miss,' Todd replied with a grin.

A few minutes later, Mrs Gibson tapped lightly at the door before entering the room. Her face was red; she wiped her brow with the back of her hand and exhaled loudly.

'You wanted to see me, Miss.'

'Yes, please take a seat. I would like you and Miss Wilson to prepare a dinner party for next Thursday evening. It's for the vicar, his two friends from Oxford, and myself. I'd like you to choose the menu and wines. And please could you check that my violet evening dress is ready for me? Oh, I haven't worn it in over a year — perhaps I should try it on to make sure it still fits?'

'I'm sure it will, Miss. You haven't put an ounce on since you came home. And it'll be nice for you to wear something other than black for a change. I know you're supposed to be in mourning for a year, but I wouldn't worry about that. It'll be a pleasure to prepare the dinner party for you.' Mrs Gibson's smile lit up her eyes which, if Phyllis wasn't mistaken, were a little teary.

'Thank you.'

Mrs Gibson hauled herself off the chair and fanned her face with her hand.

'I hope it cools down soon. We're not used to this kind of heat here,' she said. 'Opening the windows doesn't make a ha'pence of difference, there's just no air.'

After the housekeeper left the office, Phyllis sat at her desk and thought about the men who would be coming to the party. She knew so little about them, apart from that they'd been at Oxford with the vicar, and that they all shared an interest in archaeology and antiquities. It had been such a long time since she'd socialised, and she had to admit that she was excited at the prospect of meeting new people, especially when they were men from her own social class, and could potentially be suitors.

There was an air of anticipation in the Hall over the next few days whilst preparations for the dinner party got underway. Despite the continued heat, the household staff ran around with purpose. For the younger ones, it was the first event that they would witness in the grand house, and for the older ones, it would be a reminder of the good old days when Sir Thomas and Lady Margaret had entertained guests on a regular basis.

On Wednesday afternoon, Todd took the carriage to the railway station at Stanhope to meet the travellers and convey them to the vicarage at Westgate, as the vicar's trap had only two seats. When the butler returned to the Hall, Phyllis was standing at the front door.

'Is everything alright, Miss?' he asked, as he approached the house.

'Yes, thank you. I just wanted some air. What were the Oxford men like?'

'They seemed to be nice chaps — very polite and well dressed as you'd expect, but they were a little weary from the journey.'

'Yes, I'm sure they were,' said Phyllis, thinking back to her tedious trip from Harrogate in the winter. 'They'll have plenty of time to recover before tomorrow evening.'

She looked up at the sky.

'This weather looks set in to me,' said Todd.

'I'm not so sure,' said Phyllis. She sensed that the weather was going to change.

The following morning, Phyllis was anxious that everything should go smoothly. This was the first dinner party she'd held, and she was grateful for Mrs Gibson's experience in such matters. The housekeeper informed her that all of the provisions they needed for the evening meal had arrived, and that the dining room was ready. Phyllis went to check it to make sure that the table was set with only the finest china, glassware and silverware that she owned, and that the vases had been filled with fresh flowers from the garden. The windows were open and the sweet scent of honeysuckle permeated the room. She smiled, satisfied that the household staff had done everything that she had asked of them.

In the afternoon, she bathed in luxurious scented bath salts, and then Mrs Gibson styled her hair with curling tongs and helped her to dress. The housekeeper excused herself, and reappeared a few moments later with a diamond necklace.

'I've borrowed this from your mother's room,' the housekeeper said, as she fastened it around Phyllis's slender neck. 'She would have wanted you to wear it.'

It had been her mother's favourite piece of jewellery, although it had only been worn on special occasions; it had been considered too special to wear at informal events.

'There now, let's have a look at you.'

She turned around in front of Mrs Gibson, and was rewarded with another teary smile. 'Have a look in the glass,' she said, leading her by the arm. When Phyllis looked in the full-length mirror, she was shocked to see the reflection of a beautiful, young woman who looked every bit the mistress of Burnside Hall.

'Thank you, Mrs Gibson.'

She was now ready to meet her guests.

The gentlemen arrived just before seven o'clock, on horses which Reverend Dagnall had loaned for them during their stay. They dismounted in the yard and Thompson led the horses to the stables; Todd went out to welcome the guests, and was about to show them to the drawing room but, as they entered the house, they stopped when they saw Phyllis walking down the wide, carpeted staircase.

'Good evening, gentlemen,' she said.

In turn, the strangers each took her hand and kissed it, while murmuring words of greeting. The vicar was at the edge of the group and the last to greet her.

'Thank you for your kind invitation. You look very beautiful tonight, Miss Forster. That colour suits you.'

'Thank you, Reverend Dagnall. That's very kind of you to say.'

'Please, call me Timothy. Would I be too forward in asking if I could call you by your Christian name?'

'No, not at all. It's Phyllis.'

Timothy offered her his arm and they followed the butler as he ushered the group into the drawing room and offered them a seat. There was a silver salver with glasses of sherry, already poured, on the sideboard. Todd picked up the tray and offered the drinks to the guests.

As Timothy was the only one in the room who knew

everybody, he made the introductions. Gesturing to a fair-haired man of medium build, he said, 'May I introduce Alexander Wells. Alex is an estate manager at Oxford. His father owns a large part of Dorset, which we've all been to visit because it has the most magnificent ancient hill camp, with very impressive ramparts.'

'It was a great a place to hide from our governess!' said Alexander.

Phyllis joined in the laughter, as in her mind she pictured children running up the steep banks and disappearing from sight as they descended into the deep ditches, with a disgruntled teacher calling them back to the schoolroom.

The other gentleman was stocky, with dark hair, and Phyllis had noticed that he had a slight lilt to his voice. Timothy said, 'And this is Kenneth McKie. He's the only one of us that doesn't need to work for a living. He's the heir to a large estate in the Scottish borders, and he'll inherit his father's title too — meet the future Lord McKie.'

'It's a pleasure to meet you, Mr McKie. How did your interest in archaeology begin?' asked Phyllis.

'A long time ago, when I was just a wee laddie, my father took me to a magical place. Can you imagine forty-two upright stones, taller than men, arranged in a circle?'

Her eyes widened in surprise. She had seen drawings of stone circles, but never one with so many stones.

'Indeed, that is impressive.'

Todd came back into the drawing room and led the guests to the dining room. The candles in the candelabra had been lit and the room looked magnificent. Yet Phyllis noticed that it was dark considering that it was just a little after seven o'clock. Glancing out of the large windows, she saw black clouds overhead, and then a flash of lightning lit up the room, followed almost immediately by a low rumble of thunder.

The guests took their seats, commenting on the electrical storm, and continued to chat until Mrs Gibson came in to serve celery soup from a large tureen. She jumped when a loud crack of thunder sounded, and Phyllis was amazed that she didn't spill a drop.

'Timothy, how do you like living in the north?' asked Alexander.

'I love it here. The countryside is peaceful. I've visited the Roman wall built by Emperor Hadrian, and Durham city, with its wonderful castle and cathedral, and I've even started to write my book!'

'That's excellent!'

'So, what's life like as a country vicar?' asked Kenneth.

Phyllis thought this an odd question, but realised that his friends had known him for years as a student, before he had been ordained as a vicar — a role which suited him very well, in her opinion.

'Well, it's what you'd expect really. I prepare my sermons on Fridays and deliver them on Sundays, as well as performing any baptisms. Weddings are usually held on Saturdays, but I've only officiated at two since I came here. Funerals are more difficult. They can be held on any day of the week, and occur with very little notice. I'm also required to spend a considerable amount of time with the grieving families, which is dull, but I still have plenty of spare time to pursue my interests.'

'It doesn't sound much like work at all!' said Alexander, and they all laughed.

'You didn't have a calling to become a vicar?' asked Phyllis, somewhat surprised.

'No, not really. I do believe in God, and I care about my fellow men, but it's what was expected. I'm the second son in my family. My older brother will inherit my father's land and properties, so I must eke out a living for myself. My younger brothers will become officers in the army.'

The other men nodded in understanding of his situation.

'Ken got engaged last month!' said Alexander.

'Congratulations!' said Timothy. 'Who's the lucky girl?'

'We've just announced the engagement, but the union was planned years ago when we were just wains. Elizabeth is a baron's daughter from the neighbouring estate, and our parents' intention was always for our marriage to bond the estates.'

'How romantic!' said Timothy sarcastically, and then he laughed loudly.

Phyllis noticed that Kenneth didn't join in the laughter.

Instead he asked, 'Have you found yoursel' a wife yet?'

Timothy's eyes turned to Phyllis, and she looked down at her soup bowl.

'Not yet,' he replied.

The look didn't go unnoticed by his friends.

'Miss Forster would make you an excellent wife,' said Kenneth. 'She's pretty, she can manage a household, and you're obviously taken with her.'

There were a few chuckles from the men, and it was Timothy's turn to blush. Phyllis thought he looked relieved when another flash of lightning lit up the room and steered the conversation away from the topic of wives, back to the storm that was hovering over Burnside Hall.

The maids cleared away the dishes, and then the fish course was served with Hock to accompany it.

'It's trout from the River Wear,' Phyllis said proudly, 'caught earlier today!'

They all agreed that it was very tasty, and that they must do some fishing during their stay in Weardale.

The main course was venison with redcurrant sauce, and vegetables from the garden, with a red Burgundy wine that Alexander seemed to like, because Todd refilled his glass several times. Phyllis and her guests concurred that the cook had presented them with an excellent meal.

By the time the venison course had been eaten, the lightning strikes were coming thick and fast, and everyone turned their chairs towards the windows to watch the impromptu show.

Mrs Gibson served the desserts, and the men ate their trifle without comment as their attention was on the spectacular display. Suddenly there was a loud bang followed by a thud. Not more than three hundred feet from the house, a large oak tree had fallen to the ground and the remains of its trunk were on fire.

'Well, I never!' said Timothy.

'Shall we put out the fire?' asked Kenneth, as he got to his feet. But then the heavens opened and sheets of rain fell to the ground.

'No need, Kenneth,' said Timothy. 'The rain will douse the flames.'

Todd entered the room and ushered them back to the drawing room, where he served port. The guests relaxed in armchairs, some of which they moved to face the windows.

Kenneth and Alexander talked enthusiastically about their visit to the Natural History Museum in London, which had opened earlier that year, but they stopped talking and watched in fascination when forked lightning illuminated the night sky.

Phyllis sat and studied the men. Timothy and Alexander were eligible bachelors, and Kenneth was betrothed, but not yet married. Not one of them appealed to her as a potential husband, she realised. She had been entertained by their good-humoured company throughout the evening, but there was no physical attraction to any of them.

She wondered how people knew when they'd found the right person. Was it simply a case of finding someone you liked, and hoping that you'd fall in love, given time? Was love at first sight a real phenomenon, or something that just happened in romance novels? For Phyllis to commit to marriage, to live with a man for the rest of her life, and to be intimate with him, she would have to be sure that he, whoever he was, was the right person for her. She put down her glass of port; she'd had enough to drink.

Mrs Gibson came to her side, and whispered, 'Miss, the gentlemen can't possibly ride back to Westgate in this rain. Shall I have the girls prepare rooms for them?'

'I hadn't thought about them having to ride home. I suppose the groom could take them back in the carriage, couldn't he? But then their horses would still be here.' She heard herself rambling, and hated that the alcohol had dulled her senses so that she couldn't think clearly about the problem. She was usually so decisive.

'You're right. They can't possibly go out in this weather. Have three rooms prepared, and send a message to the stables that the horses won't be needed tonight. Thank you.'

Mrs Gibson nodded as she left the room.

'Gentlemen, you must stay tonight. I can't let you leave in this frightful weather.'

'That's very kind of you, Phyllis. Thank you,' said Timothy.

'How thoughtful!' said Kenneth. 'Thank you.'

Alexander nodded to show his appreciation.

The storm continued for several hours, and they all commented that they had never seen anything like it. Kenneth said, 'If we were in Ancient Greece and this storm hit, we'd think the gods were angry wi' us. We'd be thinking about all the things we'd done that could ha' upset them.'

'Now there's an idea. What have we done that could have upset them?' said Timothy. 'Come on, spill the beans everyone.'

'Seriously, Timothy?' chuckled Kenneth. 'You're a man of God. You can't believe in pagan gods, even hypothetically speaking.'

Phyllis stopped listening to the conversation because she was still pondering the question about what they could have done to upset the gods, or God, Himself. There had been the body in the cave, disturbed after many years at peace, and then there was her friendship with a shepherd that seemed to upset everyone.

When Phyllis saw Kenneth stifle a yawn, she said, 'Thank you for a most enjoyable evening, gentlemen. I believe it's time to retire. Todd will show you to your rooms.'

Todd, who had been standing outside the door, came in and waited patiently while thanks were given for a lovely evening, and then the gentlemen followed him upstairs. Alexander turned and winked at Phyllis as he left the room.

Did Alexander like her? Or had he simply had too much to drink? Alexander Wells, estate manager, son of a Dorset landowner. Her father would have approved of him. He was a fine-looking man, but she wasn't attracted to him in the slightest. She'd always preferred men with dark hair — like Ben's dark mahogany hair that had coppery streaks running through it when the sun shone on it.

Phyllis was shocked as it dawned on her that she found her shepherd much more attractive than any of these well-bred gentlemen.

She went upstairs to bed and, on her way, she heard a commotion in the east wing. She walked along the corridor, and turned the corner to see Alexander with a servant girl pressed up against the wall, obviously against her will, as she was trying her hardest to push him away.

'Let her go,' Phyllis said with authority.

Alexander looked sheepish and pushed the girl away. The girl ran past Phyllis and down the main staircase. It didn't matter to Phyllis that she hadn't used the servants' staircase; at least the girl was safe.

Alexander walked slowly towards Phyllis, his eyes devouring her body, and she felt disgusted by him.

'You're a very beautiful woman, Miss Forster. Would you like to take her place?'

'Absolutely not!'

'That's a shame,' he said with a lecherous smile, 'we

could have had some fun.' He staggered back down the corridor to his room.

'And you, Mr Wells, will leave here first thing in the morning!' she shouted after him.

Mrs Gibson appeared by her side.

'Hannah told me what happened. Are you alright?'

'Yes, I'm fine. Ask Todd to make sure Mr Wells leaves first thing in the morning — and tell the girls to lock their doors tonight.'

'Yes, Miss.'

Mrs Gibson walked Phyllis back to her room, helped her to undress and bade her goodnight. When she left, Phyllis turned the key in the lock and climbed into bed. The storm rumbled on in the distance, but it was not the noise or the flashes of lightning that kept sleep at a distance that night. Her mind was troubled by her houseguest's behaviour. Yes, she knew that gentlemen sometimes messed around with girls in service, but that didn't make it right, and she felt responsible for her servants' welfare while they worked for her. Once again, she felt the burden of responsibility that came with being mistress of Burnside Hall. Until Alexander Wells was off her property, she knew she wouldn't settle

At breakfast the next morning, her guests appeared one by one, but there was no sign of Alexander, and Phyllis was pleased that Todd must have sent him packing at first light as she had asked. When she'd finished eating,

Timothy asked to speak with her for a moment in private; she took him into the drawing room and closed the door behind them.

'I must apologise on behalf of Alex for what he did last night. He behaved inappropriately, and he begs for your forgiveness. Unfortunately, I'm ashamed to say that this is not uncommon behaviour for him. He seems to lose his inhibitions when he's had a little too much to drink.'

'His behaviour upset me a great deal last night, and I asked my butler to ensure he left the house this morning. Has he gone?'

'Yes, but he woke me before he left, and asked me to speak with you. It would be most inconvenient if the two of you remained in disagreement during his stay. We intend to begin the dig in the cave today, and that too is your property.'

'I understand what you're saying. I will tolerate his company on one condition — he must agree to stay sober. Is that clear?'

'That's very generous of you, Phyllis. You have a kind and forgiving heart, my dear.'

He took her hand and lifted it to his mouth, and kissed it gently before leaving the room.

Phyllis stood for a while looking out of the window. A sunbeam broke through the dark rain clouds and a beautiful rainbow appeared in the sky. The storm had passed and the weather was changing for the better.

Chapter 26

Westgate
July, 1881

At the end of his shift, Davey Bell was tired and weary. Nothing interested him anymore, and everything felt as though it was an enormous effort. Walking through the stone-lined tunnel with his head down, his feet dragging though the water, he looked up and saw the light at the end of the tunnel, and he wanted to laugh. Was he going mad? He wished there was a light at the end of the tunnel, because he couldn't see how things could get better; he was cursed and Lottie was dead. That was that.

Another team of men were following him out, and when they stepped into the warm sunshine together, one of them slapped him on the back, and said, 'Cheer up! It might never happen.' The other men howled with laughter as they went in the direction of the pub.

Davey felt like punching the man, but he couldn't be bothered. Instead, he slowly made his way to the churchyard and sat on the grass beside a small grave under the eaves of the church. He reached over and pulled out a weed from the turf, tossing it behind him without thinking about what he was doing, and he wondered, absentmindedly, why all the children were buried close to the church. He seemed to ponder this question for quite some time before he realised that one of his lads was standing beside him. Looking up at the sky, the sun was fairly low and he guessed he'd been there an hour or more.

'Mother says your tea's ready and you should come home.'

'Aye, alright.'

They walked home together in silence, because neither of them knew what to say. He was a bad father, he knew that. Why didn't he love his sons as much as he'd loved his daughter? But he didn't know the answer, that's just how it was.

When Davey and his son arrived back at the cottage, Martha was serving out dinner and she carried a couple of plates across to the table.

'Sit down and eat it before it gets cold,' she said, as she went back to fetch the other two. In her rush to pick up the plates, the hot stew slid over the edge and onto her wrist. She shouted loudly and Davey was immediately by her side. He took the plates from her and quickly put them onto the table, and poured some cold water into a bowl and placed it on the table too.

'Put your hand in there,' he said, and when she didn't move, he put his arms around her and manoeuvred her to her chair. 'Sit down, you'll be alright,' he said soothingly. He sat next to her and took her hand, and then he lowered it into the water and held it there.

'Eat yours, lads. Don't wait for us,' he said to the boys.

'It stings,' said Martha, after a minute or two. 'How could I have been so stupid, spilling the dinner like that? There's not enough for all of us now.'

'Don't worry about that,' said Davey. 'Just so long as you're alright. That's what matters.'

'I'll be fine, Davey, I've had worse burns than this afore. Let go of me hand. We should eat what's left before it gets cold.'

Davey got up and washed his hands before sitting at the table again and, looking at his wife and two boys, he realised that he'd hardly been aware of them since they'd lost Lottie. He'd been so tied up in his own grief to think about how it was affecting them. He picked up his fork and scraped some of his dinner onto Martha's plate, and then began to eat the delicious meal of stew and potatoes. At least now that he was back at work, his family had some decent food.

'So, what have you lot been up to today?' he asked his sons.

Martha looked up in surprise, and smiled as he listened to the lads talk enthusiastically about their day at school, and playing by the river afterwards. She'd been worried about Davey; he'd been so withdrawn of late and hadn't shown any interest in anything, and he'd been so quiet. Thankfully, it looked like he was feeling a bit better.

After dinner, Davey sat in his chair, smoking his pipe for a while, deep in thought, oblivious to the clicking of Martha's knitting needles.

'Do you fancy a walk?' he asked. 'It's a nice night.'

'Aye Davey, I do.'

She stuck the ball of wool onto the end of her needles, to hold the knitting in place, and tucked everything away into a basket beside her chair. By the time she stood up, Davey was already standing by the door, holding out his arm to her, and they went out onto the front street.

They walked leisurely up the hillside to where there was a wooden seat that had a beautiful view of the village below.

Sitting side by side, she took his hand and looked at him, thinking that he'd aged in the last couple of months. Grey hairs had appeared at his temples, and lines around his eyes.

'What is it?' he asked.

'It's good to have you back, love,' she said.

'I'm sorry, I know I've not been good company lately, but I couldn't help it. I don't know what was wrong with me,' he said, shaking his head.

'I can tell that you're going to be alright now, and I'm glad of it.'

Davey turned to the woman he loved, took her into his

arms and held her close. He whispered, 'Thank you, hinny. Thank you for everything.'

Chapter 27

Burnside Hall
July, 1881

Over the next few weeks, Timothy and his friends spent most of their time at the quarry, carefully scraping away sediment from the cave floor, and cheering loudly whenever they uncovered something from the muddy deposits. For much of the time, Phyllis thought they looked as though they'd been wrestling in the mud, so dirty were their clothes, and hands, and faces when they returned to the Hall in the evening. After they'd washed and changed, they examined their finds and discussed them at length, debating what the objects were, and what they may have been used for in the distant past.

The current item that had them enthralled was a piece of polished bronze and, because it appeared to have a sharp edge, they thought it might be part of a blade from a sword or dagger. As Phyllis listened to their conversation, she wished that Ben could be with them. He was interested in the past, and she imagined that he would enjoy listening to and disputing their hypotheses but, in reality, she knew that he would never be accepted into this group. Even her servants had turned their noses up at him when she'd invited him in for a drink. What would these wealthy, educated men think of him? They were so used to ignoring servants that they probably wouldn't even notice his presence. If introduced, she had no doubt that they would immediately move on. He was so far beneath their station that he didn't even deserve their consideration. Yet he had shown her more kindness and understanding than anyone else since she'd returned home; she could tell that he genuinely cared about her.

'Phyllis, you look miles away,' said Timothy.

'I'm sorry.'

'Are we boring you terribly with all this talk of weaponry?'

'Certainly not!' she replied, and then, noticing the mantle clock, she said, 'Good heavens! It's seven o'clock. Cook will have dinner ready. Shall we go through?'

The men were on their feet before Phyllis rose from her seat, and she led the way to the dining room, where they waited for her to be seated before they took their own places at the table.

Dinner at the Hall had become a regular event and, more often than not, the men stayed overnight. It was much more convenient for them than travelling back to Westgate each night, and they had commented that the food at the Hall was much more to their liking. Alexander had kept to his promise and not touched a drop of alcohol since that first night, or any girls for that matter. Phyllis enjoyed their friendly banter; it felt as though the place had come back to life through her new-found friends. She would miss their companionship when their summer holiday came to an end.

The next day was a beautiful summer's day with very little breeze. The men had invited Phyllis to come to the cave and see their work for herself. She wore a lemon dress and straw hat, in the hope that they would keep her cool. She walked to the quarry with Timothy and his friends, passing the sweet-smelling hay meadows where men stacked loose hay into pikes; hay-making was later than usual because of the changeable weather, but at least, Phyllis thought, there was a good crop and the weather seemed to be settled enough for them to gather it in.

Kenneth and Alexander climbed up the ladder quickly, in their rush to continue excavating the cave floor. Timothy remained on the ground, and offered to help Phyllis climb the ladder, but she said that she would prefer it if he went in front so she wouldn't hold him up. Secretly, she was concerned that her dress was not suitable for climbing ladders, and that her legs may be on show to anyone who climbed up behind her.

When she joined them, they were using trowels to remove thin layers of silt and she watched them in fascination, at first expecting that they would find something any minute, but by the time an hour or more had passed, they'd found nothing at all. She wondered about all of their conversations which had made digging sound exciting and such fun, for she was finding it tedious to watch.

'I'll go back and have some refreshments brought up for you. I'm sure you'll appreciate a cool drink and a few sandwiches.'

Without waiting for a response, she left the cave and carefully descended the ladder, before marching home. She breathed a sigh of relief when she entered the stone building; it was much cooler inside. She ordered Miss Wilson to prepare some food and drink, and sat for a while by the open window in the music room. When she had recovered from the heat, she played a short piece on the piano, to fill in time, before making her way back to the quarry, followed by two maids carrying picnic baskets.

She called up to the men, and they joined her on a grassy mound, where they sat down to eat. Phyllis had a sudden urge to look up, perhaps a movement had caught her eye, and she saw Ben standing in the shade of a tree watching them.

'Stay still,' whispered Timothy. 'There's a wasp on your collar. Let me rid you of it.'

She had never been fond of wasps, but she wasn't scared of them either; if she left them alone, she had found that they left her alone, but she stayed still as Timothy moved closer and lifted his hand to her neck, quickly flicking away the offending insect. She thanked him for his help, and then looked back to the hillside. Ben was no longer by the tree and her eyes scoured the slope until she found him; he was walking up the hill with the sheepdog, his back to her.

After a pleasant meal, they returned to the cave. Kenneth was about to resume his position by the trench, when he turned to Phyllis and said, 'Would you like to try?'

'Alright, I will,' she replied with a smile. She glanced down at her pale dress and realised how inappropriate her choice of clothing had been that morning. Seeing her hesitation to kneel in the mud, Kenneth took off his jacket and placed it on the ground where he'd been working.

'Thank you,' she said. 'That's very kind of you.'

She knelt down, and moved the trowel slowly and shallowly, as she had seen the men do, and after a few minutes, she began to enjoy herself. Time passed amazingly quickly, and it didn't seem long before she heard a metallic clank. She looked at the excited faces surrounding her.

'You've found something!' said Kenneth.

They all gathered around her as she uncovered the object and held it out for their scrutiny.

'What is it?' she asked.

Timothy took the object and wiped off the mud with

his hands. Alexander passed him a handkerchief, which he used to clean the artefact.

'What do we have?' asked Alexander.

'I believe it's a bracelet,' said Timothy incredulously. 'A bronze bracelet, to be precise.'

'Beginner's luck!' said Kenneth.

The find gave them hope that they would discover more items of interest, but by the end of the afternoon, nothing else had been found.

That night, as Tom kept watch over the quarry, Ben patrolled the fields around the Hall. All was quiet, except for the sound of voices and laughter coming from the dining room as he passed. Ben was feeling relaxed because the animals were sleeping peacefully in the surrounding fields, and he knew that they would be restless if there were any intruders nearby. He stood for a while at the corner of the building, looking out over the hills and at the almost full moon in the clear, starry sky. A bat flew silently overhead, catching moths drawn to the lamps glowing in the windows.

Ben heard footsteps on the path at the side of the Hall, and he listened intently; the sound was getting louder, someone was approaching. Rather than look around the corner of the house to see who was there, he waited patiently for the person to step out in front of him, so he would have the benefit of surprise when he confronted them. Slowly, he edged forward to apprehend the person, and when he saw a shadowy figure, he reached out and grabbed — a woman.

Phyllis shouted loudly.

'I'm so sorry,' Ben said, quickly releasing her from his grip and stepping back. In the moonlight, he could see that she wore a low-necked evening gown in a pale shade of purple; the colour suited her. She looked beautiful. Before that day, he'd only seen her wearing black clothes that blanched her skin and emphasised the dark circles under her eyes. She'd looked pretty in the yellow dress she'd worn earlier in the day and, with a stab of jealousy, he thought that the vicar must have liked it as well because he hadn't been able to keep his hands off her.

'No harm done,' she said, although her voice was a little shaky.

'What are you doing outside?'

'I wanted some fresh air. It's hot inside, and my guests are smoking cigars. Anyway, I thought it would be safe out here with the Felons guarding the place, and I can see that I was right.'

Ben smiled; he thought the way she was trying to justify why she was there was sweet.

'You don't need an excuse to come out and see me,' he said cheekily.

'I didn't!' she exclaimed, and then when she realised that he was teasing her, she nudged his arm and said sarcastically, 'That's very funny.'

Ben returned his gaze to the hillside, and was amazed

by what he saw. A green glow had appeared on the horizon.

'Look over there.'

'What is it?'

'The northern lights.'

They gazed in awe as waves of green and pink light filled the night sky, lighting the heavens in their mystical dance.

'I've never seen them before,' said Phyllis. 'They're beautiful.'

'I've seen the lights before, but not like this, not with so many colours and so much movement.'

They were so engrossed in the aurora that they didn't notice Timothy had joined them, until he spoke.

'So, that's where you've got to. And who is this chap?' he said sternly.

'Timothy, this is Featherstone — my shepherd. He's also one of the Felons I was telling you about, and he's on duty tonight.'

'You'd better come back inside, dear. You shouldn't be out here at night.'

Ben could see that Phyllis was torn between staying with him or going back with Timothy, but she took the vicar's arm and walked away with him, looking back at him apologetically. Timothy's voice carried in the still night air and Ben heard him warn Phyllis about the dangers of being alone with a common man.

Ben wasn't totally naive; he knew that some people

thought they were better than others, but he was insulted by the assumption that working-class people couldn't be trusted. There were bad people in all walks of life, and Ben had learnt the hard way that some of the worst came from the gentry. But he didn't want to get worked up about that again — not now.

In the short time that he'd spent with Phyllis that evening, they'd shared a very special moment and there was no way he would let the vicar's comment spoil it. The lights in the sky dimmed to a faint glow on the hilltops as he went back to roaming the fields around Burnside Hall, wondering how Phyllis could tolerate such pompous company.

A week later, on a beautiful day with hardly a cloud in the sky and just a hint of a breeze, Phyllis, Timothy, Kenneth and Alexander sat on a large rug in the garden, munching on a picnic of sandwiches, pastries and cakes, and drinking chilled champagne.

'It's quite a spot you've got here, Phyllis,' said Kenneth. 'I mean, as far as archaeology goes. That bracelet was a pretty little thing.' He put his hand in his trouser pocket and pulled out a shiny bronze bracelet that looked nothing like the one they'd removed from the ground. 'It's yours by right, and we'd all like you to keep it.'

'Thank you.'

'I canna believe this is our last day here,' said Kenneth. 'We're leavin' the morrow on the early train.'

'This is the perfect way to end our stay, after all, we have spent most of our time at the Hall,' said Alexander. 'Thank you, you've made us extremely welcome here, and I'm sorry we got off on the wrong foot.'

'Oh, don't worry about that. You've been on your best behaviour since then,' said Phyllis with a chuckle. 'You're welcome back, anytime, so long as you stay off the booze.'

'I'd like to thank you too,' said Timothy, 'for allowing my friends and I to take over your property. It really has been a most enjoyable summer.'

Kenneth proposed a toast to their hostess, and the men raised their glasses to Phyllis.

Chapter 28

Burnside Hall Estate
August 1881

The glorious twelfth was not such a glorious day. It started cold and dull, and by mid-morning, much to everyone's surprise, there was a light dusting of snow on the heather-covered moors.

Phyllis had asked her gamekeeper to organise the shoot, and to lead the shooting party up onto the fell. It was something she knew little about, because her father had never allowed her to take part. Her brother, Henry, should have been managing the estate; he'd been primed for the job his whole life. But as the estate owner, she thought she should attend, so she donned her warmest clothes and a stout pair of boots and set out onto the moors with thirty men who had paid good money to shoot her grouse.

Because of the low stock levels, she had decided to limit the shoot to just one day because the red grouse numbers had been seriously depleted by the late frosts. She knew that her decision would have a detrimental effect on the estate's income for the year, but if she allowed more shoots to take place, there was a chance that the bird population might not recover in time for next season, or even longer, which would lead to more substantial losses in the long term.

Phyllis had never considered Reverend Timothy Dagnall to be a sporting man and had been surprised when he'd asked to accompany them, but he looked confident handling a shotgun as he walked by her side through the coarse grasses, bracken and heather covering the uneven ground.

At a distance, she saw Featherstone up on the fell, obviously checking on the sheep as he usually did, but no doubt he'd be keeping an eye on their proceedings and making sure that none of his flock was injured by stray lead shot. She hoped that they'd be safe, but she couldn't blame Featherstone for being concerned; she'd seen some of the men handling their weapons earlier and had doubts as to their capabilities — and that was before they'd had a drink. At midday, they would partake of a large picnic, and would most likely empty several barrels of ale and a cask of whisky. She dreaded to think what their aim would be like come the afternoon.

The party eventually arrived at the shooting butts — six low, stone-walled, circular structures, built in a straight line across the moor — and the men divided themselves up into smaller groups and took their places. The beaters

— young boys from the village — were dispatched to flush out the game birds from their cover, and it wasn't long before a shot was fired. Phyllis covered her ears — the noise was so loud. She looked up, but the shot had missed its target, and she was secretly pleased as she watched the moorhen fly to safety.

However, it wasn't long before a retriever brought back the first casualty of the day, dangling from its mouth, and dropped it at his owner's feet. Phyllis watched the same thing happen time and time again, and the blood and the noise and the smell made her feel faint. Timothy noticed that she looked pasty, and sat her down against the stone wall.

Phyllis sat with her head down, wishing that she'd stayed at home. She hadn't realised how barbaric it would be, and how much the men would enjoy killing the birds. She really didn't want to stay any longer and, deciding she would walk back, she caught Timothy's attention.

'I'm not feeling well, so I'm going home.'

'Righto!' he replied cheerfully. 'I hope you feel better soon.'

'Is it safe for me to go? I won't get shot, will I?'

'Of course not, the guns are all pointed this way,' he said, pointing up the hill. 'You'll be perfectly safe.'

'Alright, I'll be off.'

He didn't seem to notice her leave because he already had his eye on another target.

Phyllis set off down the hill alone, walking as quickly

as she dared, to get away from the sound of guns and the cries from injured birds. Her head ached and her stomach churned. When she saw Ben approaching, she didn't know if she was glad that he was there or not.

'Is everything alright?' he asked.

'Yes, thank you.'

'I didn't expect you to leave so soon, that's all.'

'It's no business of yours, really, but I wasn't feeling well.'

'I'm sorry. Can I walk you back?'

Phyllis looked up the hill to the shooting butt that she'd recently vacated, and could see Timothy, his gun raised, concentrating on his prey higher up the fell — he wasn't even watching to make sure she got down safely. None of the others in the group had noticed her leaving, and it struck her that she could have passed out and nobody would have known.

'Thank you, Featherstone, that's very kind of you.'

He held out his arm, and she took it, glad of the support as they walked across the rough ground and down the steep slope to Burnside Hall, chatting casually about the unseasonal weather and the upcoming shows. When they reached the gates, he released her arm and walked a little further away from her, but he made sure she got to the front door safely.

'Thank you, Featherstone. I appreciate your help.'

'I hope you feel better soon,' he said, as he tipped his cap at her and walked towards the kitchen door.

Phyllis went inside, took off her cloak, and sat by the fire in the drawing room.

'Oh, my word!' said Mrs Gibson, stopping suddenly in the doorway, 'You gave me quite a fright, Miss. I didn't expect anyone to be in here. What are you doing back so soon?'

'To be truthful, I don't have the stomach for shooting and killing. I'm afraid that's one part of the estate's business that I will have to delegate. My father would be so disappointed in me, leaving after just an hour.'

'No, he wouldn't,' said the housekeeper firmly. 'He'd have said it was a man's business. You're doing a good job of running this place, so don't you go having any doubts.'

'Thank you, Mrs Gibson.'

'I'll get you some tea. It's cold out today, you must be frozen.'

After Mrs Gibson had left, Phyllis stared into the flames and thought about Timothy and Featherstone — the two men who played a significant part in her life, two men who couldn't be more different from one another.

Timothy had been born into an aristocratic family and had never wanted for anything in his life. He'd had a classical education at Oxford and was a man of the cloth. His interest in the past was almost obsessive, and she was certain that he'd achieve his aim of writing a book on the subject. He was witty and paid her attention, and although she'd known him for months now, she never felt as though he knew her, not really.

On the other hand, Featherstone, born into a poor, working-class family in Weardale had attended the village school where he'd learned to read and write, and he worked as a humble shepherd. He was younger than Timothy by several years, yet he seemed wiser, and as much as she had tried to hide her true self, she knew that he'd seen through her act and understood her completely.

So why was Timothy considered a suitable match for her, but not Featherstone?

Chapter 29

St John's Chapel
August, 1881

Ben had spent the best part of two days trimming and cleaning the tup and ewe that he'd chosen to take to the show at St John's Chapel. Looking them over, he thought they stood a good chance, although there would be some tough competition. He'd agreed to meet Thompson and the dairyman in the yard, as they were taking some stock up to the show as well, and when he saw them, all primped and preened, he was glad that he'd put on a suit for the occasion. They walked up to St John's Chapel together.

When they arrived at the showfield, Ben took his sheep to the pens and looked over the other sheep in the neighbouring pens. He knew that the Milburn brothers posed the biggest threat, because their stock had been bred from Mr Peart's flock, which had been as good, if not better, than Sir Thomas's. He saw Joe Milburn checking out the pens too, and he went over to have a word with him while they waited for their classes to be called to the ring.

'Morning, Joe,' said Ben.

'Morning. It's a canny day for the show.'

'It's not bad.' Looking at Joe's pen, Ben said, 'Do you fancy your chances, then?'

'Well, I don't know really. The tup I've brought wasn't me first choice. The best one went lame yesterday. Just typical, isn't it? The day before the show.'

'Aye, that's sheep for you,' said Ben knowingly. 'How's Connie?'

'Driving me crazy!' said Joe, laughing. 'But she's well. She was upset this morning because she couldn't come to the show. She used to love the riding classes. I told her that she needs to settle herself until the bairn comes and that she'll have to wait until next year.'

The cattle classes ended and the sheep were up next, so the farmers and shepherds prepared their animals for the ring. Starting with the ram class, they formed a line, and one by one they paraded the tups around the ring. The judge looked them over, feeling their backs, shoulders and rumps, and Ben's tup was chosen as the best in class. He was grinning from ear to ear, and both Joe and Tom gave him a pat on the shoulder in congratulations.

After a lot of deliberation by the judge, the ewe class was won by Joe Milburn's yearling ewe, with Ben's two-year-old ewe a close second. As they were leaving the ring, Ben noticed Phyllis walking with the vicar, and they were heading towards the sheep pens. They arrived back at the same time. Ben greeted her as he secured the ewe back in her pen.

'Are these my sheep?' she asked with a smile.

'Aye, they are,' he said proudly.

'Well done! I saw our tup win his class. That's down to all your hard work. I hardly recognised him, or you for that matter,' she said smiling, 'dressed in a suit. You've had your hair cut too.'

'Thank you,' he muttered, as his cheeks reddened. But despite his embarrassment, he was pleased that she'd noticed.

Timothy had been standing behind Phyllis, and he hadn't acknowledged Ben in any way. Addressing Phyllis, he said, 'That's quite enough. Let's get away from these smelly animals.'

Ben noticed Phyllis's slight hesitation as she took the vicar's arm, and said, 'Goodbye, Featherstone,' and then she walked away with him.

Ben wondered what she saw in him. As far as Ben could see, the vicar was a stuck up, selfish man. He didn't treat Phyllis with any respect and he certainly didn't deserve her.

Chapter 30

High House Farm, Westgate
September, 1881

It was Friday evening and Ben was looking forward to having his tea at High House Farm. He filled a bowl with cold water from the tap and took it into the kitchen, where he stripped off and washed himself. He put on some clean clothes, combed his hair and set off up the path, with Bess by his side.

When he reached High House Farm, Lizzie opened the door before her son had time to knock.

'I saw you coming, lad,' she said with a smile, and held the door open for him. 'I've been waiting to see you all day. How are you?'

As he entered the kitchen, he said, 'I'm fine, thanks. You?'

'I'm feeling grand.'

He noticed that she had regained a little weight and didn't look as frail as she had done when she'd moved in. Also, the lines on her face appeared to be less pronounced and her skin had more colour.

'You look grand as well,' he said sincerely.

Mary called over to them, 'We're about to serve out so grab a seat.'

The children overheard, and Josie, Tommy and Matt rushed to their chairs in anticipation of their meal. Ben smiled because he knew how they felt; the smell of roast beef in the kitchen was making his mouth water and he couldn't wait to eat either. He pulled out a heavy wooden chair for his mother, and once she was sitting comfortably, he sat down beside her.

After Tom said grace, they all began to eat, and it wasn't long before the meal of roast beef, Yorkshire pudding, roast potatoes and vegetables was finished.

'That was lovely, Mary,' said Ben. 'By far the best meal I've had in ages. Thank you.'

'You're welcome,' she replied. 'I hope you've left a bit of room for pudding. Jane's made apple crumble and custard.'

'Aye, that sounds good.'

Matt said proudly, 'Gran's crumble is the best pudding of them all.'

'He knows how to get around you, Mother, doesn't he?' said Tom, with a laugh. 'He's a little charmer!'

There was a loud knock at the door and it flew open. Joe Milburn burst into the room, and his eyes sought out his mother.

'Connie's having the bairn,' he said, with a hint of panic

in his voice. 'You'd better come quickly.'

Jane stood up, and said calmly, 'I wasn't expecting this just yet. I'll get some things together and I'll go back with you.' Looking at Mary, she said, 'I think you should come an' all.'

'Oh, I don't know,' said Mary. 'You know Connie's never liked me. I'm the last person she'd want there.'

'I can't manage myself, not at my age. You've had three of your own, so you know what's it's all about, and I think she'll be glad of the help — no matter what's gone on before.'

'What about Mrs Peart? Couldn't she give you a hand?' asked Mary.

'You know as well as I do that Mrs Peart's a good woman, there's none better, but she's useless where blood's concerned. She'd be to pick up off the floor!'

'Aye, I suppose you're right. I'll come over after I've cleared up here.'

Lizzie said, 'Me and Ben will clear up and see to the bairns. Just get yourselves over there and see to the lass.'

Joe had been listening by the door, his toe tapping impatiently, and he said, 'Hurry up, please. We need to get back. Mrs Peart's beside herself with worry.'

Tom went to his brother and, placing a hand on his shoulder, he gave him a knowing nod. He'd gone through the same thing every time Mary had borne a child. He stood in the doorway and watched Joe help the two women onto the cart and then climb up himself. They set off at speed and were soon out of sight. Tom closed the door and returned to his seat at the head of the table.

'I want some pudding,' said Matt, his bottom lip protruding.

'Don't worry, lad. I'll get you some pudding,' said Lizzie, taking over the kitchen duties. Ben helped her to serve out and carried the bowls to the table. The children ate their crumble happily, oblivious to the significance of Joe's visit. The adults, on the other hand, were fully aware of the implications and, as delicious as the food was, they did little more than pick at it.

Mary heard Connie's cries before she crossed the threshold at Springbank Farm, and Mrs Peart rushed out of the door to meet them. 'Thank the Lord, you're here,' she said.

'How long has Connie been in labour?' asked Jane.

'The pains started about three hours ago. They're getting worse, so I don't think the baby will be long now.'

Taking control, Jane said to Mary, 'You check that we have everything we need, and I'll go and see how she's getting on.'

'I'll wait in the parlour,' said Mrs Peart. 'Shout if you need me.'

Joe paced up and down in the kitchen as the women went about their work. Mary filled the kettle and put it on the stove to boil, and then scurried around gathering everything that they might need for the birth.

Jane came back downstairs to see Mary rushing around, and she said gently, 'She's not pushing yet. There's no rush.'

'Does she know I'm here?' asked Mary.

'No, I didn't mention it.'

'Well, I'll stay down here out of the way unless you need help. I don't want to upset her, not tonight.'

Joe sat down in the wooden chair by the window, but stood up again almost straight away and resumed his pacing.

'You're no use in here, Joe,' said Jane. 'Get yourself over to High House and have a drink with Tom. It'll take your mind off what's going on.'

'No, Mother. I want to be here.'

'Well, go and keep Mrs Peart company in the parlour. Take a bottle of sherry and some cards with you. She likes a game of whist.'

'Are you sure nothing's going to happen for a while?'

'It'll be a while yet, son.'

Joe nodded, and headed towards the parlour, raising his eyes to the ceiling as another loud scream pierced the silence. When Jane climbed the stairs to return to Connie's bedside, Mary noticed the look of relief on Joe's face.

'Mary!' screamed Jane.

At the panic in Jane's voice, Mary ran up the stairs, unsure of what to expect.

'The baby's coming now!'

'What's she doing here?' said Connie breathlessly. 'Get her out!'

'I need her to help, and so do you!'

Connie didn't say any more. She seemed to withdraw into herself and concentrate on birthing her baby — deep breaths interspersed with guttural groans as she pushed the infant from her body. It wasn't long before Mary saw the baby and she knew instinctively that something was wrong. Jane picked him up and held him with his face down, and rubbed and slapped his back to try and clear his airways, willing him to breathe, but it was no use; the baby boy was stillborn.

Connie asked, 'Where's my baby?'

Jane looked at Mary and shook her head.

Connie tried to sit up and blood gushed from between her legs. She fell back onto the bed. Jane passed the baby to Mary, and returned her attention to Connie. She did what she could to stop the bleeding, while Mary wrapped the baby in a sheet and placed him in Connie's arms.

'I'm very sorry,' said Mary.

Tears welled up in Connie's big blue eyes and began to roll down her cheeks.

Seeing that Connie was still bleeding heavily and Jane had not been able to stop it, Mary rushed to the top of the stairs and shouted, 'Joe!'

Joe appeared at the bottom of the stairs with an expectant look on his face, which changed suddenly the moment he saw Mary's grave expression. 'You'd better fetch the doctor, and quickly,' she said quietly.

Joe ran from the house without closing the door behind him, and moments later she heard a horse galloping away from the farm. Mary went back into the bedroom, where Connie was gently rocking her baby. 'It's a boy,' she said, with a faint smile. 'Joe will be pleased it's a boy.'

Jane took Mary to one side, and whispered, 'I've never seen bleeding like this afore. I hope the doctor can stop it because there's nothing more I can do for her, God help her.'

'She does know the baby's dead, doesn't she?' asked Mary.

'She did. But I'm not so sure anymore. I'm afraid we might lose her too. I'm going to get Mrs Peart. She should be with her, just in case.'

Mary noticed that Connie looked pale, and went over to the bedside. She put her hand on Connie's brow; her skin felt cold and clammy.

'Connie?'

Connie looked up and smiled dreamily. 'Mary...you came back. I'm sorry for being mean to you.'

'I know.' Mary held her hand, and said, 'Rest now. The doctor's on his way.'

Connie clung to her baby, but gradually her eyes closed and her breathing became steadier.

Jane and Mrs Peart came into the room and Mrs Peart walked over to Connie. Being careful not to look at the stained sheets at the bottom of the bed, she held her daughter's hand, stroked her hair, and kissed her pallid cheek.

'Connie, love, I'm here,' said Mrs Peart, taking hold of her hand.

Connie's eyelids flickered open.

'Joe's gone for the doctor. They'll be here soon. Let me see my grandson.'

Connie carefully pulled back the sheet from her baby's face.

'He's beautiful. You've done ever so well, love,' said Mrs Peart, with glassy eyes.

Connie smiled blissfully, and said, 'Thank you, Mother.'

Her eyes closed and she drifted off to sleep. The women waited and waited for the doctor to arrive, but the house remained silent. Jane began to clear up, and Mary followed her lead.

Mrs Peart sighed audibly. 'Where are they? They should have been here by now, shouldn't they?'

Jane shrugged. 'Maybe the doctor was out.'

Mary noticed Connie's breathing was shallow, and she said a little prayer for her. They had known each other for years, and were sisters-in-law, but they had never been friends, far from it at times. Even so, she had never wished her ill.

Connie's brow was cool to the touch, so Mary placed a blanket over her to keep her warm. Mrs Peart said to her daughter, 'There now, that's better, isn't it?'

The women stood around the bed, listening to her shallow breathing, hoping that the doctor would arrive soon. A few minutes later, Connie Milburn took her last breath.

They all knew that she'd left them, but none of them said anything because it would make it real. Eventually, Mrs Peart said softly. 'She still looks beautiful, doesn't she? Our Connie has always been beautiful.'

Through the haze, Mary heard male voices downstairs, and she realised that Joe had returned with Dr Rutherford. She left the room and walked down the stairs as if in a trance, aware of the doctor running past her with a worried expression on his face, and Joe's eyes searching for hers. When she reached the bottom, she knew she had to tell Joe what had happened. She lifted her eyes to meet his. He was standing in front of her, waiting desperately for news. The anguish in his eyes was unbearable.

'I'm sorry, Joe. We lost them both.'

The anguish turned to shock, and then to despair as the news sank in.

'The baby,' Mary swallowed loudly, 'a little boy, was stillborn, and then we couldn't stop the bleeding.' The tears running down her face were for the loss of two young lives, and for the heartbreak that her words were inflicting on this man. 'I'm so sorry,' she whispered.

Joe grabbed Mary and held her tightly, and she felt him

start to sob, huge racking sobs, and she could do nothing to ease his pain, except hold him.

Chapter 31

Burnside Hall
September, 1881

Phyllis was playing a soulful sonata by Beethoven when Todd interrupted her.

'There's a message for you, Miss.'

She took the note from the silver tray, and thanked him. Waiting until he had left the room, she opened it and, not immediately recognising the neat handwriting, she glanced at the signature before reading it.

My dear Phyllis

It is with the deepest regret that I must inform you that my darling daughter, and your dearest friend, Connie Milburn, passed away yesterday morning after giving birth to her child, a beautiful baby boy who was sadly born sleeping.

Their joint funeral will take place at St Andrew's Church on Monday morning at ten o'clock.

Yours sincerely

Mrs A Peart

Phyllis scrunched up the paper and threw it onto the burning coals in the fireplace. How could this have happened? Connie was such a lively, vibrant person — she couldn't be dead. She'd been looking forward to becoming a mother for the first time, and giving her husband the child that he craved. Poor Joe. He'd lost his wife, and his child, and his hopes in one tragic day. It was so unfair that she wanted to scream at the injustice of it.

Silent tears flowed down her cheeks. She couldn't let the household staff see that she was upset, so she crept into her late father's study and locked the door behind her, and let the tears fall. The decanters in the bureau caught her eye; she went over and poured a large measure of whisky into a crystal glass, thinking that it would be what her father would have recommended — a stiff upper lip and a stiff drink had been Sir Thomas's motto in times of stress.

The amber liquid burned her throat as she drank it, and she coughed and spluttered after the first sip, but the second wasn't so bad, nor the third. Drink was supposed to numb the pain, so she'd heard, but it didn't. She could vouch for that. The heavy pain in her chest was still there, and tears were running down her face. Thinking that perhaps she mustn't have had enough, she poured herself another.

Phyllis didn't know how long she'd been sitting at her father's desk, topping up her tumbler with his scotch, before she had a sudden urge to go for a walk. As she stood up, the room began to sway, and she reached for the corner of the oak desk to steady herself. She made her way to the door and turned the brass key in the lock and opened the study door. There was nobody in the hallway as she staggered to the outer door and crossed the yard.

She traversed several fields, not sure of where she was heading; she just wanted to walk, one foot in front of the other, until the heavy feeling in her chest subsided. Connie had been her one and only friend. With Connie gone, she was all alone in the world; she had no family and no friends.

Todd and Mrs Gibson were kind to her, but they were paid to help her and see to her needs. Had anyone shown her genuine affection, apart from the people she'd lost? She thought long and hard about that, and the only name that came to mind was Featherstone. But could she call him a friend? She knew there were barriers to their friendship, but what did that matter? She really didn't know anymore. Ben Featherstone was the only person in the whole of Weardale who had shown her any kindness since her return, and she was desperately in need of a friend.

Without releasing it, she found herself walking along the track towards Shepherd's Cottage, and when she saw the house looming towards her, she decided that she would call in. She knocked at the door and, without waiting for it to be answered, she opened it and almost fell into the kitchen. The first thing she noticed was that she'd ducked down to go through the door, and then how small and dark the room was, and then her eyes focused on Ben, who was sat at the table with a mug of milk in his hand and his mouth open. His expression showed surprise or possibly shock, she wasn't sure which. He slowly lowered the mug onto the table and stood up, whilst Phyllis pushed the door shut behind her.

'Miss Forster, can I help you?' he asked.

Phyllis stood there sobbing, and didn't say a word.

Ben went to her, and placed a comforting hand on her arm.

'Featherstone...' she said.

'Yes?'

'Hold me, please.'

Ben hesitated for a second, but seeing that she was obviously distraught, he took her into his arms and held her against his chest, comforting her in the same way he would any person, or animal, in distress.

'Shush, don't cry,' he said soothingly, as he gently rubbed her back. When her sobs eventually subsided, Phyllis lifted her head from his shoulder and turned her face up to him. She attempted to kiss him, but failed, because Ben had released her and stepped back when the smell of alcohol on her breath had hit him.

'Am I so repulsive?' she asked in anguish.

'No.'

'I need someone to love me. Please.'

'No.'

Her eyes pleaded with him. 'But why? Am I so awful that a man wouldn't want me?'

Ben looked into her troubled eyes and moved closer, gently running the tips of his fingers down her cheek, he whispered, 'You're beautiful...Phyllis.'

Had she heard him correctly? Beautiful. She wanted to laugh. She knew that she wasn't beautiful; even her own mother had said she was plain. It was the first time she'd heard him speak her name, and she liked the way it sounded coming from his lips. She'd liked the touch of his fingers too. But he had refused her.

'Then, why not?' she asked, like a petulant child.

'Because you've been drinking, and you might regret it,' he said sternly, and then he whispered into her ear, 'If you'd come to me sober and of sound mind, things might have been different, but I'll not take you into my bed tonight, not like this.'

His heated look made her flush, and for the first time in her life, she felt desirable, and as disappointed as she was by his rejection, her foggy brain was telling her that he'd turned down her advances for the right reasons.

'I should go,' she said.

'I'll walk you back. It's getting dark out there.'

After he'd closed the cottage door behind them, Ben held out his arm and Phyllis took it, and she was grateful for his support when she stumbled several times on the walk back to the Hall. Neither of them was aware of the shadowy figure that watched them from the riverside.

When they reached the corner of the house, Ben stopped and smiled at her warmly. 'You'll have a bad head in the morning,' he said, 'but please don't have any regrets about tonight. I think none the worse of you for having a drink after what's happened.'

'You know about Connie?'

'Aye, our Mary was attending her. It's tragic.'

Tears threatened to spill from Phyllis's eyes again, as she said, 'Thank you... Ben. You're a good friend.' Before he had time to reply, she kissed him quickly on the cheek and turned away. He watched her walk, a little unsteadily, back to the house.

Phyllis woke the next morning with a thumping headache. Ben had been right, she thought. She opened her eyes slowly and closed them again immediately. She must have slept late because Mrs Gibson had already been in to open the curtains.

Visions of the night before came back to her, and she pulled the covers over her head as though she could hide from what had happened. Had she really offered herself to him? Had she been so desperate to feel the warmth and comfort of another body that she'd been willing to sacrifice her virginity? How could she possibly face him after that? She was filled with guilt and shame.

Then the words he had whispered in her ear came back to her, 'If you'd come to me sober and of sound mind, things might have been different.' She blushed deeply as she realised that Ben had wanted her, and she was grateful that he'd been a gentleman. He could so easily have taken advantage of her in her drunken state.

And then she recalled the reason why she'd been drinking in the first place, the reason she'd been so upset. Connie was dead. She knew that it was true, but it was still difficult to comprehend.

She tentatively got out of bed and, while she was dressing, there was a knock at the door.

'It's just me,' said Mrs Gibson before she entered the room, 'I've brought you a nice cup of tea.'

Phyllis took it gratefully; her mouth felt dry and tasted foul.

'Where did you get to last night? We searched everywhere for you.'

'I received some bad news, and I went for a walk to help me come to terms with it.'

'I'm sorry to hear that. Please accept my condolences; I know you and Connie were close.'

'How do you know about Connie?'

'Reverend Dagnall is downstairs. He told me when he arrived, and he's asking to see you. Should I tell him that you're not available to receive visitors today?'

'Help me with my hair, and I'll see him briefly before breakfast.'

Phyllis sat at the dressing table and watched Mrs Gibson through the mirror, as she picked up the hair brush and very efficiently smoothed and pinned her hair up into a bun.

'You look a bit pasty, Miss. I'll get some of your mother's rouge to give your cheeks a bit of colour.'

'Thank you, but there's no need. Please show him into the parlour and tell him I'll be there in a few minutes.'

'Right you are, Miss.'

When the housekeeper had gone, Phyllis looked at the reflection in the mirror. The face looking back at her was gaunt, and the eyes, red and puffy from crying, had dark shadows beneath. Her mother would have been horrified that she was going to receive a visitor when she looked in such a state, but Timothy was a vicar, and she was sure that he would understand her grief at losing her best friend. She took a few sips from the teacup before going downstairs.

Timothy had been waiting patiently in the parlour and stood to greet Phyllis as she entered the room.

'Good morning,' he said, as he took her hand in his, and kissed it. She noticed the fleeting look of surprise on his face when he glanced up.

'Good morning,' she replied.

'I heard about the death of your friend, and I thought you might like some company. I'm sorry if I'm wrong; I'll leave right away if you'd prefer to be alone.'

'Please stay and have some tea.'

'Thank you.'

Mrs Gibson carried in a tray and poured the tea into porcelain cups, and then left the room. Timothy said, 'I know you and Constance were friends. Her death must have been a shock to you?'

Phyllis flinched slightly at the use of her friend's full name; everyone knew her as Connie, and it was clear that he didn't know his parishioners very well to make such a mistake. His pale blue eyes watched her intently.

'Yes, it was a shock.'

'Grief can be a dreadful thing. How are you coping with it?'

'I'm fine, thank you.'

'I can see that you're not fine, Phyllis. I can see that you've been greatly upset by it. I wish there was something I could do to help. If I can offer you any comfort, I would be pleased to be of service.'

His words reminded her of the previous night when she had gone out to seek comfort, in a very wanton manner. Why had she gone to Ben and not Timothy? Surely in those circumstances, she should have thought about talking to a vicar, but it had never crossed her mind.

'The fact that you thought of me and came to visit is a comfort,' she said, with a small smile, desperately wondering how she could turn the conversation away from her bereavement, because it was too new and too raw to talk about, and she was fighting hard to keep her emotions under control.

'Have you seen Joe? How's he taking it?' she asked.

'Oh, the husband. Yes, I spoke with him last night about the funeral arrangements. He's putting on a brave face as one would expect, but the poor man must be heartbroken. Will you be attending the funeral on Monday?'

'Yes, I'll be there.'

'You know, once this business is over, I would very much like it if you would come to the vicarage for dinner one evening. It might help to cheer you up.'

'That would be nice. Thank you, Timothy.'

As she showed Timothy to the door, she noticed a letter on the doorstep. Bending down to pick it up, she saw it was addressed to 'Miss Forster', and she desperately hoped that it wasn't more bad news; she couldn't cope with any more bad news. Taking the letter to her study, she sat down to read it, and when she'd finished her hands began to shake. She put it on the desk and stared at it.

Have you no shame?
You spent the night in his house!
The cost for my silence
£100
Hide it under the white stile.
No police.

Chapter 32

Westgate
September, 1881

When Phyllis's carriage pulled up outside the church, the sky was heavily laden with dark clouds that threatened rain. Ben watched her walk up the path and go into her family pew, without speaking to anyone. He followed her into the church and sat near the back, from where he could see her. Outwardly she looked strong, but he knew that inwardly she was falling apart, and he felt for her; she'd lost her only friend, and she didn't have any family to give her the support that she so desperately needed. At least when they'd lost Kate, he'd had his mother to share his grief.

Ben had been shocked when Phyllis had turned up at his cottage that night, drunk, and without her usual inhibitions, so unlike the high and mighty business woman that she tried to be. When her hair had come loose and curled around her neck, she'd looked pretty, and younger. The sorrow in her eyes had drawn him to her, because he knew that feeling well and he didn't want her to suffer in the same way that he had. He would have been happy to hold her and comfort her all night if that's what it would have taken to ease her pain, but he couldn't have given her what she'd wanted. He couldn't deny that he'd been tempted; she was an attractive woman, but he knew that she'd have regretted it afterwards, and she would never have forgiven him. He would rather have her as a friend than have no contact with her at all.

Mary Milburn and his mother came and sat next to him, greeting him solemnly because of the occasion. While they sat in silence, the church filled up and the organist began to play a slow march. The pallbearers — Joe and Tom Milburn, and Isaac and Jacob Rowell — carried a wooden coffin, covered with beautiful roses, and placed it at the front of the church, and then they sat down on the front pew for the service.

Mrs Peart was sitting next to Joe, her face set like stone, with not a flicker of emotion. Ben noticed a sympathetic look pass between Joe and Phyllis, both of whom were severely upset by Connie's death.

Reverend Dagnall performed the service for mother and child and, by the time he had finished the last prayer, there was hardly a dry eye in the church. Everyone stood up and followed the coffin out into the churchyard, and watched as it was lowered into a freshly cut grave.

Phyllis was standing at the opposite side of the grave to Ben; he noticed that her hands were shaking as she dried her eyes with a handkerchief. She spotted him and for a brief moment their eyes met, before she looked away. Is that how it was going to be now? Was she going to ignore him? He hoped that he'd allayed any feelings of shame or embarrassment that she might have by walking her home that night and assuring her of his friendship. He watched her say a few words to Mrs Peart and Joe, and then she walked to her carriage without looking back.

A couple of elderly women who were standing near Ben saw Phyllis leave too, and Ben heard one of them say, 'By this time next year, she'll be wed to the widower. Money always sticks with money.'

Phyllis and Joe? Never! But the more Ben thought about them as a couple, he realised that they did have a lot in common. The thought of them together disturbed him greatly, but he couldn't see any reason why they shouldn't be together. Could the old woman's words come true?

The only place Ben wanted to be right then was up on the fell. Bess had been waiting for him on the roadside, and she went to him as he walked through the gate and followed him at a brisk pace as he strode through the village and up the hill. He needed space and solitude. There had been no peace of mind for him since Phyllis had come to him that night. Since then, dreams of her had replaced his usual nightmares, but he was still tormented because he knew he could never have her.

Ben walked for miles before reaching his favourite place where the carved stone stood, but when he got there, it was gone. There was just a hollow patch of bare earth where it had been. He stepped back in horror, and looked around to see if it had been moved to somewhere close by. Frantically, he began to search the area, but it was no use — it was nowhere to be seen. Eventually, he decided that someone must have lifted it and taken it away, but he couldn't think who would do such a thing, or why. The stone had been in that place for hundreds of years, if not thousands, and that was where it belonged.

As he hurried home, the heavens opened, and within minutes his clothes were drenched. Around him, rain stotted off the ground angrily. Ben realised that there was only one person who knew the stone was there, and that was Phyllis. He stormed across the yard at Burnside Hall and banged on the large oak door. It was opened almost instantly by Todd, who stared at the rain-soaked figure standing before him, hardly recognising him.

'Featherstone!' he said, partly in shock and partly in question. 'What's wrong?'

'Is Miss Forster in?'

He hesitated just a moment before saying snootily, 'I'm sorry, she's not at home to visitors.'

'Who is it, Todd?' Phyllis pushed past the butler to see who was at the door. 'Featherstone,' she said, matter-of-factly, 'Do come in out of this dreadful rain.'

He followed her indoors, leaving a trail of water behind

him, and they went into her study. She sat in her chair, but he remained standing by the door.

'Why did you come?' she asked.

'How dare you pretend that nothing has happened?' he seethed.

Her face turned red, thinking he was referring to the night in his cottage.

'That stone belonged up there on the fell,' he continued. 'It's part of the dale, part of our past, part of our ancestors, part of us. It should have been left where it was — where it was meant to be.'

When he stopped for breath, he looked at the stupefied face in front of him. Phyllis sat there, her eyes wide and her mouth slightly open.

'What do you think I've done?' she asked, bewildered.

'It's gone! And you are the only one I showed it to. How could you move it from there?'

Phyllis's look turned to one of alarm as she realised that she wasn't the only one who knew about it; she had shown it to Timothy, but it was possible that anyone could have stumbled across it and removed it. With her experience at the quarry, she estimated that it would have weighed about a ton, so it wouldn't have been easy to carry away. It would have taken a team of men to lift it, and a horse and cart to carry it down off the fell, at the very least — that's not something many people could organise.

'Are you going to deny it?' Ben asked spitefully.

'No.'

She would rather he thought that she had taken it, than tell him that she'd betrayed his confidence and shown his precious rock to Timothy, for no other reason than to impress him. What would Ben make of that?

'So where is it?'

'I'm sorry, but I'm not prepared to tell you.'

Ben glared at her, before leaving the room and slamming both doors on his way out.

Chapter 33

Burnside Hall Estate
September, 1881

Ben stood at the gate to the fell and looked down at Burnside Hall, admiring the building's honeyed hue in the autumnal light, and the mature trees surrounding it, dressed in red and gold. He'd always thought Weardale looked its best at that time of year. Peering at the windows, he wondered if Phyllis could see him from her favourite seat that looked out onto the hillside.

Bess nudged his leg.

'Aye, you're right, lass, we'd better get these sheep gathered up. Away!'

That was what his dog had been waiting to hear, and she immediately ran to the right, as close to the fell wall as she could, to get to the other side of the sheep without moving them. She then zigzagged across the fell, bringing the sheep together as a group and moving them towards Ben, who was holding the gate open. Before long they were following the sheep as they made their way down the slope to the valley bottom. Once they were all in the field next to the Hall, Ben closed the gate behind them.

Heading for his cottage, he said, 'Good lass. Now, let's go and get some dinner.'

That afternoon, Ben separated the lambs from the ewes and put them into a neighbouring field. There was a lot of bleating, and some ewes tried to jump the high dry-stone wall to get back to their lambs. It upset Ben to see the sheep distressed, but it had to be done. The lambs had been eating grass for weeks now, and most were as large as their mothers, and the ewes needed a few months to get back into condition before tupping time.

'Come, Bess. The sooner we get them back on the fell, the better it'll be for all of them.'

He opened the field gate, and then he and Bess drove the sheep back up the hillside, and he watched them quietly as the flock spread out over the land and began grazing the coarse grasses. Once he was sure they were settled, he walked back down again and thought about tomorrow's task, which was sorting the lambs into two groups: the ones that would stay on the estate for breeding, and the ones that would be sold at the market. He glanced across at the Hall, and thought he saw someone move away from the window in the room he believed was Phyllis's music room. Had Phyllis been watching him? But he reasoned that it could just have easily been Mrs Gibson or one of the maids that he'd seen.

The following day, Ben chose the lambs he'd like to keep and moved them into another field. When he'd finished, he hesitated by the gate. Sir Thomas had always checked the lambs over himself, before the others were taken to the sale. He knew he should give Phyllis the chance to look them over, as they were going to join her flock after all, but he really didn't want to speak with her after what she'd done. He didn't know why he felt awkward, it was her that was in the wrong, taking that stone. He swallowed his pride and walked to the Hall, and after knocking loudly on the front door, he stood back and waited, his heart beating faster than normal. The door was opened by Todd.

'I've come to see Miss Forster,' said Ben.

'I don't think she'll want to see you after you upset her the last time.'

'If she wants to see the lambs that I'll be adding to the Burnside flock, and you don't let me in, you'll be the one in her bad books.'

'Hmm.' Todd glared at him, and eventually he said, 'I'll see if she's available.'

The butler's displeasure was obvious, and Ben wasn't surprised in the least when Todd closed the door in his face. Ben stood on the step listening for any sounds inside the house and, a few moments later, he heard voices and footsteps approaching. This time the door was opened by Phyllis.

'Featherstone, what can I do for you?' she asked

primly.

'Would you like to come and see which lambs I've chosen to keep?' he asked.

'As I've no idea what I'm looking at when it comes to sheep,' she said, 'I'll have to trust your judgement.'

'Alright, if that's what you want. Will you be going to the sale tomorrow?'

'Yes, I'll be there. I'd like to see what price they make.'

'Aye, I'll see you at the sale, then.'

Phyllis turned away from the door and Todd closed it. Ben put his hand down and touched Bess's head. 'Women!' he said to her. 'That Miss Forster couldn't have been much colder today, could she? Come on, let's go and see what Miss Wilson's made us for tea.'

The next morning, Ben was up at first light. He had to make sure the lambs looked their best before he drove them up to St John's Chapel, about five miles up the dale, before the sale started at ten o'clock. The earlier they were penned, the more time buyers had to admire them, and the more likely they were to sell for a decent price.

He made good time; the lambs were penned at the market before nine o'clock and he stood by the stock so he could talk to potential buyers. There was quite a bit of interest and the time flew by; it didn't seem long before the auctioneer took the stand. Ben looked around and noticed Phyllis near the door, talking to Joe Milburn, and he watched them for a while, wondering what they were talking about. Phyllis was smiling and Joe was laughing. Perhaps they were already more than just friends?

Tom Milburn came up behind Ben and put a friendly hand on his shoulder. He said, 'It's plain to see that you're taken with her, but she's out of your reach.'

'But not out of your Joe's?' Ben retorted.

'What!' exclaimed Tom, 'Our Joe's just lost his wife, and he's not looking for another. I think the green-eyed monster's gotten into you. Your mother's right, you know, you should find a nice dale's lass to settle down with.'

Ben turned quickly towards the auctioneer when he heard that the first lot of Burnside sheep was about to be sold, and Tom stood beside him, listening closely; his lambs were yet to be sold. The bids kept on coming and Ben grinned broadly when the hammer went down.

'Well done, lad. I hope the rest do as well,' said Tom, patting him on the shoulder.

The rest of the lots continued to fetch good prices, and after the last pen of lambs was sold, Ben glanced across at Phyllis, who was smiling too. Their eyes locked for a moment, and she nodded in recognition of the fine job he'd done in rearing and selling the lambs. A slight inclination of his head acknowledged her gratitude, but he hadn't forgotten that she had taken the stone from the fell, and he couldn't forgive her for it. He wished he could fathom out why she'd done it and where she'd put it. Why was she being so secretive?

Ben watched as Phyllis turned back towards Joe and

began to speak with him again, but this time the conversation appeared to have taken a serious turn. Joe was leaning in, listening intently, and Phyllis looked to be confiding in him. Ben saw Joe put his hand on Phyllis's arm, and she smiled weakly in return, and then they left together. There was something wrong, he could sense it.

Ben stayed at the market with Tom while his lambs were sold, and he was pleased to see that High House Farm had a good year too. Ben had expected the prices to be higher than usual because farmers had suffered two harsh winters in a row, winters that had been particularly brutal on the hills, and they'd taken their toll on flocks.

When the business was all over, Ben and Tom walked back to Westgate and stopped at The Half Moon for a quick drink to celebrate their success at the sale. They sat down at a table and the barman carried over two tankards of beer, spilling a little on the flagstone floor on the way. They supped slowly and savoured the drink.

'There's nothing like a cold pint after a long, hard day,' said Tom.

'You're right there.'

'Oh! There's something I meant to tell you. I've asked The Felons to come here for a meeting on Monday night.'

'Has something happened?' asked Ben.

'It's just to find out if anyone has seen anything up at the Hall, that's all.'

'Alright, I'll be there. The normal time?'

'Aye.'

When Tom finished his beer, he yawned.

'Sale days are always hard, but I swear they're getting harder every year. I'm ready for me bed.'

'Yeah, but at least it's been a good one — my best, in fact,' said Ben, smiling.

They parted company, tired but in good spirits.

On Monday evening, Ben climbed the steps of The Half Moon at Westgate and entered the bar. He was early for the Felons meeting, so he got some ale and sat at their usual table to await the arrival of the rest of the members. They turned up one by one and joined him. As most of them were farmers, the conversation didn't stray far from the lamb sales until everyone was seated, and then Tom cleared his throat before starting the meeting.

'Good evening, gentlemen,' Tom began. 'This meeting has been called to update everyone about the situation at Burnside Hall, and to discuss any new crimes or complaints that have been made. Now, have any of you anything to report from Burnside Hall? It's been quiet when me and Ben have been doing our rounds.'

Nobody had any sightings to report, so they carried on with their meeting.

'There's been one new development,' said Joe, 'and I don't know if it's related to the other business or not, but Miss Forster told me that she was concerned about a letter she received a couple of weeks back.'

Ben paid close attention to Joe's words.

'She didn't show me the letter, but the gist of it was that someone had seen her with a man, in what looked like comprising circumstances, and having misunderstood the situation, this person is asking for a hundred pounds to keep their mouth shut. The letter said that if Miss Forster doesn't pay, they'll tell everybody what she'd been up to. I don't believe for one minute that Phyllis...Miss Forster would have done anything improper, but I think we should try to find out who sent it. This has to be stopped.'

Ben exhaled loudly. He guessed that somebody had seen Phyllis leaving his cottage that night — that could very well have looked like the two of them were having an affair, which was ironic because that is exactly what would have happened if he'd let it. He wondered if the letter, and the threat that it posed, were responsible for Phyllis's coldness towards him since that night, or whether it was simply embarrassment. Either way, he couldn't see them being on such friendly terms again, especially after she'd admitted taking his stone off the fell as well.

'Has she told Robert Emerson about the letter?' he asked moodily, upset that Phyllis had confided in Joe rather than him.

'Three letters,' said Joe. 'They said not to go to the police or she'd be sorry, so she didn't tell anyone about them. And she was stupid enough to pay the first two!

The third one was more threatening and asked for a larger sum of money, and she didn't know what to do. She told me how worried she was about it and asked me for my opinion. I told her not to do anything until I'd spoken to you.'

'What can we do to help?' asked one of the men.

They sat in silence, supping their drinks, whilst contemplating the problem in hand, and trying to come up with a solution. After a while, Tom said, 'I think she should arrange to pay the money, and when they come to get it, we'll catch them in the act.'

The men around the table murmured their consent, and agreed that Tom's plan might work. They discussed what they'd do in fine detail, and when it was all arranged, Tom asked, 'So, has there been anything else going on?'

'Aye, you could say that,' said Ben. 'Up on the fell above Burnside Hall, there was a large stone, about two feet by three feet, and it had carvings on it. It's not there anymore.'

'How could someone steal a rock that big?' asked Joe.

'I reckon it would take at least four men to lift it and a cart to carry it away. Anyway, could you just keep an eye out for it, and let me know if you see it anywhere?'

The men agreed to Ben's request, with interest, because they couldn't understand why someone would have taken a rock off the fell in the first place.

The only other complaint that had been received was

about young lads hanging around the village in the evenings, drinking alcohol and shouting obscenities at passers-by. This was an ongoing problem that all of the Felons, as well as the local constabulary, tried to control, but they agreed that young lads were young lads and that there was little they could do to stop them.

By the time they ordered another round, Ben noticed that the miners by the bar were getting rowdy and, from the few words he could make out above the din, he realised that they were talking about Phyllis Forster. He strained to hear more, and he heard phrases like 'miserable bitch', 'two peas in a pod' and 'cut from the same cloth'. They were likening Phyllis to her devil of a brother. She was nothing like Henry!

That was it, he'd heard enough. Ben stood up, a little unsteadily, and went over to where the men stood by the bar, and said, 'What did you say? Phyllis Forster is nothing like Henry.'

'On first name terms, are we?' one of the miners mocked. 'Frosty Phyllis is a fancy filly.'

Laughter filled the room, and another man chipped in, 'I wouldn't mind a ride on her!'

Ben grabbed him by his jacket, and said in a low voice, 'Outside, now.'

Tom came over and put a hand on his arm. 'Ben, he's not worth it.'

'They can't get away with talking about her like that, she doesn't deserve it.'

'Aye, alright. But if I see it getting out of hand, I'll put a stop to it. You're one of the Felons and we've got a reputation to uphold.'

Ben heard what Tom said, but at that moment he didn't care, he was so angry at the way they'd been talking about Phyllis that all he could see was red. He wanted to hit somebody so much — and this man was asking for it — and Ben was going to teach him a lesson that he wouldn't forget.

Outside on the road, with a circle of onlookers surrounding them, the two men squared up to each other. The miner obviously had some wrestling experience because he tried to grab Ben in a wrestling hold, but before he could, Ben raised his fist and punched him hard on the jaw, sending him reeling backwards. Somehow, he kept his footing and moved forward once more. This time Ben's fist connected with the miner's nose, and he fell to the ground with a dull thud, putting a hand over his nose to stem the bleeding.

As Ben looked up, he saw a horse and trap parked along the road, and Phyllis was looking directly at him with a look of horror on her face. Nothing could have sobered him up faster. He wanted to explain that he'd done it for her, but the vicar had already driven the horse on, and they were rapidly disappearing from view.

'That's enough,' Tom said, as he led Ben away from the crowd. 'You did what you had to. You stood up for her. But it's time you were going home now.'

Without saying a word, Ben began to walk back down the road to his cottage. He wasn't angry any longer, but the feeling he had was almost as bad. He wasn't sure what it was, but he thought it might be dread. Why had Phyllis been there? Why did she have to see what he'd done?

When he got back, he turned on the outside tap and held his hand in the flow of cold water. His knuckles were sore and swollen, and he knew that by tomorrow they would be bruised. The one consolation he had was that the other fella must be feeling a lot worse.

'Did you see that!' said Timothy, as he drove his trap towards Eastgate. 'They behave like animals when they've had a drink, and they're not much better when they're sober.'

Phyllis had looked to where the disturbance was, on the road outside The Half Moon, and she'd focussed on a face she'd instantly recognised amongst the crowd. Featherstone. She'd been shocked to see him squaring up to a man that looked to be almost twice his size. Why on earth would he be fighting outside the inn? She'd always considered him to be a quiet man, who kept himself to himself, not a trouble-maker. Although he wasn't as large as his opponent, she'd seen that he had won the fight. When the big fellow had fallen to the ground, Featherstone looked up and their eyes had met briefly. But she hadn't been able to decipher the meaning in his look, and she hadn't had time to think about it because

Timothy had begun to rant.

'Filthy animals, the lot of them,' he said. 'They should be locked up for that kind of behaviour. Where's that policeman when you need him?'

'Robert Emerson?'

'Is that what he's called?'

'Yes.'

Phyllis was surprised that Timothy hadn't known the constable's name; he'd been the vicar at Westgate for six months now, and Robert was a regular member of the congregation.

She said, 'My father used to get on well with the locals. He always had a kind word for them, and helped them when they needed it. I was wondering, there's a lot of hardship at the moment. Do you think I should give the miners who are out of work a little money to tide them over? I hate to think of the children going hungry.'

'Hmm, I wouldn't if I was you. If you give them a little, they'll expect more and more. You don't want them knocking at your door and demanding money or food, do you? My father has a firm hand and only gives out money to those who work for it. He won't let anyone take advantage of him.'

'But it's not that they're idle — there just isn't any work for them, with the mines closing. And some can't work — old miners who can hardly breathe because the dust has damaged their lungs, and a few who've suffered dreadful injuries that have left them crippled.'

'That's not your problem, dear. That is what the workhouse is for. If men are unable to bring home a wage, for whatever reason, the workhouse will take them in, and their families as well, and give them a roof over their heads and food to eat.'

'The workhouse is a last resort!' said Phyllis adamantly. 'My father would have stepped in and helped decent people well before they got to the steps of the workhouse, and I think I should do the same.'

'On your head be it, but don't say I didn't warn you. You can't trust these people.'

'I have no idea what you're talking about. Most of them are good people. In fact, there are many times that the Forster family have relied on them for help.'

'Phyllis, dear,' he said, as he pulled up the horse in the yard and turned to look at her. 'I think you're mistaken. The people around here don't like your family. For some reason there's a deep resentment, and I doubt very much that they would accept your charity. I urge you to think carefully before you get involved with them.'

'What is it that you've heard?'

'Nothing specific, but they don't speak well of you, or your family. I'm sorry to be the bearer of bad news.' He shrugged.

Phyllis stepped down from the trap, without saying farewell to Timothy, or inviting him in for refreshments. As she entered the house, her mind was troubled; she went to the study where she could still feel her father's comforting presence.

She wondered how on earth she could have had feelings for a man who drank to excess and brawled in the street like a commoner, and then it hit her, as fond as she had been of Ben, he was a commoner. The two of them were poles apart in society, and she should never have taken an interest in him. Had her parents still been alive, she would never have spoken to the man. She'd allowed herself the liberty of thinking that she wasn't Phyllis Forster, the daughter of Sir Thomas Forster and mistress of Burnside Hall, and that she was simply a dale's lass interested in one of its men. But not anymore! There was nothing attractive about a drunken lout that fought on the street, and she would waste no more time thinking about him.

Phyllis was shocked to think how close she'd come to ruining everything, and she thanked God that he'd refused her advances that night and had turned her away. She was so angry at herself. She'd made a foolish mistake in letting down her guard in front of Ben, and she vowed that from now on she would never let that happen again.

The blackmail letters came back to mind and, leaning on the desk, she put her head in her hands. Someone had been there that night. Someone had seen them together and assumed that they were lovers, and now they were threatening to expose her secret. She scoffed. That was nothing less than she deserved for going to his house, full of drink, and begging him to take her, like a brazen slut.

She had considered paying the ransom again to prevent her secret from becoming common knowledge, but she knew that they would keep sending notes, and asking for more money each time. Would there ever be an end to it? She had desperately wanted to confide in Ben about the letters, and ask for his advice, but she couldn't, not after what had happened.

Her anxiety had been so profound that when Joe had asked if something was wrong, when they were at the market, she'd blurted out the whole story to him. With Connie gone, and not being on good terms with Ben, she supposed Joe was the closest thing she had to a friend.

Chapter 34

Burnside Hall Estate
October, 1881

Ben could hear nothing but the howling wind as he fought to stay upright on his walk down from the fell. The sheep were huddled at the back of the dykes for shelter, and he'd considered staying there with them, but after that time when Phyllis had thought him drowned, he thought he should try to make his way back home. The gusts on the open moorland were ferocious, and twice he'd lost his footing and had fallen heavily to the ground.

He spotted a patch of white at the bottom of an old hush, and he instinctively knew it was one of his ewes that had been blown over the edge of the gulley. He carefully climbed down the steep slope until he reached her, but he was too late. She was dead. He couldn't move her, or bury her, until the weather improved, so he continued to battle his way through the storm.

Eventually he made it back to the Hall and he went straight to the kitchen to pick up his dinner; he was starving and exhausted, and it must have shown, because when Miss Wilson finished filleting a fish and saw him, she looked concerned.

'What happened to you?' she asked.

'I've just come down off the fell. It's blowing a gale out there, and I'm beat.'

'Sit yourself down and I'll make you a hot drink. Would you like some cocoa?'

'Aye,' he said, as he took off his boots and gratefully sat on a chair by the table. 'Thank you.'

Miss Wilson placed a mug of steaming hot cocoa on the table in front of him, and he put his hands around it to warm them, while he watched her brush the fish with oil and sprinkle some herbs over it.

'What are you making?'

'Miss Forster likes 'Salmon en Croute' — salmon pie to you and me.'

'What are the rest of you having tonight?'

'Mutton stew and mash.'

'Would you have a spare plate, if I came over here for tea tonight?'

'I'm sure I can make it to stretch to one more.'

'Miss Wilson!' Phyllis's voice sounded clearly from the doorway. 'I thought I heard a man's voice. Have you a man in the kitchen with you?'

Phyllis walked in and saw Ben sitting at the table, drinking cocoa, and thought he was getting cosy with the cook to deserve such favours. She said, 'Oh, it's you,

Featherstone. There's no excuse for you to linger in the kitchen. You don't eat with the servants anymore, so take your food, and go home.'

Miss Wilson looked at him sympathetically, but then Phyllis turned her attention to the cook, and said, 'And you should know better than to entertain men in the kitchen. The cost of his cocoa will be deducted from your wages.' Phyllis turned and left.

Putting his boots back on, Ben saw the look of shock on Miss Wilson's face, and he mouthed, 'Sorry,' so that Phyllis wouldn't hear him. She smiled back at him and pointed at his food. He'd almost forgotten to pick it up. So much for stew and mash, he thought. He had in his hands a small pie, meat he hoped, an apple, and a jug of milk.

Miss Wilson whispered, 'Wait.' She disappeared, returning a moment later with a large beef bone which she handed to him, saying, 'For your dog.'

'Thank you,' he said sincerely, grateful that he wouldn't need to share the small pie with Bess.

He struggled against the wind on his way to the cottage, and was pleased to close the door behind him. Bess went to her bed and he gave her the bone, which she took between her paws and started to chew. Ben sat at the table and ate his tea, and he must have fallen asleep as soon as he'd finished eating, because he was woken by a strange crashing noise, and it sounded like it was coming from the Hall.

Ben opened the cottage door and listened, but all he could hear was the wind, so he put on his coat and headed for the Hall. After knocking at the front door, he waited for several minutes but there was no answer; he knew something was wrong. He opened the heavy door and let himself in. Raised voices could be heard in a room near the kitchen, the one that the conservatory was attached to, and he walked tentatively towards it, wanting to help, but unsure if he would be welcome in the house. Miss Wilson spotted him and she came over to him.

'What's happened?' he asked.

'A tree fell on the conservatory. It's completely wrecked.'

'Is anyone hurt?'

'No. Luckily nobody was near it at the time.'

Ben saw Phyllis watching him chatting with Miss Wilson, and she approached them, her expression unreadable.

'Featherstone, what are you doing here?'

'I heard the noise and came over to see if you needed any help.'

'There's nothing we can do tonight. It's still blowing a gale out there and there's glass everywhere. You can help the gardeners clean the mess up in the morning. Until then, you should go home.'

'I'm sorry about the damage.'

'Featherstone, there's another matter I need to speak to you about. Miss Wilson, please leave us.'

When the cook had gone, Phyllis said quietly, 'There are rules about staff consorting with one another. If there is anything going on between you and Miss Wilson, I expect that one of you will find another position. Do I make myself clear?'

Ben was shocked by her bluntness. 'There's nothing going on.'

'I'm pleased to hear it,' she said, and closed her eyes briefly, before adding, 'You're both good at your jobs, I wouldn't like to lose either of you.' She turned away, and left Ben wondering what all that had been about.

By morning, the wind had died down and Ben could see the full extent of the damage. An old gnarled tree was lying across the lawn and a large branch covered the area of the glass house. Shards of glass were sparkling in the grass, and he thought it would take hours to pick them up. He worked all morning, with the two gardeners and the groom, to remove the remnants of the conservatory, while the woodsman had enlisted help from the errand boy and gamekeeper to cut up and remove the tree. He didn't see Phyllis until midday, when she appeared in the garden, and said, 'Please down your tools, and come into the kitchen. Miss Wilson has prepared refreshments for you all.'

It wasn't often that the estate workers were invited inside, and Ben noticed the looks of surprise on the men's faces as they left what they were doing and followed

Phyllis into the kitchen. She said, 'There is a mug of tea and a plate of food for each of you. Please help yourselves.'

Phyllis went around the room, and chatted with them all individually as they ate, thanking them for their help in clearing the garden; but when she reached Ben, she simply stood in front of him, and said, 'Thank you, Featherstone.'

He hated that she'd been so unfriendly towards him for so long. Was it since she'd come to his cottage after Connie's death? He wasn't sure if that was the reason for the change, or because he'd accused her of taking the stone, or because someone was blackmailing her. What he was certain of, was that things had been even worse between them since she'd witnessed the fight. If only she knew what the fight had been about, he thought, but he wouldn't be the one to tell her; if she knew what those men had been saying about her and her brother, it would hurt her deeply. He wouldn't be the one responsible for inflicting more pain on her after everything she'd been through.

It took the full day to clear the garden of debris, and it was dark by the time Ben got back to his cottage. He hadn't been to the fell that day to check the sheep, there hadn't been time, and it prayed on his mind all night that it was his job to care for those sheep. He should have left the clearing up for the rest of the men, rather than neglect his duties.

At first light, Ben and Bess got straight to work, and as soon as he reached the fell, Ben knew something was wrong. In the distance, he could see that a section of wall had fallen, the section where the sheep had been sheltering, the section where he had been tempted to sit out the storm.

He ran over as quickly as he could, and as he got nearer, he could see that the wind had blown down a stretch of wall about twenty feet long, and he could hear the tired bleat of a sheep trapped under the fallen stones. Bess quickly found her and Ben moved the stones that had her pinned to the ground. When the last one was lifted, he helped her to her feet and assessed her condition, and was relieved that no bones were broken. The ewe looked around, and then put her head down and started to graze as if nothing had happened.

'Would you believe that?' he said to Bess. 'She's been trapped for two days and there's not a scratch on her.'

He was pleased that everything else seemed to be in order, and he went to the hush to bury the dead ewe he'd found two days earlier.

When he returned to the Hall, he asked Todd if he could see Phyllis, and Todd reluctantly showed him to the study, where Phyllis sat working at the desk.

'Please, come in,' she said.

He entered the room and stood patiently until she finished her calculations. Beside the account ledger, he noticed some drawings for a new conservatory.

'Yes, what is it?' she asked.

'I'm afraid there's been some damage up on Eastgate Fell. There's a twenty-foot stretch of wall fallen. One of the ewes was trapped under it, but she was fine when I freed her.'

'I'll see to it. Is there anything else?'

'We lost one on the day of the storm. She was blown into the hush. I buried her today.'

'I'm sorry to hear that,' she said, looking contrite. 'It was a dreadful storm. I don't suppose you've read the paper?'

'No, I haven't.' Ben rarely read the papers.

'Over one hundred fishermen were lost at sea, just off the Scottish coast at Eyemouth. It's horrendous. I can't help thinking about those poor families and how they must be suffering.'

'Aye, that's terrible.'

Her icy facade had slipped, and he had a fleeting glimpse of the warm-hearted woman underneath, but it was just a glimpse. Without looking at him, she said, 'That will be all. Thank you, Featherstone.'

Chapter 35

Burnside Hall
October, 1881

Phyllis's mind was in turmoil, speculating on who the blackmailer might be. Since the last note, she hadn't been able to concentrate on anything else. It was awful to think that someone she knew would hold her to ransom over her dark secret, and she feared the consequences if that secret became common knowledge. She would have to leave the dale.

She'd refused to see Timothy when he'd visited, as she'd still been upset by what he'd said about the villagers, but when he called a second time, she thought that she should receive him. She could hear her mother's voice telling her that holding a grudge was not lady-like, and that it wasn't polite to turn away visitors when they'd made the effort to call. She smiled to herself. Lady Margaret had been a wonderful hostess.

Todd showed Timothy into the drawing room where she'd been reading the newspaper.

'Good afternoon,' she said.

'Good afternoon, Phyllis. Thank you for seeing me. I know you were upset the last time we saw one another, and it was my doing. I'm sorry.'

'Please take a seat.'

When Timothy was seated in the chair facing her, at the other side of the fireplace, she said, 'You only said what you thought I should know.'

'That's very true, dear. May I ask? Are you recovered now?'

'Yes, I'm fine. Thank you.'

'Would you like to take a walk? It's cool outside, but it's a pleasant day, nevertheless.'

'Why not?' she said. 'I've spent too much time cooped up indoors. It'll be nice to have some fresh air.'

Phyllis asked Mrs Gibson to bring her cloak and hat, and the housekeeper helped her put them on. When she was ready, they left through the front door and Timothy offered her his arm. Phyllis thought it would be rude not to take it, so she did, and he led her in the direction of the river. They walked quietly for a while, until they saw Ben working Bess in the neighbouring field. Timothy stopped to watch them.

'It's surprising what a dog can do, don't you think?' he said, admiring the way the dog moved the sheep through the narrow gate.

'Have you ever had a dog?' she asked, for she was well aware of how capable dogs were.

'I've never had a dog of my own, but my father has kennels on the estate for the hounds. We don't rear sheep on our estate in Oxfordshire, so I've rarely seen sheepdogs work like this. You'd think it could read the shepherd's mind.'

She knew that Ben was aware of their presence and was putting on a show of his skills; he was asking far more of Bess than was necessary, but she had to admit that they made an excellent team, making the difficult task of moving sheep appear easy.

Timothy was peering across the field at Ben.

'Isn't that the man I rescued you from when you went out alone after dinner that night?'

'It was hardly a rescue, Timothy, but, yes, it was him. That's Ben Featherstone, my shepherd.'

He thought for a moment, and then said, 'He looks very much like one of the men who was fighting at Westgate.'

'Do you think so? I can't see it myself. Shall we walk a little further?'

As they walked along the path by the tree-lined river, Phyllis wondered why she'd denied that Ben had been fighting. Was it because she had a good idea what Timothy's reaction would have been? He would have demanded that she dismiss Ben on the spot, and she didn't want to do that. She told herself that he was a good shepherd and it would be difficult to find a replacement for him.

Just outside the village of Eastgate, there was a wooden

bench overlooking the water, and Timothy suggested that they take a seat and have a short rest before heading back. He took off his hat and placed it on the bench beside him. Rubbing his hands over his golden hair to flatten it, he said, 'There's something that I wanted to speak to you about, if I may?'

'Of course.'

'I don't think this will come as a surprise to you, but I have admired you since we first met. When my friends were here, they pointed out to me that you and I are well-suited, and I take their opinions very seriously. Therefore, I wondered if you might like to be my wife?'

Phyllis leaned back and breathed deeply. She got along reasonably well with Timothy, but marriage? She remembered that Connie had suggested that he'd be a suitable match for her, and at almost thirty years of age she would be lucky to be asked by anyone else. She'd almost given up hope of marriage and children, and Timothy was offering her a future that she had longed for.

'Yes, Timothy, I think I would like that.'

He beamed at her and kissed her clumsily on the cheek.

'Thank you, Phyllis. I think we'll make a jolly good couple. I'll write to my parents as soon as I get home. My father will be delighted! You should tell your family too.'

Phyllis didn't respond because his comment hurt her more than she thought it should; she would have loved to be able to tell her parents that she was betrothed.

'Do you have any family?' he asked insensitively.

'Only my aunt and uncle in Harrogate, and my cousins. I'll write to them.'

'Very well. I'll come over soon so we can discuss the details and make arrangements.'

On the way home, a veil of sadness shrouded her. She wouldn't have any family with her on her big day, but she told herself that it didn't matter, and what was important was the fact that she would have a husband and, God willing, children would follow; she would no longer be alone.

That evening, Phyllis sat at her piano playing a sonata by Haydn, and when she finished, she was certain that she'd heard a man's voice outside. She went to the window and moved the curtain aside to look out, but she could see nothing in the pitch darkness of the night. She went out through the front door, and walked through the yard, heading for the front of the house, but still she could see nothing in front of her. She stopped suddenly when she heard voices in the distance.

Standing at the corner of the house reminded her of the evening when she and Ben had stood in exactly that place and watched the aurora light up the night sky. What a wonderful sight that had been! But tonight, because of a thick blanket of cloud, there was no moonlight and not a star to be seen.

She heard a shuffling noise, and somebody walked into her. Startled by the contact, and knowing someone was within reach of her, she tried to hide her fear by calling out, 'Who's there?'

'It's just me, Miss Forster. Tom Milburn. Are you alright?'

'Yes, I heard noises outside, so I came out to see what was going on. As it happens, I can't see a thing!' She laughed, and said, 'Please come inside where it's light.'

Tom followed Phyllis back to the house and they went into the study where she invited him to take a seat.

'So, what was the commotion I heard?'

'I was doing my rounds as usual when I heard a noise in the paddock at the side of the house. I couldn't see them, but I could tell that there were at least two men there because I heard two voices. I think they were trying to break into the Hall. I shouted at them, and they scarpered across the fields and headed towards the woods. I'm sorry I didn't catch them, but at least I scared them off. I don't think they'll bother you again.'

'Thank you, Mr Milburn. We keep the silver in that room. That must have been what they were after.'

'Perhaps you could keep it out of sight.'

'Yes, that's a good idea. I'll have Todd see to it. The Felons have done a tremendous job and I can't thank you all enough, although I must say, Ben is lucky to still have a job here after I saw him fighting at Westgate.'

'You saw that?' asked Tom, his eyebrows raised.

'Yes! I was shocked and sickened by his behaviour. I wouldn't have believed it if I hadn't seen it with my own eyes. It seemed totally out of character.'

'There's something you should know about that night.' Tom paused, and when he was sure he had Phyllis's full attention, he continued, 'Ben took that miner on because of what he heard him saying — about you. Ben heard him calling you names, likening you to your brother, and making vulgar suggestions. Ben was the only man in that room to stand up for you — that's the sort of man he is — so don't judge him too harshly.'

Phyllis was dumbfounded. She had totally misjudged Ben, and her treatment of him since that night had been abysmal. Instead of ignoring him, she should have been thanking him for what he had done, and singing his praises to anyone who would listen. The only reason that he'd been fighting was to defend her. That pleased her in one sense, because it meant that Ben was of good character as she'd originally thought, unlike Timothy's assessment of him, but in another sense, it distressed her because it meant that the locals didn't like her, and unfortunately Timothy had been right about that.

Until recently, the Forster family of Burnside Hall had been widely respected. It hurt her immensely to know that Henry, in just a few years, had undone what their ancestors had taken generations to accomplish. Phyllis believed it was her place to make amends and she wondered how she could possibly make things right again.

Chapter 36

Following Tom Milburn's advice, Phyllis wrote a note and left it under the stile. It simply stated a date and a place where the ransom money would be hidden. She hoped that everything would go according to plan, and that the blackmailer would be enticed into their trap.

At dawn of the day when the cash was due to be hidden, the Felons walked up to the ruined farmstead on the hillside above Burnside Hall, where Ben had spent the night of the flood. The place had been carefully selected because of its suitability for an ambush. Assuming the blackmailer would approach from the valley, there were plenty of places for the Felons to hide — two farmers stood behind the building, two men hid in the entrance to a mine, about twenty yards away and with a good view of the path leading up to the house, and Tom and Ben waited inside the ruined house.

The Felons didn't think it was likely that Phyllis would

be in danger, but they wanted to cover all possibilities, so Joe Milburn stayed at the Hall as a safeguard. To keep up appearances, Phyllis walked up to the ruined building mid-morning, carrying a small bag, and she went inside for a few minutes. She was grateful that Tom and Ben were there to greet her.

'I felt as though I was being watched when I walked up the hill,' she whispered. 'I shouldn't stay too long, just long enough to make it look like I'm leaving the money here.'

'Just keep calm, and go straight back home,' said Tom reassuringly.

'Thank you for what you're doing today. I hope they turn up and that you get them. They deserve to be punished for this.'

'We'll get them,' said Ben. 'Don't you worry!'

Ben watched Phyllis descend the hill until she was out of sight, and then he and Tom sat in silence, one on each side of the door, with their backs against the wall, listening and waiting.

Ben could hear birds calling, and sheep bleating, and even the faint rustle of grass in the breeze, but it was several hours before he heard what he'd been waiting for, the sound of approaching footsteps. Ben glanced at Tom, who had heard them too, and they quietly got to their feet, ready to apprehend the blackmailer.

The footsteps stopped. Ben could imagine the person outside, looking around to see if they were being watched, or followed. Sweat beaded on Ben's brow as he waited, ready to grab the scoundrel who had threatened Phyllis. The inside of the building darkened noticeably as the blackmailer moved into the doorway and stepped over the threshold.

Ben and Tom both moved forward at the same time and reached out to grab the cloaked figure, but they weren't quick enough. In a split second, the intruder had turned and run, closely followed by Tom and Ben. But in the meantime, the two men in the mine had come out and were lying in wait outside, and one of them grabbed the blackmailer by the arm.

The small stature made Ben think the villain was a youth, and when Tom removed the hood from the person that they held captive, Ben stepped back in disbelief. He could not have been more surprised if the blackmailer had been his own mother.

Tom and Ben marched their captive back to the Hall, with the hooded cloak firmly back in place. The front door was open and they entered the hallway, where Joe was stood at Phyllis's side. Tom took the hood in his hand and pulled it back to reveal the blackmailer.

Phyllis stepped back in horror and grabbed Joe's arm for support, not wanting to believe what was in front of her. She opened her mouth and struggled to speak, 'Mrs Gibson — it was you?'

'Aye, it was her,' said Tom.

Stoically, Phyllis said, 'This way, gentlemen,' and they followed her into the drawing room, where Tom and Ben sat on a sofa, with Mrs Gibson between them. Joe remained standing by the door and Phyllis moved to stand in front of her trusted servant.

Tom said, 'We caught her entering the building.'

'Was it you who wrote the notes?' asked Phyllis.

The housekeeper nodded her head sheepishly.

'But it wasn't your writing.'

'I disguised it. I wrote them with my left hand.'

'But I don't understand. Why would you blackmail me?'

When Mrs Gibson failed to reply, Phyllis continued, 'I gave you employment, I gave you a room in my house, and I trusted you. My parents trusted you. And this is how you repay me?'

'I wanted to teach you a lesson because it isn't right that someone in your position should be carrying on with the likes of Featherstone. It isn't proper.'

Ben glanced at Tom and Joe, who looked back at him in surprise.

Mrs Gibson continued, 'I saw you riding together on that horse that morning, clinging on to each other. The looks on your faces said it all. You were smitten — the pair of you. And if that wasn't enough, you had the nerve to invite your fancy man into the Hall for a drink. I got Todd to tell you how inappropriate that was, but did you listen? No, you didn't, because the next thing I heard is that you'd spend the night in his cottage with him.'

Ben noticed that Tom and Joe's expressions had turned to shock at that last statement.

'It was Miss Wilson who alerted me to what you were doing. She'd seen you go into his house, but I saw for myself that you walked back together, holding on to each other. Taking a workman for a lover...' Mrs Gibson shook her head, and hissed under her breath. 'You're a disgrace to your family, just like your brother was.'

Ben was livid, and Tom gave him a look which meant 'keep quiet'.

Standing tall, Phyllis replied, 'What you saw was not what it looked like. Featherstone is a friend, and that is all. There is nothing going on between us and there never has been.'

'Of course, you'd deny it, whether it was true or not.'

Ben thought Phyllis looked puzzled, and heard her say, 'I pay you well. Why did you do it? Did you need the money?'

'It was never about the money,' said Mrs Gibson. 'When you came back from Harrogate, you had every chance to make something of yourself, to restore the good name of your family, but you went and spoilt that by cavorting with him. I wanted to teach you a lesson. It's as simple as that.'

'If you were a man, I'd take you outside, right now,' seethed Ben. Tom reached over and put a restraining hand on Ben's shoulder.

Phyllis said, 'Todd will accompany you to your room where you'll collect your belongings, and then you will leave this house, and I don't want to see you again. You'll go without references, and if you ever dare to come back here, or spread malicious rumours about me or my family, I will set the constabulary on you. Do you understand?'

Mrs Gibson glared at her, before nodding almost imperceptibly.

'I said, do you understand?' Phyllis said firmly.

'Yes, I understand.'

Phyllis called for Todd, who had been standing outside the door the whole time and, following orders, he took the housekeeper away.

Tom made his excuses soon after, and he and Joe took their leave. It had been clear from Mrs Gibson's allegations that something was going on between Ben and Phyllis, and Tom tactfully wanted them to have an opportunity to discuss matters in private.

When they were alone, Phyllis perched on the edge of an armchair, and leaning forward, she said, 'I never thought that there'd be so many repercussions from the time I've spent with you. I felt awkward and embarrassed about what I did that night, but when I knew we'd been seen together, in what must have looked like a compromising situation, I was worried that your name would be tarnished by being connected with mine. I'm sorry I came to your cottage that night and caused all of this bother.'

'I'm not sorry,' he said softly, looking at her tenderly. 'I'm pleased that you did. It showed me that you trusted me.'

'I do trust you, Ben. More than anyone I know.'

Ben wanted to take her into his arms and hold her so badly that his chest hurt, but he knew he couldn't. He envied men who fell in love with women of the same class, as they could take the initiative, but the class system stopped him from doing that. If anything was to happen between them, it would have to be Phyllis who instigated it.

'You look like you could use a drink. Would you like one?' Phyllis was already walking to a walnut cabinet with three decanters standing on top of it. Without waiting for his reply, she opened the cabinet door and took out two glasses, and filled them both with brandy. 'My father used to swear by brandy whenever there'd been an upset.' She handed a glass to Ben, and took a sip from her own.

'Thank you,' he said, taking a large gulp from the glass. He thought he should leave, but it would be rude to refuse her hospitality, and he really did want to stay with her.

'Miss Wilson likes you. Did you know that?'

'Yes, I knew.'

'You know, I almost feel sorry for her — unrequited love and all that.' Her head was bowed, and she looked up at him through her lashes, 'It is unrequited, isn't it?'

'Yes, it is,' he said emphatically. 'I don't have any

feelings for Miss Wilson.'

The wistful look on Phyllis's face was too much for Ben; he put down his glass and got to his feet. Taking her hands in his, he pulled her to her feet, held her against his body and kissed her soundly. And then he left, leaving Phyllis stunned.

Chapter 37

Town Hall, St John's Chapel
November, 1881

A huge crowd gathered outside the town hall at St John's Chapel and, as soon as the doors were opened, the people made their way into the building and sat in rows of seats in the large room. When all of the seating downstairs had been filled, people filed up the steps into the balcony, or stood around the edges and at the back. The event had been well-advertised throughout the upper dale, and the turn-out was unprecedented.

Davey and Martha stood together near the front of the hall, waiting for the man he'd met in the pub to speak. Mr Walter Beaumont, who had organised the evening to give himself the opportunity to speak to the miners of Weardale, stood up, and there was an expectant hush from the audience as everyone quietened down to listen to him.

'Thank you all for coming this evening. What I have to say to you tonight will not be received well in some quarters, but say it I will! I must! The dispute between the owner of W B Lead, my brother, Mr Wentworth Blackett Beaumont, and the Ecclesiastical Commissioners, has gone on for far too long. The closure of the mines affects them very little, if at all, but it affects the people of Weardale greatly. It is you, my friends, who are suffering because of their indifference. It is you who have no work, no pay, no food on your tables. It is your children that run barefoot in the streets. It is a disgrace that my brother, despite my insistence, has not come here to see the suffering that he and his agents have created. It is a disgrace that the Ecclesiastical Commissioners have not sought a timely resolution to the dispute to relieve your suffering. Houses stand empty, up and down this dale, because your comrades have gone in search of work elsewhere, and I sincerely hope that this matter can be resolved before you too have to leave.'

A loud cheer sounded in the hall, and miners shouted their support. On the stage was an influential man who had listened to them, who had seen what was happening to them, and who cared enough to help them. He was willing to stand up against his own brother, the mine agents, and the Ecclesiastical Commissioners in order to help them — humble miners.

Davey, who had been suspicious of the stranger when they'd first met, was moved by his rhetoric and couldn't wait to hear more. He said to his wife, 'He's on our side, he is.'

'Aye, I hope he's as good as his word.'

When the hall fell silent once again, Mr Beaumont resumed his speech.

'Surely both parties are able to reach an accord without threatening mine closures. These threats are unjust, and unnecessary, and cause a great deal of distress. Gentlemen, you have been treated badly by my brother and the Ecclesiastical Commissioners, but you have been treated with gross inhumanity and impropriety by Mr Cain and Mr Rumney, and they should hang their heads in shame for what they have done. You have my word that I will do everything in my power to reopen the mines, to get you back to work, and to restore Weardale to the prosperous place it once was. And so it shall be again.'

A reporter from 'The Northern Echo' asked, 'Is it true that Mr Cain is going to sue you for making libellous accusations against him?'

'Let him try! I have not written or said anything about Joseph Cowper Cain that is not true, as God is my witness and my judge.'

Some of the miners questioned Mr Beaumont about the reasons for the dispute, and about whether or not he thought the few mines that were still open were at risk of closure as well; they wanted to know when things would be right again. Mr Beaumont's support and reassurances meant a lot to the men, and it was clear that they were grateful for any assistance that he could offer to lessen their plight.

After the question and answer session was over and the crowd had dispersed, Davey waited until he could talk with Mr Beaumont.

'That was a very good speech you gave there,' he said.

'Thank you. When I met you and your brother, he'd just lost his job, and you were fearful for yours, if I remember rightly? What's the situation now?'

'I'm still working, on short hours, but I don't know for how much longer. I can see all the mines closing before they get a deal sorted.'

'I sincerely hope it doesn't come to that, but you must be prepared, because neither side wants to back down. They're as stubborn and as greedy as each other. It's just a game to them. They don't see the consequences of what they're doing, but I do, and I guarantee you that I will make them aware of what is happening up here.'

'Thank you, Mr Beaumont. We appreciate your support.'

Mr Beaumont nodded, and took his leave.

Martha had been waiting outside for her husband to reappear, and when he came out, he put his arm around her waist, and they walked back to Westgate, full of the promises that had been made, and with serious expectations that the mines would be working again before Christmas.

Chapter 38

Burnside Hall
November, 1881

Since the proposal, Phyllis had been thinking a lot about her upcoming marriage to Timothy — about the ceremony, the reception and the first night they would spend together as husband and wife. In her mind, she had planned a small service at Westgate church, obviously with another vicar performing the duties, and a reception back at Burnside Hall. She had decided to have one of the large bedrooms at the front of the house prepared for them, and all this would happen quickly, as the sooner she was married, the more likely she would be to conceive a child; she was fully aware that time was running out for her.

There were only a few people that she wanted to invite — Mrs Peart and Joe Milburn, perhaps Tom Milburn and his family, and the staff from the house and the estate. She didn't think her aunt and uncle would want to make the journey from Harrogate to attend the wedding.

Mrs Phyllis Dagnall. The name had a certain ring to it, although she didn't think it sounded as distinguished as Miss Phyllis Forster. She'd always liked the alliteration of her old name, but no doubt she would soon get used to her new one. Taking a piece of paper, she dipped her pen in the inkwell and practised writing her signature as Phyllis Dagnall.

Timothy arrived in the middle of the afternoon and, after greeting her with a light kiss on her lips, they sat together in the morning room. He cleared his throat, and said, 'I thought we could be married at Durham Cathedral. The Bishop has married several vicars there, and it's such a wonderful building. The acoustics are fabulous.'

'Oh, I thought we'd be married at Westgate,' said Phyllis.

'That would be so impractical. The Bishop would have to travel all the way up here, and it would be further for my family too. They haven't been to Durham before, and they'd love to see the city.'

'Wouldn't they like to see where you live, and the church where you work?' she asked.

'There's not much to see, really. It's very desolate — just mine heaps, quarries and sheep. It won't be to their liking in the least. So the wedding will be at Durham, I'm pleased that's settled. Moving on, there's a nice hotel in the centre of Durham, just a short walk from the cathedral, and I thought we could have the reception there. What do you think?'

Phyllis nodded in agreement. She would have preferred to have the reception at Burnside Hall, a place that meant something to her, rather than in an impersonal hotel, but she could see that was not going to happen if the wedding was to take place in Durham, so there was no point in pursuing it.

'Perfect,' he replied. 'As you don't have parents to send out invitations, I expect that you'll do that. I'll give you a list of names and addresses for those on my side of the family. And while we're staying at Durham, I'll arrange for your personal items to be taken to the vicarage.'

Phyllis gasped. 'I can't move to Westgate. I need to be here to manage the estate.'

'Well, I must live at the vicarage. It's a stipulation of my contract.'

'I suppose I could stay with you and come here during the day.'

'You'll have duties at Westgate too. As a vicar's wife, you'll be expected to accompany me to events, to help the parishioners, to entertain...'

'But managing the estate takes up so much of my time.'

'Then we'll employ a manager to run it for you.'

'No!' The thought of somebody else taking over the management of the family estate was unbearable. It was her place to run it, as it had been her father's before her. She didn't think when she'd accepted his proposal that he would expect her to give up the Hall. 'I'll cope with the extra work somehow.'

'But Phyllis, dearest, you'll soon have children to care for. You must think about the future. I see taking on a manager as the best way forward, but I suppose we could sell it?'

'No. Under no circumstances can it be sold. I'd rather hire a manager.'

As she said the words, she felt a small part of her wither and die, but she kept control; the confusion and unease she felt inside did not show outwardly, her mask was firmly in place. After the wedding, Timothy would be the owner of Burnside Hall, and it would be his to do with as he pleased. But could she rely on him not to sell it? The Hall and estate had been everything to her when she'd returned to Weardale, but she wanted a future with a husband and children, and if that meant making sacrifices, then so be it.

'The only thing left to decide is the date,' said Timothy.

'I wondered about Christmas.'

'I couldn't possibly marry at Christmas, it's a busy time in the church. And it doesn't give my family enough notice to undertake such a long journey. May is a lovely month.' He took a calendar from his pocket and his finger traced the dates. 'Shall we say Saturday, 13th May?'

'I don't want to marry on the 13th. Could we make it the 6th?

'Of course, if that would make you happy.'

He grinned at her, and said, 'I can't believe my luck.

I'm ever so grateful that you agreed to marry me.'

Phyllis stood up and took his hands in hers and, when he rose from his seat, she stepped towards him and tilted her face up to him. He placed his arms around her and kissed her gently on the lips, and pulled her closer. She deepened the kiss and he responded, but she didn't feel anything stir in her heart. It was nothing like Ben's kiss, which had stirred her up inside and made her want more. She'd been totally lost, all reason gone, and she'd felt desolate when he'd pulled away and walked out.

But perhaps attraction and passion would come later, she thought. She remembered Connie saying that she hadn't enjoyed married life at first, but that it had improved with time. But there was a niggling doubt in her mind that perhaps she was giving up more than her family home by marrying Timothy.

Chapter 39

Davey marched home and stormed through the door of his cottage. Martha stopped sewing and looked up from her work to see his grey face.

'Whatever's the matter with you?' she asked, looking concerned.

'Something awful happened at the mine. A man died.'

'I'm sorry, love.' She put down the trousers she'd been patching, and went to her husband and put her arms around him. 'What happened?' she asked.

'Bad air. The fella collapsed and his mates couldn't get him out quickly enough. There wasn't enough air in the shaft for him to breathe and he suffocated.'

Pulling away slightly so she could look at him, she asked, 'Was it anyone I know?'

'Joe Robinson, from Huntshieldford. He was just a year or two older than me, and he had a wife and bairns as well.'

Martha got him to sit by the fire while she made him a cup of tea.

Davey sat and stared into the empty grate. He'd lost several workmates over the years, usually in rock falls or blasting accidents, but this was no accident. Robinson's death could have been avoided. No, it should have been avoided. It wasn't the first time that there'd been foul air in that part of the mine, and the managers knew that. The pressure had dropped on the barometer that morning, and they'd have known there was a high chance of bad air when the pressure was so low, but they still let the men go into the mine to work. Somebody should have stopped them.

Davey got to his feet, and paced up and down in the room for a while, contemplating the best course of action. Walter Beaumont came to mind, and he decided that he'd be the best person to talk to about it. The agents didn't listen to the miners, they never had, but they might listen to Mr Beaumont. Maybe he could get something done about the ventilation, and prevent anyone else from dying in the same way.

After his tea, he told Martha that he was going out. He'd heard that Walter Beaumont was lodging at the inn at Eastgate, and that's where he found him. He was sitting at a table in the bar, alone.

'Mind if I join you?' Davey asked.

'As you wish,' replied Walter sullenly.

The innkeeper shouted over, 'What would you like to

drink?'

'A beer, please.'

Davey sat opposite Walter and waited in silence for the man to bring his drink to the table. If Davey hadn't met Walter before, he would have thought he was a solitary sort of fellow that didn't like to talk.

The barman handed him a tankard and he took a sip, and then he said, 'It's just that something happened today at work, and I wondered if there was anything that could be done about it.'

As Davey related the details of the accident, he noticed Walter's attitude slowly change from indifference to interest and, by the time he'd finished, he had his full attention.

'This is a worthy cause indeed, and I'll do my utmost to help,' Walter said, holding up his glass and smiling brightly.

'Cheers,' said Davey.

'Sorry, I wasn't good company when you came in,' said Walter. 'I don't know what comes over me sometimes. But you've cheered me up. Thank you, good man. You will hear from me shortly.'

Davey gulped down the rest of his ale and headed for home, a little puzzled by Walter's behaviour. But at least he'd come around and promised that he would try to help, and Davey was pleased that his faith in the man hadn't been misplaced.

Just a week later, Walter Beaumont called another

public meeting in the Town Hall at St John's Chapel to discuss the dangerous working conditions in the Weardale lead mines. The room was full of miners and their families wanting to hear someone take their side.

They listened intently as Mr Beaumont queried the coroner's verdict of accidental death in the case of Joseph Robinson, and he said in no uncertain terms that the dead man should not have been allowed to work that day in a shaft with such poor ventilation and foul gases. He stood up for hundreds of miners that day, and pleaded for their right to work in fresh air.

At the end of the meeting, Walter received a standing ovation; he had earned the admiration and respect of even the most sceptical dale's men.

Davey stood proudly throughout the meeting with Martha at his side, watching the proceedings, and wondering at the positive things that could be achieved, all because he had voiced his concerns to Walter Beaumont. For the first time in months, he actually felt good about something he'd done, and he smiled to himself as he cheered along with the rest of the crowd.

The next morning Davey woke early and leaned over onto Martha's side of the bed.

'Are you awake?'

'Aye, I know I should be getting up.'

'You're alright for a bit longer. I just wanted to tell you something. This year, I've done a lot that I'm not very proud of, and it's a horrible feeling that keeps eating away at me. The meeting last night made me realise that I can do more with me life, you know, I really can make a difference in this world.'

'And how are you going to do that?' she asked, as she sat up in bed.

'By preaching. I want to spread God's word and help people make the right choices in their lives. Our Jack took the wrong path, and he led me astray for a while an' all. I just want to do something I'll be proud of.'

'Davey Bell, you're full of surprises. I never thought I'd see the day that you'd want to be a preacher,' Martha chuckled. 'I've had to drag you into that chapel for years.'

'Aye, I know, but after all these years, I think I've finally seen the light that they keep going on about. I'm going to go and have a chat with the minister today. I've never felt this excited about anything in years.'

Martha, fully awake now, smiled at her husband.

'You've always been a good man, Davey, and I'm glad I married you.'

He pulled her into his arms and kissed her, wishing that he didn't have to get up for work.

Chapter 40

High House Farm, Westgate
December, 1881

Mary was alone at High House Farm. After breakfast, Jane and Lizzie had taken the children out to search for things to make Christmas decorations with — pine cones and holly and such like. Tom was up on the fell checking on his sheep. She'd almost finished polishing the parlour furniture when she heard someone knocking at the door. She put down her cloth, and ran through to the kitchen to find Joe standing there. His face was pale and the hands that held his cap were shaking.

'What's wrong?' she asked.

'It's Mrs Peart. I can't wake her up. I think she might be...'

'No, she can't be,' said Mary in disbelief. She grabbed her coat from the hook behind the door and joined him outside, but she could only see his horse in the yard. 'Didn't you bring the cart?'

'Damn it! I rushed over in such a hurry, I didn't think.

Would you mind riding back with me?'

He mounted the brown mare and reached for Mary's hand to help her up. For a second, Mary thought to decline, but the look of desperation on his face made her take his hand and get on the horse. He held her tightly against his chest as the horse cantered to Springbank Farm. Mary was thankful that the journey was short, and it wasn't long before he carefully lowered her to the ground.

Leaving the horse fully saddled and untethered in the yard, he walked briskly into the house, with Mary following close behind, and they both ran up the wide staircase and into Mrs Peart's bedchamber, a room Mary remembered well from the time she'd worked there as a housemaid.

Mary rushed to the old lady's bedside, but she could see that she was too late to help her. She held a cold hand in hers and a tear ran down her cheek. Mrs Peart looked so peaceful, all the lines in her face seemed to have disappeared, and if Mary had ever doubted that there was an afterlife, she no longer did. She imagined Mrs Peart reunited with her husband, whom she had loved dearly, as well as with Connie and her little grandson. In fact, she thought Mrs Peart looked happier now than she had done since Mr Peart's death.

Joe stood quietly behind Mary, and she turned to him, and whispered, 'She's gone.'

Joe opened his arms and she embraced him. They'd

both miss this wonderful woman so much; she'd been a part of their lives for so long. As her son-in-law, Joe had lived in the same house with her for years, and Mary had known her since she'd gone to work for her as a girl, and since then, they'd become neighbours and friends.

Joe released his hold on Mary and looked down at the body.

'I don't understand it. She was fine last night when she went to bed,' said Joe, looking for answers as to why this dreadful thing had happened. 'We had our teas together in the kitchen, and she said she was looking forward to Christmas at your place, with the bairns.'

Joe's eyes were glassy with tears.

'At least she didn't suffer,' said Mary, trying to comfort him. 'You'd better go and fetch the doctor. He'll need to see her. And when Jane gets back, we'll come over and lay her out.'

'Aye, I'll go and fetch him now. Thanks for coming, Mary.'

'We're family, Joe. You can depend on us if you need anything.'

He hugged her again before leaving the house and mounting his horse.

Mary walked home, quietly reflecting on the past, about the Pearts and about everything that had happened since she had gone to work there when she'd still been a young and foolish girl.

About an hour later, she went back with Jane, and they

arrived at the house just as Dr Rutherford was leaving. Outside the farmhouse door, Mary asked, 'What was it that took her, doctor?'

'Her heart,' he replied. 'It appears to have stopped while she slept. A peaceful way to go.'

'May she rest in peace,' said Jane. 'Mrs Peart and me were neighbours for over thirty years, and I can honestly say there wasn't a bad bone in her body. The poor woman didn't have much to live for though, after she lost Connie and the little 'un. She had nobody left.'

Joe stood brooding in the doorway, and said in a low voice, 'That's enough, Mother.'

'I'm sorry, Joe. I'm not thinking straight. I know you miss them as well.'

The doctor bade them farewell and rode off down the farm track, and Mary and Jane went inside to do their work.

As there was no woman at Springbank Farm to prepare a funeral tea, Mary and Jane stepped in to help, and mourners were invited to High House Farm after the service at St Andrew's Church. Mary was surprised by the number that showed up, and she had a busy afternoon serving tea and refreshments, and chatting to acquaintances whom she rarely saw.

Despite having a great deal to do, Mary noticed that Joe was particularly quiet, and she was concerned about him. In just a few months, he'd buried his mother-in-law, his wife and his child. That was a lot of death for anyone to cope with. She'd watched him shake hands with everyone as they'd come in and he'd accepted their words of condolence, but he'd had little to say in return. She made a mental note to ask Tom to keep an eye on him.

Phyllis Forster was one of the last guests to arrive at the house, and Mary noticed that her eyes were red, and that she carried a handkerchief in her gloved hand. Phyllis was another one who had suffered from too much grief in her life, she thought. Seeing Joe and Phyllis together, Mary wondered if there was any truth in the rumour that they might get together. Phyllis was nowhere near as beautiful as Connie had been, but she was extremely wealthy, and young enough to give him children. She wouldn't rule out a marriage between them in the not too distant future.

Mary could see Ben sitting with his mother, but his eyes were on Phyllis as she talked with Joe, and Mary felt for him. He was obviously taken with Phyllis, and it was clear that he was jealous seeing her with Joe, and there was little doubt that he would get his heart broken. Poor Ben.

Mary disliked funerals and the effect that they had on her; they made her morose. She couldn't help but remember all the people that she'd loved, and lost, over the years, and it made her worry about losing her nearest and dearest. She chastised herself, and told herself to stop being so silly.

People lingered for an hour or two, and after most of the mourners had left, Mary invited Joe to have a glass of sherry with the family. The mood was melancholy; Mary's thoughts had shifted to Mrs Peart, and she wondered if the others were thinking about the dear old lady too. This was quickly confirmed when Joe refilled his glass, and made a toast to absent friends.

'Absent friends,' they all replied, as they raised their glasses in the air.

In an effort to cheer everyone up, Jane and Lizzie led the group in song and, before long, they were all singing together; even Joe joined in. After an emotionally intense day, either the music or the sherry successfully lifted their spirits.

When it was time to leave, Joe had had a little too much to drink, and Ben offered to see him home. They put on their coats and went outside into the cold night air. They walked for a while in silence, and then suddenly Ben said, 'You know Phyllis Forster, I've heard your names connected. Is there anything in that?'

'No, you've heard wrong. There's never been anything between me and Phyllis. We both loved Connie, and that's that. I don't intend marrying again,' and then he almost spat out the words, 'Not ever.'

'But it hasn't been long. Give it a few years and you might change your mind.'

'No! No, I won't. God didn't see fit to give me a bairn,

and he took me wife away from me as well. I couldn't go through that again.'

'But you're still a young man. What are you? Mid-thirties? You could still have a family with another woman.'

'I don't feel like a young man,' he said wearily. 'When I was a young man, I dreamed about owning this farm, and of having a beautiful wife and a house full of bairns. I wanted too much, and I didn't care who I hurt to get what I wanted. I can see now that I was greedy and selfish, and God has punished me for it. Just look at what I'm left with — this bloody farm and an empty house. That's what I deserve. Nothing more.

'I'll tell you something, lad. It's people who are important in this life, not property, or land, or money. Years ago, I made a mistake. I followed my dreams instead of listening to my heart. I've often wondered how different me life would have been if I'd chosen a different route back then. Listen to me. Never take people you love for granted, Ben. Never.'

Ben walked by Joe's side until they reached the farmhouse and he watched Joe disappear inside, and as he walked back to his cottage, he mulled over Joe's words. Joe had been adamant that he wouldn't marry again and Ben had believed him when he said that he had no interest in courting Phyllis, and for that he was grateful. He felt for Joe, though, the poor fella.

Chapter 41

Burnside Hall
December, 1881

'The Reverend would like to speak with you, Miss,' said Todd. 'He's most insistent.'

Phyllis put down the book she was reading and smiled at her butler. 'Please show him in.'

A few moments later, Timothy marched into the room, his face red and his eyes troubled. He fiddled with his necktie as he paced the room, before sitting in the armchair on the opposite side of the fireplace. He drummed his fingers on his knee.

'Are you alright?' asked Phyllis.

'No! I am not alright.' He stood up and walked over to the window.

'Please tell me, what's wrong?'

'How could you, Phyllis?'

Phyllis racked her brains. How could she what? Had Timothy heard something about her and Ben? She stood up and composed herself, before saying, 'What are you talking about?'

She saw Todd hovering at the door, but waved him away.

Timothy turned to her. 'You never told me about your brother!'

'What! You didn't know?' she asked in astonishment. 'I thought everyone knew about Henry.'

'You've made me look such a fool. I can't marry a woman whose brother committed murder!'

Phyllis's jaw dropped open and she fell back into her chair. Timothy was calling off the wedding because of Henry. Could she ever escape what he did? She had never hated her brother more than she did at that moment, and if he had still been alive, she would have killed him herself!

'I've asked the Bishop if I can take some time off work to visit my family in Oxfordshire. But Phyllis, I can't forgive you for your dishonesty. You deceived me into marrying you!'

'I did no such thing!'

She heard a scuffle outside the door and suddenly Ben burst into the room and stood directly in front of Timothy.

'How dare you speak to her like that?' Ben said angrily. 'She's not to blame for what her brother did.'

Phyllis felt a tear run down her cheek as she watched Ben defend her once again.

'What has this got to do with you? Get out!' shouted

Timothy.

'It's you that will be leaving.' He glowered at Timothy in such an intimidating way that showed he meant what he'd said.

Timothy looked to Phyllis for support, but she simply said, 'See him out, Featherstone.'

Phyllis's thoughts and emotions were in turmoil. How could Timothy not have known about Henry. He'd lived in the dale for almost a year. Surely someone must have mentioned it. She'd felt gutted when he'd called off the wedding — or was it that she thought she *should* feel gutted? Was she even disappointed?

And to confound things even further, Ben had appeared out of nowhere, and he, a mere shepherd, had taken the higher moral ground over a vicar who had wrongly accused her of dishonesty. She was so grateful that Ben had risen to her defence. Realising that Ben had returned to the room and was standing before her, she raised her eyes.

'Sorry,' he said, 'I was waiting in the hall to have a word with you, and I overheard what that pompous idiot said.'

'Thank you, I'm glad you were there.'

Thank you for standing up for me, she wanted to say, and thank you for getting rid of him. It seemed as though she was always thanking Ben and would be forever in his debt.

'Is it right? Were you going to marry him?' Ben asked.

'Yes, I was,' she said sadly. 'He proposed and I accepted, and we were to be married in May.'

'Do you love him?'

'No.'

'So why? Why him, when you could have your choice of men?'

The question hit a nerve. 'Could I?' she replied. 'Could I, really? As you can see, I'm fighting off suitors with sticks!' She turned her face away.

'I'm sorry, I didn't mean to upset you. It's just that you deserve someone much better than him, someone who'll love you and respect you for who you are — someone who doesn't give a damn about Henry.'

She couldn't help it. She couldn't stop the tears from flowing down her cheeks and, to her horror, she sobbed loudly. Her marriage was off and her hopes for a husband and a family had been dashed, and Ben had just said the nicest thing that anyone had ever said to her. She felt an arm around her shoulder, and she turned instinctively towards Ben, who held her against his chest until her crying stopped.

He placed a cotton handkerchief into her hand, and she wiped her eyes and blew her nose.

'Thank you,' she said again, and then smiled.

'You're easy to please, if all I have to do is give you a hankie,' he joked.

She poked him in the ribs with her elbow, and they laughed as they moved apart.

'Seriously though,' she said, 'I'm so glad you were here this afternoon.'

'Glad I could be of service. Are you sure you're alright?'

'Yes, I'll be fine. Thank you.'

A few days later, Ben was surprised to hear a knock at the door, and when he opened it, he found Phyllis standing there, smiling at him. He was intrigued as to why she had called on him so early; she must have left the house at sunrise to catch him before he started work.

'Good morning, Ben.'

'Morning, to what do I owe the pleasure?'

Her eyes sparkled with excitement; and he thought she looked very different from the austere woman who had returned to Burnside Hall almost a year ago.

'I know where your stone is!'

Ben raised his eyebrows, and asked 'You didn't take it?'

'No. But I know where it is. Mr Milburn came to see me last night and told me that one of the Felons had seen it at the vicarage in Westgate — in Timothy's garden!'

'Why would he take it off the fell?'

'He's interested in antiquities and such like. He's writing a book about the ancient people of Weardale and he probably wanted to include a sketch of it.'

'It must be put back where it came from,' said Ben, with feeling.

'I agree,' said Phyllis. 'We'll need a horse and cart, and some strong men. I'll have Thompson prepare one of the plough horses, and I think the gardeners will be pleased to come along — there's not much for them to do at this time of year.'

'Alright, let's go!'

Phyllis rode Samson alongside the cart and, when they reached Westgate, the men jumped down from the cart. Phyllis and Ben marched to the vicarage and knocked loudly at the door, which was answered by a middle-aged woman who asked if she could help them.

'We've come to see the vicar,' said Ben.

'He's not here.'

'When will he be home?'

'Not for another week. He's gone to visit his parents down country somewhere.'

'Thank you.'

The door closed, and Phyllis looked at Ben.

'What shall we do now?' she asked.

'What we came here to do — we'll get the stone and take it back with us.'

With difficulty because of its size and weight, the men moved the stone from its temporary resting place, and lifted it onto the cart. The bottom of the boulder was fairly flat, so there was no need for them to tie it down. They made their way slowly back towards Burnside Hall, and then veered off up the track towards the fell.

Phyllis rode ahead, and stopped when she came to the spot where the carved stone had been. The groom pulled up the horse and cart beside her.

Once again the men began the arduous task of moving the large rock to the bare patch of earth from where it had been removed. Once it was in position, they stood back and admired it. The men soon jumped back onto the cart and returned to the Hall, leaving Ben and Phyllis alone.

Ben looked at her; some of her hair had come loose and it was blowing in the icy breeze, her cheeks were rosy and she was beaming.

'Thank you,' he said, grateful that the stone, that meant so much to him, had been found and that Phyllis had been instrumental in bringing it back. 'But if it wasn't you who took it, why did you let me think it was?'

'It was my fault. I told Timothy about it and I felt bad about that. But it's back where it belongs now, and so am I,' she said, looking around at the beautiful view. 'Mrs Peart warned me that it might be difficult for me to stay here after everything that had happened in the past, and she suggested that I should sell up and move away.'

Ben's heart started to beat faster, and he stepped closer to her and put his hand on her arm.

'You're not going, are you?' he said, with something akin to panic in his voice.

'No, quite the opposite, in fact. I've decided that there's nowhere I would rather live than here in Weardale.'

Ben grinned. She was staying in the Hall. He wished things were different though, and that he'd been born a gentleman so he could tell her how he felt about her. But as a lowly shepherd, being friends with her was more than he could ever have expected; he would have to be content with that.

'Ben, you don't need to say a word. Your eyes speak for you.'

Did she know how he felt? She held out her hands to him and he took them in his and looked at her in awe.

'There's something I'd like to say to you,' she said, looking into his eyes. 'I stand before you sober and of sound mind. Age doesn't matter, class doesn't matter, and the past doesn't matter. The only thing that matters is that I would rather spend the rest of my life with you than anyone else. We can build a future together and finally lay the past to rest. What do you say, Ben? Will you marry me?'

She was looking at him expectantly, waiting for an answer.

He leaned forward and kissed her gently on the lips, and then said, 'Yes, I love you and it would be an honour to marry you. Somehow we'll make this work.'

He took her into his arms, pulled her close and kissed her firmly until he felt her relax into him. They held each other for the longest time, until the sun began to descend in the sky, and then they made their way down from the fell, hand in hand, with Samson and Bess walking behind.

Chapter 42

Town Hall, St John's Chapel
December, 1881

A large crowd huddled together in the Town Hall to hear Mr Walter Beaumont's update on the situation with the mines, and the news was not good. An air of despondency hung over the room, and Phyllis felt it keenly. She knew there must be something she could do to help, but what?

At the end of the meeting, Phyllis walked to the front of the room, with her back straight and her head held high. She said something to Mr Beaumont that the audience couldn't hear, and then turned to face the crowd and addressed everyone in the room in a clear and compassionate voice.

'I am Phyllis Forster of Burnside Hall, and I am no enemy of yours.'

She looked around the room at the miners, their wives and families, and could see the distrust and suspicion in their eyes. Some seemed perplexed that a woman would have the audacity to speak at a public meeting. Ben watched her with fascination, wondering what was coming next, and she smiled at him reassuringly.

'I am very sorry about the current situation with W B Lead and the predicament in which you find yourselves. And now we hear that the last mine is to close. This is a first for Weardale. Never before, in living memory, have there been no mines operating in the dale. Many families have already left their beloved Weardale in search of work, and those that remain are suffering greatly through lack of money. I cannot sit back and do nothing while you and your children are slowly starving.

'I, myself, will petition the Ecclesiastical Commissioners and Mr Beaumont, and urge them to end this impasse, as my father would have done if he had still been with us.'

She noticed that several heads bowed in respect at the mention of her father, and this gave her hope that her next words would be well received.

'Words cannot express how sorry I am for the misery and suffering caused by my brother, but please don't confuse me with him. I am nothing like him. I am a Forster of Burnside Hall, and like my father before me, I want the best for the people of Weardale.

'We are but a few days away from Christmas. On Christmas Day, the doors at Burnside Hall will be open to you. There will be food on the table, and gifts for the children, and you are all welcome to come and join us. I hope you will put the past behind you and accept my offer of hospitality.'

The crowd began to murmur, and she saw people nudging their partners. Tom Milburn started to clap and others followed his lead, and before long almost everyone in the room clapped their hands together in thanks to the generous and humble lady that stood before them. Some of the women wiped their eyes, relieved that their families would have more than just bread or potatoes for their Christmas dinner.

Phyllis made her way back to Ben and she could see that he wanted to hug her but, because they were in a public place and news of their impending wedding had not been released yet, he took her hand and squeezed it gently. The look in his eye told her that he was proud of what she'd done.

When they were back at Burnside Hall, sitting together in the music room, Ben asked, 'So, when did you decide to do that?'

'Not until I was there, listening to Mr Beaumont. Somebody has to do something to help those poor people, and it's my place to do it.'

'I'm just surprised, that's all, after everything that's been said about you and —'

'Nobody could be expected to put that behind them and move on when I hadn't myself, and I have you to thank for helping me to do that.'

'I would do anything for you, you know that. I love you.'

'I love you too.'

Ben stood up, took her hand and pulled her up beside him, and kissed her. She moved closer and kissed him more passionately. He gently pulled away, and said, 'How about New Year's Day for the wedding? A new year and a new start.'

Phyllis was so incredibly happy. She wanted this man as a husband, and as soon as possible. 'Yes! I would love that.' She hugged him tightly.

'That's settled then.'

On Christmas morning, Phyllis rushed around to make sure that everything was ready for the Christmas party. The kitchen staff had prepared food for one hundred guests, and she had wrapped the sweets for the children herself. She looked anxiously at the clock — it was noon already, now all she could do was wait. Half an hour later, nobody had appeared and Phyllis was growing concerned. What had she expected? That there would be a queue at the door? But what if nobody came? How embarrassing would that be!

As if she had summoned them herself, a cart pulled up outside, followed by a trap. Tom Milburn and his family stepped down, and Ben helped a woman alight the trap. As they came into the hallway, Tom and Mary introduced their children to Phyllis, and then Ben introduced her to his mother.

'I hear you made a good impression the other night,' said Lizzie.

'Thank you. I do hope so.'

Lizzie looked at Ben, and then leaning in towards Phyllis, she said, 'You've made a good impression on my lad, too.'

Phyllis blushed.

'Mother, will you come in here for a minute?'

'Aye, lad.'

Lizzie followed the couple into the music room. Phyllis closed the door behind them, and then unconsciously took Ben's hand for moral support. He closed his hand around hers and smiled down at her.

'Mother,' Ben said, without any preamble, 'Phyllis and I are going to be married.'

If Lizzie was surprised by their news, it didn't show. She smiled warmly, and said, 'Now that I've seen the two of you together, I can see that you're right for each other. God bless you both.'

She hugged her son and then his bride-to-be, and stepped back and smiled at them both.

Phyllis was amazed that Mrs Featherstone had accepted the news so well, and she said, 'Ben's a handsome, kind and wonderful man, and I have you to thank for that.'

'You do what you can. Our Ben's not had it easy, but neither have you. No good can come from dwelling on the past, and I'm pleased to see that you're both looking to the future now. I'm so glad that you've found each other.'

Ben kissed his mother on the cheek, and said quietly,

'Thank you.'

When they went back into the grand hallway, they were astonished by the volume of noise coming from the dining room and the drawing room — the sound of people talking and laughing, and children shouting and giggling.

'You've done it!' Ben said. 'You wanted to fix things between the Forster family and the locals, and I think you've done it!'

Phyllis grinned in delight as she walked around the rooms and greeted her guests. A man with a scarred face approached her, and stood awkwardly beside her until she'd finished opening a present for a small child.

'Miss,' he said, 'The name's Davey Bell. Please will you give me a minute of your time and hear me out?'

Phyllis nodded, and said, 'Go ahead, Mr Bell.'

'I want to apologise for what me and me brother did. It was us that shot one of your hares up on the fell earlier this year. Our families hadn't had any meat to eat in weeks, and we shared it atween us all.'

'I can sympathise with how hard it must have been for you, but that doesn't give you the right to take what doesn't belong to you.'

'I know that, Miss, and I'm heartfully sorry for it, but that's not all. It was me brother that was arrested for taking that piece of gold out of yon cave.'

'I heard the guilty man fled from the area and that he's still not been found.'

'Aye, he disappeared one night, and left his wife and

baby behind. We've not heard anything from him since. We don't know where he's at, but the police won't stop looking for him until he's found.

'But there's something else you should know an' all. He wasn't alone in the cave that night; I was with him. Ever since we uncovered the skull, nothing's gone right for us. The next day, I came down with the 'flu, and we lost our bonny little lass to it. Our Jack got arrested, but ran off and left his wife and bairn and now he's a wanted man. Even the weather's been out of kilter! I've learnt me lesson, and I've changed me ways. I've become a preacher. I just wanted to tell you that I'm sorry for what I've done, and to ask for your forgiveness, but I'll understand if you want to set the constable onto me.'

'Mr Bell, it sounds like you've suffered quite enough. If you had come to me and asked for food, I would have gladly given it. You know what you did was wrong, and I don't expect that you'll do it again, so I forgive you. What was your daughter's name?'

'Lottie. Charlotte May Bell.'

'I'll pray for her soul to rest in peace.'

She held out her hand to him and he shook it warmly.

'Thank you, Miss. If there's ever anything I can do for you, just ask.'

As Phyllis watched him walk over to his pregnant wife and two sons, her heart ached for their loss. Ben came and stood by her side, and asked, 'What was that about?'

'That family lost their little girl — it's so terribly sad.'

'Aye, it's sad. But it's no use dwelling on things you can't do anything about. Come on next door, the bairns are about to sing some carols.'

She followed him through, and as she listened to the innocent voices singing 'Silent Night', she couldn't help but think that she might have a child of her own soon, maybe even by next Christmas, and that gave her a warm feeling inside; she smiled to herself. Looking around the room, she noticed that quite a few faces were turned towards her and most of them were smiling too.

The party was a huge success and everyone who attended left with their bellies full and kind words for their hostess. Phyllis had not enjoyed a Christmas so much since she was a child.

Chapter 43

When Phyllis woke up, she couldn't believe that it was her wedding day, a day that she'd longed for but thought she'd never see. She bathed in the morning before breakfast, and brushed her hair until it shone, and then tied it up in a much more elaborate style than she usually wore, and she had to admit that it looked well.

Mary Milburn kindly came over to help her get ready. Phyllis slipped into her mother's wedding dress, which she believed had been made for her grandmother, and Mary fussed about her making sure that it hung correctly, and then she fastened her mother's diamond necklace around her neck.

'Something old, something new, something borrowed, something blue,' said Mary. 'It'll bring you luck. What do you have that's old?'

Phyllis opened her dressing table drawer, took out the bronze bracelet and slipped it onto her wrist.

'What about something new?'

'All of my undergarments are new.'

'Something borrowed?'

'My mother's necklace.'

'No, that belongs to you now, so it's not borrowed.' Mary took a silver ring off her little finger. 'Wear this. I'd like it back after the wedding though, it's not worth much but it has sentimental value. It's the only thing I have of my mother's.'

'Thank you. And do you have any ideas for something blue?'

'I stitched a small blue flower onto your petticoat when you were in the bath,' she said, grinning.

'Thank you. I couldn't have done this myself.'

'You're welcome, and you look stunning.'

Phyllis brushed off the compliment, and asked Mary to check if the carriage was waiting by the door.

Phyllis sprayed a little perfume on her wrists and took a last glance in the mirror at Miss Phyllis Forster. The face looking back at her was smiling, and she knew it was a genuine smile because she had never felt so happy and sure of herself in her life. When she returned to the Hall later that day, she would be Mrs Phyllis Featherstone, and that was a name she was thrilled to take, and it had the alliteration that she'd always liked. She was ready.

Tom Milburn and his family met Ben at Eastgate, and give him a lift down to St Thomas's Church at Stanhope.

In Stanhope market place, he jumped down off the cart and helped his mother down.

'Thanks, lad.' Looking at him from head to toe, Lizzie reached over and straightened his collar, and said, 'You look very handsome.'

He offered her his arm, and he walked up the path to the church door, where the vicar, Reverend Longstaff, was waiting for them.

'Good morning, Mr Featherstone. It's a lovely morning for your special day.'

For once, Ben hadn't noticed the weather, and he looked up at the clear blue sky.

'Aye, it's a bonny day, but it's cold out here. Come in and sit down, Mother.'

They sat in the front pew on the right of the aisle, the groom's side of the church, and the Milburn's followed them, Tom sitting next to Ben and the children in the pew behind them. Ben sat patiently while people filed into the church and filled the pews. Finally, the vicar came in and stood by the altar, from where he nodded at the organist to begin to play, and he gestured to Ben to come and stand beside him at the front of the church. He was pleased to have Tom, his best man, by his side.

Mendelssohn's 'Wedding March' sounded loudly in the large Norman nave, and everyone turned to look at the bride walking up the aisle on the arm of Joe Milburn, who'd been delighted when she'd asked him to give her away. He looked as proud as any father leading his daughter down the aisle would have done. Behind them walked Mary Milburn, Phyllis's matron of honour.

When Ben saw Phyllis, he was astonished by how beautiful she looked. Her chestnut hair was piled up on top of her head, and a delicate lace veil was held in place with pearl pins. Her face was radiant, and the lace dress that she wore clung to her body, not leaving much to the imagination. Ben couldn't take his eyes off her.

When she reached the altar, Joe kissed her on the cheek and left her standing next to Ben. The vicar began the service with the usual preamble, and Ben didn't really hear the words until it was time for them to say their vows, and suddenly everything came into focus.

'Do you, Benjamin Featherstone, take Phyllis Margaret Forster to be your lawful wedded wife? Will you love her, comfort her, honour and protect her, and, forsaking all others, be faithful to her as long as you both shall live?'

Despite Ben's initial misgivings about his feelings for Phyllis, and the unorthodox way in which she had proposed, he had no doubt in his mind that he was doing the right thing in marrying her.

He said, 'I do.'

When Phyllis looked up at him, there was so much love in her eyes. She answered the vicar's questions with an enthusiastic, 'I do.'

Tom took a gold ring from his pocket and handed it to the vicar, who blessed it, and passed it carefully to Ben, who placed it on Phyllis's finger. When the vicar finished speaking, he said quietly, 'You can kiss her now.'

Ben took her in his arms and kissed her gently on the lips, and earned a huge round of applause from the congregation. They then walked hand in hand up the aisle to the door. When the door was opened, the grins on their faces were replaced by looks of shock. The path through the churchyard was lined with people and there was a crowd almost filling the market place. The dale's people had turned out in force to see the wedding of Miss Phyllis Forster, mistress of Burnside Hall, to Ben Featherstone, who was one of their own. Tears of joy sprang to her eyes as they walked back to the carriage, with confetti, rice and good wishes being thrown at them.

Before they embarked on their journey home, Ben threw some coins out onto the cobbles for the children, and then he helped Phyllis into the carriage, climbing in after her and sitting by her side. They left to cheers and words of congratulation, and a few lewd suggestions too, as they waved at the crowd until they were out of sight.

'I can't believe they came,' Phyllis said, in amazement. 'Their support on our wedding day is more than I could ever have hoped for.'

'I have everything that I ever hoped for right here,' he replied, kissing her lovingly.

Back at Burnside Hall, Ben helped Phyllis out of the carriage and carried her to the door, and for the second time he crossed the threshold with her in his arms. But this time she was his wife.

Epilogue

High House Farm, Westgate
June, 1882

Phyllis sat back in the trap and watched her husband as he carefully turned the horse onto the track to High House Farm. She could hardly believe that it was six months since their wedding, and she had never been so happy in all her life.

As they pulled into the farmyard, they were met with shouts of welcome from the children, and Tommy and Matt ran up to greet them.

'Can we see to your horse, Ben?' Tommy asked.

Tom and Mary had come to the door, and Tom nodded to Ben, so Ben handed the horse over to them.

Tom said, quietly so that only Ben and Phyllis could hear, 'Thanks for that. Our Tommy's keen to work with horses and it's good practice for him.'

'Come inside,' said Mary. 'Your mother's helping Josie in the kitchen. They're making a birthday cake for Jane — she's sixty today!'

They followed Mary into the kitchen, where Lizzie and Josie were busy decorating a cake, and Jane was trying to join in.

'You can't help,' said Josie. 'It's your birthday so you have to let us do it.'

Phyllis said, 'Many happy returns, Mrs Milburn.'

'Thank you. Sit down on here. Would you like a cup of tea, or something cool to drink?'

'Tea would be lovely, thank you.'

Josie shouted, 'I'll make it.'

'Thanks, lass,' said Jane, and then to Phyllis, she said, 'They won't let me do anything today. I'm glad you've come because I hate sitting around with nothing to do.'

Ben was still standing by the door, and Phyllis noticed a look pass between him and his mother, and then Lizzie smiled a knowing smile. She came over to Phyllis and said, 'So, I'm going to be a grandmother! When is it due?'

'November, I think. But how did you know?'

'I can read Ben like a book,' she said.

Tom and the boys came in together, and Phyllis realised that he must have been supervising his sons with the horse, and was grateful to him.

Matt said to Ben, 'We're going to have cake!'

'I know. I chose a good day to visit, didn't I?'

Ben leaned forward and picked up the little boy, and then he tickled him until he squealed and laughed in his arms. He put him back down and Matt ran away, with Tommy chasing after him, threatening to tickle him too.

Phyllis could never have imagined that she would be part of such a large and happy family.

Joe Milburn knocked quietly at the door before coming in.

'Morning, Joe,' said Tom.

'Good mornin', it's a beautiful day for mother's birthday. Where is she?'

As he asked the question, Jane came out of the pantry, and said, 'Joe, thanks for coming over.'

He went to his mother and gave her a hug and a kiss on the cheek. 'Happy Birthday, Mother!' He went over to the kitchen table and said, 'This cake looks good enough to eat. I wonder who made it?'

Josie said proudly, 'I did!'

'I thought so,' he said, winking at her. 'I can't wait to try some.'

Mary said, 'Everyone's here now, so Jane, why don't you come and cut the cake.'

'At last, you're letting me do something,' she laughed.

Jane cut the cake and placed small pieces on plates for Josie to hand out to the guests, and then the family.

Lizzie said, 'I put a coin in, so mind you don't swallow it!'

'Did you put a thimble in, as well?' asked Jane.

'No, I would never do that.'

'Why not?' asked Josie.

'If you get the piece of cake with the thimble in, it's said that you won't ever marry.'

'It's just a load of old nonsense,' scoffed Tom.

'I found the coin!' said Josie, 'What does that mean?'

'That you'll be wealthy!' said Lizzie with a smile.

Phyllis was amused by the boys' discussion about what they would spend their sister's money on if she was rich — houses, and horses, and carriages. She had all of those things, but she would gladly swap them for what this family had — each other.

Joe and Tom discussed the miners, who were apparently much happier now that the mines had reopened and they were back at work. She knew that the Ecclesiastical Commissioners had backed down, and she hoped that her letter may have helped them to realise the damage that they'd wreaked by their stand-off with the mine owners.

She heard Joe say, 'They've only just got back to work, and already the miners are raising funds so they can put up a plaque at St John's Chapel to thank Walter Beaumont for everything he's done.' She would have to find out who was collecting the funds and make a donation.

'You'll never guess what I heard,' said Jane. 'The new vicar up at Westgate's leaving already. He's got a job down in the south — near where he grew up, so they say. He'll not be a big miss up here though because he never really fitted in, did he?'

Ben caught Phyllis's eye and smiled at her.

'Oh, I have a birthday gift for you, Mrs Milburn.' Phyllis

reached into her bag and pulled out a package wrapped in brown paper, and handed it to Jane.

'Thank you, lass.'

Phyllis smiled to herself. Jane had called her lass, rather than Mrs Featherstone, or Miss, and she took that as a huge compliment coming from a daleswoman. Whether it was for helping the miners, hosting a Christmas party for the dales people, or marrying a local lad, she didn't know and she didn't care, because whatever the reason, she had finally been accepted.

Author's historical note

In 1881, Weardale's main industry, lead mining, was in a desperate state. The price of lead had plummeted two years earlier, and it didn't recover as it had after previous slumps. This was due to cheap imports of lead. The largest mining company in Weardale at this time was W B Lead, owned by Mr Wentworth Blackett Beaumont. So, by the time this novel is set, in 1881, many of his mines had already closed. However, this wasn't the only factor leading to unrest in the miners. Mr Beaumont was in dispute about royalties, with the Ecclesiastical Commissioners who owned the mineral rights, and their extended disagreement resulted in more miners being laid off. Also, a recent change to the pay system by Mr J C Cain, a mine agent at W B Lead, meant that some miners received little or no subsistence money, which they had relied on in the past. The miners held strikes in 1881 and 1882. The following year, the Beaumont family withdrew from lead mining in Weardale, and the mine leases were taken over by the Weardale Lead Company.

Mr Walter Beaumont was a quite a character. Standing up for the Weardale miners against his elder brother earned Walter the highest respect from the miners, and they erected a plaque to him at St John's Chapel. The unfortunate story of Joseph Robinson, who died due to foul air in the mine, is true, and Mr Walter Beaumont held a meeting in December 1881, where he questioned the coroner's verdict of accidental death, and called for miners to have the right to free air. He was quite outspoken about his brother and the mine agents. Mr Cain tried, but failed, to press criminal charges for libel against Mr Walter Beaumont.

As a result of the declining lead industry, the population in Stanhope Parish fell from 10,330 in 1871 to 8,793 in 1881, quite a substantial reduction in just ten years. Many Weardale people emigrated during this time. On 16th October 1879, the sailing ship *Margaret Galbraith* left London for Dunedin. On board were 145 passengers, almost 60 of whom were from upper Weardale, seeking a new life in New Zealand.

Farming was fraught with difficulties during this period too. The agricultural depression meant farmers were unable to make enough money from their produce to pay their rents. They campaigned for a reduction in rent, but not all landlords were willing to give any relief, so many farms were abandoned through necessity. In 1882, 'The Wear Valley Farmers' Club' was set up to give local farmers a bigger voice. Market prices for lambs fluctuated depending on weather conditions, and prices in 1881 were good. Wool prices, however, steadily declined during the second half of the nineteenth century due to imports flooding the market. Agricultural shows were a highlight of the year and farmers took the competition very seriously.

Scarside quarry and cave are fictional, but they reflect the limestone geology and prehistoric archaeology of the area. A large collection of Bronze Age weapons and tools was discovered at Heathery Burn Cave, near Stanhope. The site was excavated between 1859 and 1872 by Canon William Greenwell, who described the artefacts as 'one of the most valuable discoveries ever made in Britain of weapons, implements, ornaments, and other things belonging to the Bronze Age'. Most of the finds are in the British Museum. There are references to cave fish worldwide. Because of the permanently dark conditions underground, they are usually small, white, and some even lack eyes.

Poaching was rife in the dales when the miners didn't have enough work. Surrounded by grouse moors, the temptation to hunt for food must have been irresistible. The River Wear is home to trout and salmon. Tickling trout was a common method of fishing, especially by poachers, because no equipment was necessary. Thomas Martindale's 1901 book, 'Sport, Indeed', describes how trout tickling was performed in the River Wear:

The fish are watched working their way up the shallows and rapids. When they come to the shelter of a ledge or a rock it is their nature to slide under it and rest. The poacher sees the edge of a fin or the moving tail, or maybe he sees neither; instinct, however, tells him a fish ought to be there, so he takes the water very slowly and carefully and stands up near the spot. He then kneels on one knee and passes his hand, turned with fingers up, deftly under the rock until it comes in contact with the fish's tail. Then he begins tickling with his forefinger, gradually running his hand along the fish's belly further and further toward the head until it is under the gills. Then comes a quick grasp, a struggle, and the prize is wrenched out of his natural element, stunned with a blow on the head, and landed in the pocket of the poacher.'

The weather throughout 1881 was extreme and, at times, unseasonal. There were severe blizzards early in the year, one of which left around 100 people dead and blocked rail tracks with huge drifts, dozens of feet high in places. When temperatures began to rise in early March, there had been a continual blanket of snow in many parts of the Durham dales for nineteen weeks. The accumulation of melting snow on higher ground, combined with torrential rain, led to drastic flooding. William Thwaites, a watchmaker, and Richard Gargate, a gamekeeper, were killed on 9th March when a bridge spanning the River Tees at Barnard Castle was washed away.

References

Bowes, P, *Weardale: Clearing the Forest* (1990: P Bowes)

Forbes, I, *Whar a candel will not burn...* (1996: Durham County Council)

Hunt, C J, *The Lead Miner's of the Northern Pennines* (1970: Augustus M Kelley, New York)

Milburn, T A, *Life and Times in Weardale 1840-1910*, (T A Milburn)

Rowley, M, *Weather in History 1850 to 1899* AD [Accessed at: http://premium.weatherweb.net/weather-in-history-1850-to-1899-ad]

Sanderson, F, *Life and Times in Victorian Weardale: The Letters of Francis Vickers* (2018: Frank Sanderson)

Whetham, E H, *Livestock Prices in Britain 1851-93* [Accessed at: http://www.bahs.org.uk]

The Great Flood in Weardale, *Newcastle Courant* (April 1st, 1881)

Terrible Thunderstorm, *The Northern Echo* (July 7th, 1881)

Monthly Weather Review (1881, September)

Also by Margaret Manchester

The Lead Miner's Daughter

It is 1872 when Mary Watson, a lead miner's daughter, leaves her childhood home to work at Springbank Farm. She soon meets a handsome neighbour, Joe Milburn, and becomes infatuated with him, but is he the right man for her?

Mary's story is woven into a background of rural life and crime in the remote valley of Weardale. Not one but two murders shock the small community.

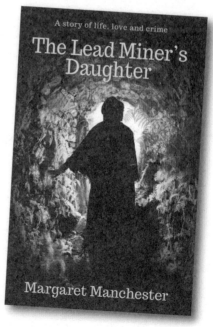

Find yourself in the farmhouse kitchen with the Peart family, walking on the wide open fells, seeking shelter underground and solving crimes with PC Emerson as this intriguing story unfolds.

Will the culprits be brought to justice? Will Mary find true love?